SCANDAL IN FAIR HAVEN

Also by Carolyn G. Hart

DEATH ON DEMAND
DESIGN FOR MURDER
SOMETHING WICKED
HONEYMOON WITH MURDER
A LITTLE CLASS ON MURDER
DEADLY VALENTINE
THE CHRISTIE CAPER
SOUTHERN GHOST
DEAD MAN'S ISLAND

SCANDAL IN
FAIR HAVEN

CAROLYN G. HART

BANTAM BOOKS

NEW YORK · TORONTO · LONDON · SYDNEY · AUCKLAND

With love to my son, Philip.

ACKNOWLEDGMENTS

I would like to thank Joan Hess, Chris and Ellen Myrick, and Corinne Stoddard for their very good suggestions, and my agent, Deborah C. Schneider, for her encouragement and insight.

SCANDAL IN FAIR HAVEN

1

always opt for life.

Even when it's desperately hard to do. Even in the midst of death and travail.

That's why I walked up the stairs from the intensive care unit, where my friend Margaret was struggling to survive, to the second floor of the hospital.

I'd first found my way upstairs in mid-morning, seeking respite from the life-and-death drama that unfolds—inexorably—in the lounge that serves the intensive care unit.

I'd slipped quietly out of the waiting area as a weary surgeon in bloodstained scrubs slowly walked toward a mid-thirties man and woman. Their faces flattened in grief as he came reluctantly closer. The doctor's rubber soles squeaked against the marble floor. It was the only sound until the mother began to moan. Cars and youth and alcohol.

I didn't want to see those parents grieve. It hurt too much.

So I slipped away, up the antiseptic gray stairs to the second floor and the maternity ward, where life was beginning.

Yes, there could be heartbreak here too.

But not this April afternoon.

One of the babies, a little boy, scrunched up a red, puckered face and began to cry, the utterly unmistakable mew of the newborn. God, how precious life is. I thought of my family, of my grandchildren.

It wasn't the kind of nursery I'd expected, of course. But the only constant in life is change. A brisk nurse explained to me what appeared to be the dearth of babies. Babies today don't stay in the nursery in bassinets with cards affixed, Baby Boy Jones, Baby Girl Smith. Today's babies are in the room with their mothers, right from the first.

Sensible, of course.

They spend only brief periods in the nursery, for weighing, for checking.

I wandered down the hall. Many doors were open. I had other glimpses of new babies, new mothers, new adventures beginning.

I returned to Margaret's bedside much refreshed.

The nurse moved near. "She's conscious now, Mrs. Collins. Don't let her talk much."

Margaret's hand was quiet and cool in mine. Her eyes fluttered open.

"You're doing fine." I spoke quietly. "I talked to the doctor. No major damage to the heart muscle. The surgery was successful."

Her breathing was shallow, her lips bluish.

"Henrie O . . ."

My late husband Richard gave me, Henrietta O'Dwyer Collins, that nickname. Richard used to say I packed more surprises into a single day than O. Henry ever put in a short story.

"Be quiet now, Margaret. Rest."

She licked her lips.

I reached for the plastic cup with ice shavings, gently spooned a cool mound on her tongue.

Margaret swallowed, closed her eyes in thanks.

The visiting period was over.

This time when I walked upstairs, it was during the shift change. A flurry of scrub-clad attendants, nurses, nursing assistants, doctors, orderlies, passed me.

So why did I notice the bone-thin woman who stood in the hallway?

Her face was hidden behind a curtain of long, straight hair as she looked down at the infant cradled in her arms.

A pale blue receiving blanket and a tiny hand. That's all I saw within the protective embrace. Faded green scrubs sagged against the woman's bony shoulders, exposed her thin wrists. A stethoscope dangled around her neck.

I'd passed dozens of men and women similarly attired since I brought Margaret to the hospital late last night in the throes of a heart attack.

I watched as she—nurse? nurse's aide? doctor?—passed the nursery.

She picked up speed.

Her scuffed black leather flats slapped against the floor.

Faster. Faster.

She reached the stairs, gave a swift look behind.

And saw me.

I didn't hesitate.

"One moment, please." I held up my hand. Imperiously, if you will. And strode quickly toward her.

She stood frozen, her face impassive, her arms curved tight as steel bands around that small, helpless bundle.

With every step I took, I became more certain of my suspicions.

I'll never forget looking into her eyes, dull green eyes flecked with amber and despair. Straggling light hair, darker at the roots, framed a gaunt, hollow-cheeked face. Her mouth was slack, loose, straight lips that had long ago forgotten how to smile. A pulse throbbed in her throat.

I held out my arms.

Her shoulders sagged. Tears edged down her wan cheeks. Slowly, as if the tiny creature were too heavy to be borne, she handed me the precious mewing bundle.

She whirled away, yanked open the door, plunged into the stairwell. Before the heavy door eased shut, I heard the clatter of her shoes on the cement stairs.

My arrival in the nursery caused a stir, of course.

The alarm went out immediately.

And a sobbing new mother held her baby—tiny six-pound James Allen Wilson—cradled in the sanctuary of her arms.

The head nurse caught me as I walked toward the stairs. Her ruddy face was touched with paleness, her commanding voice wavered. "They found her in the parking garage. The police are on the way. She'll be charged with attempted kidnapping." The nurse stopped, swallowed, briefly closed her eyes, blocking out the frightful vision of what might have been, what almost was. "God. We're so grateful. But how did you know? How on earth did you know?"

I looked down and pointed at the head nurse's Reeboks.

"The scrubs were right. She had a stethoscope. But have you ever seen anyone who works in a hospital wearing thin-soled leather flats?"

"Christ." The nurse was forty-five, stocky, with an air of certitude. She cleared her throat. "I probably shouldn't tell you. We have a doctor who wears stiletto heels. Thank God you didn't know."

I left it at that.

But it wasn't simply the shoes, the wrong shoes. It was the almost half century I spent as a reporter. Body language tells so much. Without ever seeing her, I knew the stiletto-heeled doctor exuded assurance, command.

The rigid back of the kidnapper shouted fear.

And if I'd been wrong? So? I don't embarrass easily. And I've learned to play my hunches. For good or ill.

It was a good day all around. They moved Margaret out of intensive care and into her room. I was relieved enough to pick up my regular schedule the next morning, my last class before spring break.

I still find it hard to see myself as an academic. Probably because I'm not an academic. But it is my pleasure to serve on a rather unique journalism faculty, one that employs retired professionals rather than degree-laden and experience-poor academics. The professors at this small college, nestled in the wooded rolling hills of southern Missouri, are people who have crafted ads, waged campaigns, worked public relations magic in the wake of industrial fiascos, and covered wars and famines and jugular politics for all kinds of media. Our students might not have contact with academics flourishing in the sanitized arena of juried journals (*You kiss my ass, I'll kiss yours*), but they are exposed to how the media world really works.

I carried a small box of divinity when I visited Margaret in the afternoon.

She looked much better, her color improved, her eyes clear. Margaret has such a civilized face. I've seen its counterpart on tapestries in Brussels—an aquiline nose, almond-shaped eyes, a soft, rosebud mouth.

I waved away her thanks for my vigil. I know how much a hand clasp matters when life hangs in the balance. Not as much as oxygen, but more perhaps than Margaret's beardless young doctor realized.

She'd heard from her night nurse about yesterday's excitement.

"Henrie O, only you!"

"You would have noticed in an instant." It wasn't simply a modest disclaimer. Margaret, also on the general news faculty, was a longtime INS correspondent in Paris. Very little escapes her.

"Perhaps. In any event, you've earned your holiday." Her soft mouth looked stubborn.

We'd planned, before illness struck, to spend the spring break at Margaret's cabin in the Cumberlands. I'd looked forward to our trip eagerly, our departure planned for Saturday morning. I dearly love Tennessee and never pass up an opportunity to visit there. Margaret grew up in Chattanooga, and the cabin had been in her family for years. Now there was only Margaret and a nephew who lived near Nashville.

I sat up straight. "Margaret, I didn't think! Your nephew—I should call him."

"No, no. No need. There's nothing Craig can do and I don't want to bother him."

Funny how much you can read into words when you are my age. Margaret and I have a here-and-now friendship. We enjoy driving into St. Louis for art shows (everything from Turner to Monet to Klee), discussing politics (if you think today's press coverage is savage, take a look at Charles A. Dana's editorial invective in the New York *Sun* in the 1880s), and sharing discoveries of new books (Margaret likes poetry, I prefer nonfiction).

We don't spend our lives in the past.

But we know the outlines of each other's lives, our husbands, where we'd worked and lived, what we'd written. She was a widow too. She and Paul had no children. Her sister Eileen died several years ago. Margaret's only family was Eileen's son, Craig. I'd seen family photos scattered about Margaret's house as photos are scattered about mine.

And she didn't want me to call her nephew about her heart attack and surgery.

"He's been very involved with his wife and her family since he married." Her eyes slipped away from mine.

Translation: No time for an elderly aunt.

I let it drop. I pulled out the box of divinity and a new paperback.

Margaret smiled her thanks, then once again looked stubborn. "Now, I don't want any heroics here, Henrie O. You go ahead tomorrow and take the holiday as we'd planned it. I don't need to have my hand held. And several friends from the altar guild have phoned. They'll be by."

I let myself be persuaded.

Margaret was fine, was going to be fine.

And I was eager for my holiday.

A peaceful week in the Cumberlands in a solitary mountain cabin.

What could be more restful?

2

 drove through Nashville at dusk. It is a city I love, elegant and southern, a city of church spires and country music tour buses, glittering new glass office buildings and treasured antebellum mansions, boot factories and insurance empires, towering oaks and ghostly gray limestone. I stopped for dinner at Houston's, an old favorite near the Vanderbilt campus. The restaurant was jammed, as always on a Saturday night. It was almost nine o'clock when I reached my turnoff from Highway 24E some eighty miles south of Nashville.

I had no trouble finding the cabin—Margaret's map was excellent —though it was several miles to the east and far up a rutted gravel road. Not a gleam of moonlight penetrated the canopy of trees that interlocked above the twisting lane. My headlights stabbed into the darkness, disappeared into the night.

In the glow of my lights, the cabin had a deserted, bleak appearance, one wooden shutter hanging on a hinge, pine needles thick on the rock path. I pulled around to the side, squeezed my MG between two pines.

I was tired from the full day's drive and the stress of Margaret's illness and my hospital vigil. I did take time to breathe deeply of the cool pine-scented air, to welcome the embrace of country silence, but within a few minutes I'd unpacked the car—my luggage and provisions for a week—washed my face, made up one of the twin beds, and tumbled into it and a deep, satisfying sleep.

I wake like a cat. Shifting in an instant from deep sleep to full alert.

Adrenaline pumped through me. The noise that jolted me awake —the metallic rattle of the front doorknob, the faint screech as the door swung in—was startling in the silence, but perhaps even more shocking was the sudden blaze of light from the combination living room-kitchen, illumination that spilled in a harsh swath into the bedroom.

The layout of the square cabin was simple.

The front door opened into the small living room and kitchen area. The bedroom door—which I'd left ajar when I went to bed—was to the right of the front door. I'd had no reason to close the door. I was alone in the cabin.

But not now.

There was no possible good reason why someone was inside the living room of Margaret's cabin, between me and the only exit.

Except for the single bedroom window.

At bedtime I'd managed, with a struggle, to raise the window almost an inch for a breath of fresh cool night air. It hadn't been easy. The window'd obviously not been budged in years.

The intruder would certainly hear if I tried to get out that way, assuming I could wrestle the window any higher, which I doubted.

That left the front door. And my late-night visitor.

I was already moving, easing over the side of the bed, grabbing my key ring with its attached Mace canister and my small travel flashlight from the nightstand.

The Mace canister? Of course. Women, old or young, pretty or ugly, sexy or plain, are always at risk. At home. At work. In hotels. On the highway. Daylight or dark. Every woman knows it.

I uncapped the cover to the Mace, gently touched the trigger with my thumb. My hand trembled.

The wooden floor was cool beneath my bare feet. Shoes. I'd run faster with shoes.

I fought indecision and knew it was a form of panic. Thoughts, incomplete, inchoate, whirled in my mind. Shoes . . . door . . . Mace . . .

But first I must know who was there.

I reached the open bedroom door with only one telltale creak of the boards.

I've trod a good many dangerous paths in my life. I've learned to look hard at faces.

The old saw instructs that pretty is as pretty does. The converse is equally true. The discontented droop of a mouth, the venal gleam in an eye, the obsequious curve of lips, the angry lift of a chin—oh, yes, faces tell tales. And dangerous men have in common an air of reckless abandon. They are not bound by any rules, man's or God's, and they will kill you without qualm.

I had to see the face of my intruder.

He slumped in the room's single easy chair, his dark eyes wide and staring, focused on nothing.

His face surprised me. It was slender, almost delicate for a man. It reminded me of tintypes of Robert Louis Stevenson, oval with deepset eyes, a small, gentle mouth, a high-bridged nose. In his mid-thirties. Despite the bristly stubble fuzzing his cheeks, my intruder had a thoughtful, civilized, almost professorial look. But he appeared desperately tired. More than that, his face retained a kind of incredulous astonishment, like the single survivor of a road smash surveying the crushed cars and mangled victims.

His long, lean body sagged with despair. He wasn't dressed for the part of a housebreaker. He wore a glen plaid cotton shirt, stylishly pleated khaki slacks, tasseled burgundy leather loafers. But his right trouser leg was soiled, some kind of dark stain.

And I had the elusive, teasing sense that I'd seen him somewhere before. Somewhere . . .

Faintly a motor rumbled from the road.

He jerked upright, every muscle tensed, his pale, strained face frozen in panic.

The roar grew louder, nearer.

He scrambled to his feet.

The car rattled closer, closer. And then it was by. The sound receded.

He drew his breath in, gulped it. His hands were shaking.

I saw him clearly now in the light. All of him—including his left shirt-sleeve.

I stared at the sleeve, at the blackish substance that discolored it. It was quite different from the stain on his trousers.

Blood.

Viscous thick blood had dried to a dark crust above the cuff.

A wound?

He didn't move like an injured man. His left fist was tightly clenched. The instinctive tendency of an injured member is to go limp, thereby putting the least possible stress on pain-racked flesh.

Abruptly his fight-or-flight stance relaxed. The young man turned, stumbled wearily to the chair, and flung himself down.

I slipped away from the door, edged silently across the bedroom. I was wearing cotton shorts and a T-shirt, my favored garb for sleep. My suitcase and gym bag were on the floor near the bathroom. I fished out a pair of sweats and my Reeboks. I placed the Mace canister handily on the edge of the bed, then slipped into the sweats, pulled on athletic socks and the running shoes. Maybe it took me forty seconds.

I crept quietly back to the open door. He hadn't moved.

My husband Richard always warned me against snap judgments. But I don't waste time, and I don't waver between choices.

I stepped out into the living room. "Excuse me. Could you possibly be in the wrong cabin?"

I did, of course, have the Mace in my right hand, ready to spray, and I was on a direct line to the front door.

His head jerked toward me. The remaining color drained from his face. He turned a sickly hue. I thought he was going to faint.

He struggled to his feet, staring at me as if I were the first witch in *Macbeth*.

I know that at times I can be intimidating. I have a Roman-coin profile, dark hair silvered at the temples, jet-black eyes that have seen much and remembered much, and an angular body with a lean and hungry appearance of forward motion even when at rest. However, surely not witchlike. Oh, the right age perhaps, but I feel that I look especially nonthreatening in baggy gray sweats and running shoes.

"Oh, my God, who are you? What the hell are you doing here?"

"Henrietta O'Dwyer Collins," I replied crisply. "I'm a guest of Margaret Frazier's. So I might ask the same of you."

He swallowed jerkily. "A guest . . . oh, Christ. If that isn't my frigging— Sorry. God." He looked past me toward the bedroom. "Where's Aunt Margaret?"

Aunt Margaret. Of course. That's why he looked familiar. That aquiline nose and small, full mouth.

I slipped the keys and Mace canister into the pocket of my sweats.

Craig. Margaret's nephew. "I'm sorry to say she's in the hospital. A heart attack and bypass surgery. But she's . . ."

He wasn't listening.

I felt a quick flare of anger. No wonder Margaret had resisted notifying him.

"I believe she is going to recover quite nicely, in case you're interested."

His eyes blinked. He heard my anger. It took a moment for him to make the connection. "Aunt Margaret . . . oh, I'm sorry." Blank dark eyes finally focused on me. "She's real sick? I'm sorry." He gave me a shamefaced look. "And I'm sorry I scared you. I didn't mean to. Truly, I didn't know you were here. I'm Craig. Craig Matthews."

He lifted a slender, well-manicured hand to massage his temple.

The emerald in a thick yellow-gold ring glittered like putting-green grass on a sunny day.

The bloodstain ran from just above the cuff to his elbow.

He followed my glance.

There are many kinds of silence. Companionable. Hostile. Angry. Shamed. Defeated.

And frightened.

His handsome face crumpled, a mixture of horror and pain and disbelief. He shook his head. "I didn't kill Patty Kay. I didn't do it." It was a husky, broken whisper. Gingerly, he touched the crusted blood with his right hand. His fingers quivered.

His denial echoed in my mind. What had I stumbled into? *I didn't kill Patty Kay.* Did he say it again or did the shocking, frightening phrase simply pulse in my mind?

No wonder Craig Matthews wasn't worried about his aunt. No wonder his demeanor was terrified.

I tensed like a runner awaiting the starter's pistol. My hand closed again around the slender Mace canister. Margaret's nephew or no, if he took a step toward me . . .

Instead, he backed to the chair and sank into it again. Dully, he looked up at me. "You know Aunt Margaret?"

I said nothing.

He blinked; his mouth twisted in a small embarrassed smile. "Sorry. I can't hold anything in my head. You said you were her guest. Sure."

He was a man in shock. Talking about the price of chicken feed while the sky fell.

He shook his head, as if struggling to clear it, then once again got to his feet, as if belatedly remembering his manners. "I'm sorry. Awfully sorry. I woke you up, frightened you. I didn't mean to. I mean, I didn't see your car. But I didn't look. And it was dark . . . I'll leave."

But once on his feet, he simply stood.

"Where will you go?" I took my hand out of my pocket. I was in no danger from this scared, disoriented young man.

". . . Chattanooga, I guess. I've got an old friend there."

"Do you need a friend?"

"I've got to talk to somebody. I'm in trouble. Big trouble."

He'd whispered, *I didn't kill Patty Kay. I didn't do it.*

Yes, I thought, he probably was in a shitload of trouble.

Killers come in all shapes and sizes. And it is domestic violence that can surprise you every time.

He didn't look like a man who'd killed a woman.

I wasn't afraid of him.

I know when to be scared.

He glanced toward the door, then back at me. His shoulders sagged. "I don't know what to do. I don't know what the *hell* to do."

There was the tiniest suggestion of a plea in his voice, perhaps a flicker of hope in his eyes.

I knew what I was hearing, the tones of a man accustomed to letting someone else run the show.

I wondered when I'd been transformed from a Shakespearean witch to a succoring figure. If he were older, he would know better than to assume age renders its possessor harmless. But he was seeing me now as not only harmless but someone to help. The friend of his aunt.

I'd spent a lifetime among take-charge men. I'd butted heads with most of them. But even while insisting upon my rights and prerogatives, I'd admired their verve and spirit and, yes, the automatic masculine presumption of each and every one that by God, I'm in charge here. It's a factor that makes news pools a living hell for real reporters. The testosterone level among newspapermen beggars description. As a class, it's also true of lawyers.

So winsome I'll-leave-it-up-to-you types don't impress me.

But I hadn't spent a lifetime asking questions to be able to ignore what was obviously a life-and-death drama. And this was Margaret's only living family, the son of her beloved sister.

He was gazing at me with pleading spaniel eyes.

It wouldn't hurt to talk to him. Talk didn't commit me to anything. Not a single damn thing. After all, my night's sleep was already ruined. Moreover, I had to find out if I could help Margaret's kin.

And, yes, I admit it, I wanted to find out what had happened to Patty Kay. *Who, what, when, where, why, how*—they pulse in my blood and in my brain. Maybe I should have them scored on my tombstone. Or, *She Came, She Asked, She Wrote.*

So that's how it began for me.

I said, "Who's Patty Kay?"

"My wife."

"What happened to her?"

The dazed, uncomprehending look returned to his eyes. "I came home and—and I went in the house and called out. But she didn't answer. I went upstairs. She wasn't anywhere. But she'd told me to come home. I mean, I thought she had. There was this message from her. But maybe it wasn't from her because—"

I held up a hand. "Wait a minute. You came home." I didn't yet know where "home" was. There was so much I didn't know. But it was critical to keep him focused. "You looked for Patty Kay. What happened then?"

"I went in the dining room. Everything was ready for the party." Again disbelief flared in his frightened eyes. "We were going to have a party tonight. The table was set. The china. The silver. Crystal. Perfect, the way Patty Kay always has everything. So I thought she was probably in the kitchen and just hadn't heard me. She cooks—Patty Kay always cooks everything herself. She doesn't believe in having it done by a caterer. She always laughs and says she's a better cook than any caterer. And she is. So I thought she was in the kitchen and I went in there and that's when I knew something was wrong, really wrong. Cheesecake was all over everything."

"Cheesecake?"

"Patty Kay's cheesecakes are famous—chocolate wafer crumbs and butter and creme de menthe and . . . Somebody'd taken the cake pan and thrown it up and there was stuff on the ceiling and the cabinets and the floor, and the pan with the chocolate—the one on the stove—had burned black. The smell was awful. And there was creme de menthe splashed on the floor and a whole bottle of creme de cacao emptied out too. I mean, it scared me. What the hell was going on? And Patty Kay wasn't anywhere. Then I saw the back door was open. I wasn't really thinking. I started for the door, too fast I guess, and I skidded and slipped." He looked down at his trouser leg. "Got the stuff on my hands too. The liqueur. I picked up a towel and wiped my hands off, then I went out the back door. Everything looked okay, like it always did." His voice lifted with remembered astonishment. "The deck and the pool. And nobody was out there. That meant Patty Kay had to be in the playhouse—if she was anywhere. So I ran down there."

He came to a stop. His fingers gripped the worn sides of the armchair.

"What did you find?"

Just for an instant his eyes met mine. They were worried, uncertain, frightened—and sickened. "I—" He yanked a handkerchief from his pocket and wiped his face. "I've got to have something to drink."

I went into the kitchenette, grabbed a glass, and filled it with tap water. He was close behind me. But I wasn't frightened. He scarcely knew I was there.

I held out the glass to him.

He took it and drank in long, greedy gulps. He slumped down at the rickety pine table. Sweat beaded his face. An unhealthy reddish flush overlay the paleness.

I took the seat opposite him.

I didn't repeat my question.

But we both knew it wasn't going to go away.

He didn't look at me. He spoke as if each word were a burden. Was he picking his way or was the recollection too painful?

"I ran down the path. The playhouse door was partially open. But when I pushed, it didn't move. I kept shoving and shoving. Finally I squeezed inside." He shuddered. "You don't ever think that something like this can happen to you. Not—not murder."

He stared down at the table, but I knew that wasn't what he saw.

"The door wouldn't move because Patty Kay was bunched up on the floor behind it. I got down on my knees. I lifted up her head"— His voice cracked. His fingers sought his blood-encrusted shirt—

"and her face . . . there was blood—" He buried his face in his hands.

"Why didn't you call the police?"

His hands fell away. His head jerked toward me. "How'd you know—"

"You're here. You ran. Why?"

"Because—" His eyes flickered away.

I leaned forward.

"The siren. I heard a siren. Coming closer and closer. I knew it was coming there."

"Why did you run?" I insisted.

His fingers plucked at the bloodied sleeve. "I don't know." There was just a trace of sullenness in his voice. "God, wouldn't you? Come home, find your wife bloody and dead. Hear the cops coming. Why? Why were they coming? And they always blame the husband. Pick up a newspaper, any newspaper. You read about it almost every day. You know that."

I knew it better than he imagined.

But with good reason.

So often, so very often, death wears a familiar face.

Of course, those statistics are changing. We live now in a drive-by-shooting society. More and more often death is a stranger. That's why the homicide solve rates have plummeted.

"They'll put me in jail." Fear lifted his voice.

"They certainly will if they pick you up as a fugitive, Craig. You must go back."

Like a bereft child, he looked at me. "What am I going to tell them?"

"Whatever your lawyer advises you to tell them."

"Lawyer?"

"Don't you have a lawyer?"

He shrugged. "Not me. Patty Kay does. Mr. Fairlee."

I felt like a kindergarten instructor. "Call him."

Craig massaged his temple. "He doesn't like me."

I waited.

"He—he thought Patty Kay and I got married too quick." He didn't look at me.

Something interesting there. Why shouldn't Patty Kay's lawyer like him?

"You must know other lawyers."

Craig's head jerked up. "Oh, yeah, sure. One of the guys I play poker with. I'll call him." He looked around the room.

"I've got a cellular phone in my car. I'll get it."

When I came back into the cabin with the phone, he took it obediently.

He held the handset tightly, punched in the numbers. "Desmond, this is Craig. Listen—" He broke off, his eyes widening.

When he spoke again, his voice shook. "No, no, I haven't seen the news. No. Oh, God . . . no, no, I didn't do it, I tell you. I didn't kill her. I don't know what happened. I found her this afternoon, and" —he swallowed and nodded—"yeah, yeah, I want to come home but" —he shuddered—"no, no, I didn't run away. I—I was supposed to—I came to see my aunt. She has a cabin near Monteagle. I was upset, I didn't know what to do. So I thought I'd talk to my aunt."

He carefully did not look my way.

I watched him with a good deal of interest. Quite a nifty little liar under pressure.

". . . in the morning at your office? Yeah, I can be there by nine. You'll talk to the police for me?"

I could imagine the lawyer's call: "My client is quite willing to cooperate with the authorities . . . in shock from the brutal slaying of his beloved wife . . . fled the scene of such horror to seek family support . . . surely that's an understandable human reaction, nothing sinister at all . . . will be willing to talk with the police at my office at . . ."

Unaware, of course, that Patty Kay's husband's clothing was bloodstained, and dealing with an obviously affluent member of the community and without eyewitnesses, the police would be patient.

When he ended the connection, my visitor reluctantly turned to face me.

"Your aunt?" I asked quizzically.

His eyes slid away. "Sorry." Then he visited me with a rueful, studiously charming glance. No doubt it had worked for him for a long time. Now it was habitual. Only with women, of course. "Aunt Margaret's all the family I have. I wish you were my aunt too," he said in a rush.

It was designed to evoke sympathy.

It didn't.

But Margaret is my friend. There was no way she could help her nephew now.

I could.

He took a deep breath, started to push back his chair. "Well," he said awkwardly, "thank you for helping me. I'll go now. There's a motel—"

"That's all right. You can sleep on the couch."

He accepted. Which didn't surprise me.

And stood by while I made his bed. Which didn't surprise me either.

As I turned to go to the bedroom, he said, "Listen, thanks for everything, Mrs. . . ." He didn't remember my name. But then, he had plenty on his mind.

"Mrs. Collins. My friends call me Henrie O."

"Henrie O. That's nice. Good night, Henrie O."

This time I did close the door to the bedroom behind me. I also wedged a straight chair beneath the knob. I may sometimes be a soft touch.

I'm not a damned fool.

3

I wouldn't have been surprised if he'd slipped away in the night. That was my first thought when I awoke. I had no confidence in Margaret's nephew. But Craig Matthews still slept heavily on the couch, his hair tousled, one arm flung over his face, the blankets dragging the floor. He looked vulnerable and utterly innocent.

Isn't that true of all sleeping creatures?

I can shower, blow-dry my hair, and dress in twelve minutes. When I came out into the living area, Craig was struggling awake.

"I'll get breakfast," I told him briskly. "You'll find shaving cream and a fresh disposable razor in the bathroom. All I can offer in the way of clean clothes is a sweatshirt." It would be large enough because I like them loose and floppy. Clean trousers I couldn't provide.

I'd not brought provisions for visitors, and I incline to a rather spartan breakfast—cereal, applesauce, and coffee. It isn't that I hoard fat grams, but life is a trade-off, and I'll take a hot fudge sundae later in the day over buttered toast anytime.

When Craig joined me, he looked a good deal better than the night before. He still wore the stained trousers, but the sweatshirt was a great improvement over the bloodied shirt. Yet, even freshly shaven and after a few hours of sleep, he still had the air of a stunned survivor.

It didn't, given the fare, take us long to eat.

I refilled our coffee cups.

"It's all so crazy," he blurted out. "I can't believe I'm here. I can't believe what happened to . . ."

I looked sympathetic. I wondered if I was serving as a practice session.

"I was at the store."

"Store?"

"Patty Kay's bookstore."

Hmm. Not *our* bookstore. *Patty Kay's* bookstore.

"Where?"

He looked at me blankly.

"What town?"

"Oh. Yeah. Sure. We live"—He paused, I knew, because Patty Kay no longer lived—"in Fair Haven."

I was familiar with it. Fair Haven is some twenty miles south of Nashville on Hillsboro Pike. It is not only one of Tennessee's loveliest old towns, it is one of its wealthiest. There is a great deal of old money in Fair Haven, and lots of new.

I glanced again at his slacks. Stained or not, they were expensive and well cut.

"Is that how you earn your living? Running the bookstore?"

It shouldn't have been a difficult question.

"Well . . . I mean, I run it for Patty Kay. I used to teach but . . . Actually, she has—*had* lots of investments."

"So the bookstore doesn't have to make money." I know those kinds of booksellers, wealthy people who love books.

"Oh, no. Patty Kay wants"—another sober pause—"always wanted to make money."

Certainly. No one appreciates money more than the rich. But they can afford to indulge hobbies until they become profitable.

"So you were at the bookstore. When?"

"Yesterday afternoon. It was a regular Saturday. Busy. I answered the phone a dozen times. Then somebody hung up when I answered. I didn't think anything about it. A wrong number. Happens sometimes. It rang again. Another hangup. Then I was waiting on a customer. One of the clerks—Amy—answered the next ring. After I made the sale, Amy came over. She said Patty Kay wanted me to pick up a basket of fruit at a shop in Green Hills, then hurry home. So I drove to the shop—"

"Just like that? No, 'Will you please' or 'Could you . . .' Did Patty Kay order you around all the time?"

He didn't like that. His voice became defensive. "She didn't order me around. But, sure, she asked me to do things."

"And you did them."

"Sure. I mean, why not?"

That wasn't for me to say. But, despite all the lip service to androgynous work roles in today's liberated marriages, from my observations most women still handle the domestic chores, and, when they don't, there is a good deal of charm exercised in shifting them. I didn't hear any echoes of charm here.

So what kind of marriage did Craig and Patty Kay Matthews have?

The police would want to know.

I was beginning to have some ideas.

"All right. You went to pick up the fruit."

Puzzlement puckered his face. That, or some artful Method acting. "They didn't have an order. I thought there was maybe a mixup. So I called home—"

Ah, what a dutiful errand boy—

"—and the machine came on." His eyes brightened. "Listen, they'll remember that at the deli, won't they? Patty Kay must have already—" He broke off.

CAROLYN G. HART   22

Because he didn't want to remember? Or did he remember only too well?

"So you started home?"

"Well, I had them fix up a fruit basket. Just in case."

This fellow didn't want to face his wife without a basket of fruit. Not if she wanted a basket of fruit.

It was further proof of the power Patty Kay exercised over him. I could imagine the cold, jaundiced eyes of a cop listening to this. Margaret's nephew would come off as henpecked at best. Resentful at worst?

Margaret.

"Craig, before you leave, you should phone your aunt. It certainly won't do for her to hear about Patty Kay's death on the morning news. And it will reassure her to speak—"

He abruptly plunked down his cup. Coffee sloshed out. "Yeah, I know. That would be best." He shoved back his chair. "But there isn't time. I told Desmond I'd get to his office by eight. I've got to leave right now, *right* now, to make it. Why don't you call? Tell her everything's going to be okay."

And he was grabbing up his soiled shirt and heading for the door.

I followed him.

He yanked open the door of a new metallic green Porsche that glittered like emeralds in the early morning sun slanting through the branches of a hackberry. I pegged the cost of the car at around $75,000.

Funny, how some people spend their money.

Pots and kettles. After all, how many people does a stained glass window feed? Moral judgments appear easy. Quicksand looks solid. Try walking on it.

The motor growled to life. "Yeah, I've got to drive like hell. But I want to thank you—"

"No problem."

"Uh—"

I could have finished it for him, but I didn't.

"Uh—if the police want to talk to you. I mean, I told Desmond you were my aunt."

Yes, indeed he had.

A quick little lie. But wasn't it simply human nature to try to put a good face on running away? However, it wasn't Craig's only lie.

The trouble with lies is how easily they can be exposed and the mass of detail that must be remembered to deceive successfully. Last night, distraught over his wife's murder, embroiled in telling me what had happened, caught up in talking to the lawyer who made it clear that his flight had made him a suspect, Craig had repeated the lawyer's query, . . . *in the morning at your office? Yeah, I can be there by nine.*

How easily, how quickly this morning Craig changed the time so that he would not have to call his aunt.

Was he afraid that somehow, some way, he would reveal himself to Margaret? Was he fearful of an emotional outburst on her part? Or on his?

I could guess all morning. All I knew with certainty was this young man's penchant for untruths.

And he was asking me for help, asking me in effect to join in a lie.

Why should I?

He looked young and vulnerable. His rosebud mouth drooped. His woeful eyes pleaded.

Margaret's nephew, her only living kin.

Oh, hell. "Honorary aunts aren't unusual. I suppose I could be your Aunt Henrie O."

He shifted the gleaming auto into reverse, flashed me his winsome, charming smile.

As the Porsche's smooth roar faded in the distance, I shook my head. I had a strong sense that Craig Matthews's accomplished smile wasn't going to be enough to help him this time.

And he'd left me the task of calling Margaret. I wondered how often he fobbed off unpleasant tasks on those around him.

Margaret's voice sounded stronger.

I handled it as well as I could, making it clear at the outset that Craig was en route to see the authorities.

"Murdered . . . Henrie O, how dreadful." A thoughtful, somber pause. "He'll be a suspect." It wasn't a question.

"Yes." Margaret and I know the world too well for sugarcoating.

"I met her only twice," Margaret told me, because she knew I needed her help. "A vibrant personality. Forceful. Direct. Quite wealthy. The kind of woman you'd love or hate. No halfway measures. Of course, she married someone like Craig. . . . Nice, but weak. That's the truth about him, Henrie O. Craig isn't strong enough to kill anyone."

Sometimes crimes are committed because the perpetrator is weak. I didn't say so.

But Margaret knows me well. "Henrie O, please. Look out for him. I'll get a lawyer—" Her voice rose.

"Don't borrow trouble, Margaret. Craig's on his way to see a lawyer right now. Perhaps the crime will be quickly solved. Don't worry, I'll keep on top of it."

After I hung up, I didn't take the leisurely ramble in the woods I'd anticipated with such pleasure. Instead, I drove to a gas station/convenience store on the highway. I picked up the Sunday newspaper.

Back at the cabin, I poured another cup of coffee and opened the paper. I looked first at the two-column photograph of Craig Matthews and a strikingly attractive woman in her late thirties. She was slender and athletic, dark-haired with a vivacious smile and a bright, challenging look. Behind her was a pavilion and a lake.

The cutline read: IN HAPPIER DAYS—*Craig Matthews and his wife, Patty Kay, are pictured at the annual Walden School fall picnic last September. Mrs. Matthews, 38, was found slain in their exclusive Fair Haven home on Saturday.*

This story was circumspect:

SOCIALITE DEAD
IN POSH MANSION;
HUSBAND MISSING

Mrs. Craig Matthews, the former Patty Kay Prentiss, was found dead at shortly after 5 p.m. Saturday in her Tudor mansion in Fair Haven.

Alerted by an anonymous phone call, Fair Haven police

found the body of the thirty-eight-year-old socialite in a pool
of blood in the estate playhouse, well known as the scene of
many charitable functions.

Police Chief J. T. Walsh declined to describe the cause
of death. An autopsy is scheduled Monday by the state medical examiner.

Police said repeated efforts to contact Mrs. Matthews's
husband were unsuccessful. A clerk at Books, Books, Books,
the bookstore owned by Mrs. Matthews, said that Mr. Matthews left the store Saturday afternoon, reportedly to pick
up a fruit basket to take to the Matthews home. The couple
apparently had planned to host a dinner party at their home
that evening. Police said the dining room table was set and
preparations for the dinner were under way by Mrs. Matthews when she was slain. Some guests arrived to be greeted
by the police.

Mrs. Matthews was the eldest daughter of a well-
respected and long-established Tennessee family. The first
Prentiss arrived in Fair Haven in 1843. Family members
have included judges, lawyers, physicians, and legislators.
Her father, the late Merriwether Prentiss, served as mayor of
Fair Haven for three terms in the 1970s.

Mrs. Matthews's first marriage, to Stuart Pierce, ended
in divorce. In addition to her husband, Craig Matthews, she
is survived by her daughter, Brigit Pierce, and her sister,
Mrs. Willis Guthrie, both of Fair Haven.

Hmm. Craig hadn't mentioned his stepdaughter, Brigit. Where
was Patty Kay's daughter on a Saturday afternoon? Had Craig run
away, perhaps leaving the girl to discover her mother's corpse? But no,
an anonymous phone call summoned the police. Why hadn't Craig
mentioned Brigit?

It would be interesting to know what the anonymous caller said
to the police.

The Monday-morning update showed a change in tone:

MATTHEWS TELLS POLICE
WIFE WAS ALREADY DEAD

Craig Matthews admitted to police in a Sunday interview that he discovered the body of his wife, Patty Kay Matthews, in their Fair Haven home Saturday afternoon but made no effort to contact authorities.

Desmond Marino, Matthews's attorney, said his client was distraught by the gruesome discovery and he left the home in a daze and went directly to the vacation residence of an aunt, seeking family support. "His aunt urged him to call me and he did so at once. Mr. Matthews was completely shaken and unable to cope with the tragedy. It came as a complete surprise to him that he was being sought by the police. As soon as he realized the situation, he agreed at once to return for an interview and did so Sunday morning. I have here a brief statement from him for the press."

Statement to the press by Craig Matthews: "I came home Saturday afternoon with a fruit basket I thought my wife had ordered. I entered the house. Patty Kay didn't answer my call. I looked upstairs, then downstairs. When I went into the kitchen, I knew something bad had happened. Our kitchen had been vandalized. I ran outside. The playhouse door was open. I found my wife's body there, on the floor. I knelt and tried to lift her and then I knew she was dead. There was blood everywhere. I didn't see a weapon.

"It was such a shock, I ran outside. I don't know what I was thinking, but I wanted to go for help. I got in my car and drove to my aunt's vacation cabin. I have tried to be helpful to the police. I know of no reason why anyone would murder my wife. I ask anyone who has any information to please report to the police or to my lawyer, Desmond Marino."

Marino declined to answer further questions, saying his client was doing everything possible to help the authorities.

Police Captain J. T. Walsh said the investigation was continuing.

Funeral arrangements for Mrs. Matthews are pending.

I put down the paper and dug my Sony Walkman out of my gym bag. I turned it on, found a Nashville news station. It came as no surprise a few minutes later when the announcer said that Fair Haven police had arrested Craig Matthews late Sunday evening. They had charged him with murder in the death of his wife.

I reached for my cellular phone, then paused. I had a decision to make.

What was I going to tell Margaret?

More important than that, what—if any—action was I prepared to take?

I was not surprised at the arrest.

But an arrest didn't mean Craig Matthews was guilty.

I found it intriguing, to say the least, that Craig received two phone calls at the bookstore where the caller promptly hung up.

Aaah, so what, the pro-police view would demand. Who said those phone calls occurred?

Craig Matthews.

But when the clerk answered, there was a message for Craig to pick up the fruit basket and bring it home.

Sure, the police could respond. Mrs. Matthews called. The lack of a basket could simply have been a mistake at the deli. Or perhaps Patty Kay thought she'd ordered the basket and hadn't. There could be lots of explanations. The fact that the store had no record of an order was no proof that the phone call to the bookstore was part of an elaborate plan to frame Matthews.

Because either Craig Matthews was guilty of his wife's murder or he'd been cleverly lured to the death scene.

To me, the strongest argument for Craig's innocence was the Johnny-on-the-spot phone call that brought the authorities to the site just after Craig arrived home.

It wouldn't impress the police.

Police everywhere receive a lot of phone tips. The calls can be accurate as hell, but the callers are not necessarily involved in the crimes they report. Many anonymous tipsters are semi-good citizens. They want to see justice done, but they definitely don't want to get involved.

A simple scenario could account for that phone tip: A neighbor observed Craig's arrival at the house, perhaps heard a noisy quarrel, and called.

A variation on that theme could account for the call even if Craig's story was true: A neighbor came to the house before Craig arrived, found Patty Kay's body, then scurried off to call the police but avoid involvement.

So the phone tip could have occurred whether Craig was guilty or innocent.

But clearly the phone tip could have been part of a clever plan to frame Craig.

I made my decision.

When I called Margaret, I didn't tell her not to worry. She wasn't a fool. But I promised to help Craig.

I changed from my holiday slacks and cotton top to a crimson linen suit with a jewel-necked jacket and a pleated skirt, a crisp white blouse, and matching red pumps. As a fashion writer I once knew would have trilled, "Faux pearl earrings and necklace completed the ensemble." If I do say so myself, I looked elegant and absolutely trustworthy. It took me five more minutes to pack, then I was on the road to Fair Haven and traveling fast.

At the outskirts of Fair Haven, I stopped at a convenience store and bought the afternoon paper.

This headline was crisp:

POLICE ACCUSE
CRAIG MATTHEWS
OF WIFE'S MURDER

Police arrested Fair Haven businessman Craig Matthews, 29, late Sunday evening for the murder of his 38-year-old wife, Patty Kay, after teenage hunters found a pistol linked to her slaying in the brush several hundred yards from Highway 94 near Snell.

Fair Haven Police Chief J. T. Walsh revealed that Mrs. Matthews was shot three times.

Sheriff Coby Trent said Snell residents Michael Bettis, 15, and Jimmy Graham, 17, were shooting squirrels late Saturday afternoon when they saw Matthews discard an object after he stopped on a country road near Highway 94. Sheriff Trent said, "The boys saw the suspect, whom they later identified as Mr. Matthews, get out of a green Porsche carrying a bundle. He unwrapped the bundle, looked around to see if he was observed, then threw a gun into the brush. Mr. Matthews then got into his car and drove off. The boys found the gun and brought it to us."

Chief Walsh said the weapon had been wiped, but the laboratory found a partial print on the bottom of the trigger guard that matched Matthews's right index finger. The bullets which killed Mrs. Matthews were shot from this weapon, the chief said.

Fair Haven attorney Desmond Marino said his client is innocent of the crime.

The murder of the well-known socialite on Saturday shocked residents of the historic community twenty miles south of Nashville. Next-door neighbor Carl Jessop said, "I don't believe he did it. Craig's a really nice, mild-mannered guy. He and Patty Kay got along real well. This has got everybody nuts. Nobody around here even locks their doors in the daytime. But now my wife's scared. Who'd want to shoot Patty Kay?"

Several neighborhood residents declined to be quoted, but their reports tallied with that of Jessop. All appeared shocked and surprised at Matthews's arrest.

Services for Mrs. Matthews will be at 10 a.m. Wednesday in St. John's Episcopal Church. The family requests no flowers. Memorials may be made to Walden School.

Craig had said: *There was blood everywhere. I didn't see a weapon.*

Now eyewitnesses claimed they saw him toss away the gun that killed his wife.

Obviously, another lie by Craig.

So what else was new?

In Craig's recital to me there was no mention of a gun or that surreptitious stop.

I didn't feel quite that I had been played for a fool. But I certainly had to accept the fact that Craig Matthews had been less than candid.

The police would argue that the only reason to lie would be guilt.

But it could be fear, came the whip-quick thought.

I lifted an eyebrow. Somewhere within me lurked a champion for Craig Matthews.

Craig Matthews. A civilized, delicate face. And frightened eyes. Not a very truthful man. The police discoveries surely augmented that judgment.

All right. But there were facts in his favor. And being a liar can indicate either poor character or stupidity, but it hardly equates with being a murderer.

I'd driven fast. I was glad. If anything could be done for Margaret's nephew, it had to be done quickly.

As a reporter I learned some horrifying truths about our legal system. I don't call it our system of justice. It is, instead, an often haphazard process relentlessly affected by the participants, who can be bright, stupid, indolent, industrious, incompetent, or brilliant.

If you question that, read some true crime books. Or go down to the courthouse and sit in on a murder trial. Either exposure should scare the bejesus out of you.

Bottom line: The cops wouldn't be trying to clear Craig; they would be busy amassing evidence so the D.A. could get a murder conviction.

I wasn't a cop. Or a private detective.

But there's no law against asking questions.

For whatever reason.

4

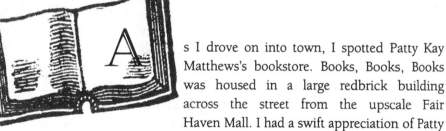

s I drove on into town, I spotted Patty Kay Matthews's bookstore. Books, Books, Books was housed in a large redbrick building across the street from the upscale Fair Haven Mall. I had a swift appreciation of Patty Kay's abilities as a businesswoman. Malls aren't it in the 1990s. Separate shops with plenty of parking and easy access definitely are.

It was another couple of miles on tree-shaded Henry Avenue to the turnoff that led directly to the heart of old Fair Haven. As I neared downtown, plenty of bronze plaques attested to protected historic homes, both antebellum and Victorian. I parked near the town square. As always, I'm stiff when I first get out of a car after traveling. I gingerly stretched, admiring the worn granite statue of a Confederate soldier and the recently painted brickfront buildings, the colors ranging from apricot to gray to mauve.

I stopped first at a small cottage with a gilt sign proclaiming the Fair Haven Historic Society. I came out with maps, a history, and a quick summary of the efforts that had gone into refurbishing downtown and making it a tourist mecca. Patty Kay Prentiss Matthews's name was all over the brochures.

Fair Haven can't compete historically with neighboring Franklin, of course, home of the Carter House which was so central to the anguishing Battle of Franklin. Five hours of fierce fighting on November 30, 1864, resulted in 6,552 Confederate dead, 2,326 Union dead. But Fair Haven has its own grim stories of war, including brave women who carried information past Union troops beneath hoopskirts and a handsome Confederate spy hung by the Yankees while a sobbing maiden looked on.

Today Fair Haven's nineteenth-century main street was home to antique stores, funky little shops selling everything from handmade quilts to homemade jams and candies, and, of course, to Fair Haven's most prestigious law firms.

The offices of Desmond Marino, Counselor at Law, were on the second floor of a mauve brick building at the corner of Main and First. I opened the frosted glass door and stepped out of the nineteenth into the late twentieth century.

Sometimes it's hard to tell the office of a successful lawyer from the reception area in an upscale funeral home. The same ice-toned gray predominates in the drapes, walls, and carpets, enlivened occasionally by a discreet flash of gold in a vase or painting. The subliminal message is that silver and gold are our ultimate objective, whether in the streets of heaven or on those of earth.

Desmond Marino's Oxxford suit was gray too, with the merest hint of a muted crimson stripe. His Hermès tie was jovial in comparison, a vivid carmine with a gold medallion pattern. One of those absurdly expensive watches glittered on his left wrist.

Marino had an interesting face, part monkey, part raccoon. A bright intelligence was apparent in the coal-dark eyes, wily caution evident in his careful smile.

Not that Marino was smiling overmuch after the initial though suitably muted (the circumstances) warmth of his greeting to Craig Matthews's aunt (me) after his secretary, slim and blond in a gray silk sheath, showed me in.

I hoped to find out a great deal from Desmond Marino, but there was one urgent question.

"Where is Patty Kay's daughter?"

"Oh, Brigit's okay. She's home."

"In that house. By herself?"

Desmond Marino looked surprised. "She lives with her dad. Didn't you know that?"

Fake aunthood obviously was going to have many pitfalls. "Oh, I suppose I misunderstood a recent letter from Craig. I thought Brigit had moved back with her mother and Craig."

"Not likely."

I needed to get away from this subject pronto. I managed a smile. "I'm so glad I misunderstood. So there's no one at the house now?"

"That's right. Unless I can get bail for Craig."

"What are the chances?"

Marino waggled his hand. "Maybe so, maybe no. Judge Lehman's hard to figure. We're on his docket for tomorrow. The thing of it is, Craig's in a tough spot, Mrs. Collins. Not only did the police find the murder weapon where he'd dumped it, they've got the shirt he wore that day and it's—"

"Bloodstained. I know."

"The gun is his, one of a pair of Smith and Wesson .38 handguns he and Patty Kay owned. And his footprints are all over the place in the kitchen and the playhouse."

"How about Patty Kay's footprints?"

The lawyer looked puzzled.

I was patient. "In the kitchen. Are her footprints in the mess from the cheesecake? And how about on the path to the playhouse?"

"That damned cheesecake."

It wasn't responsive to my questions but the exasperation in his voice intrigued me. I would pursue it in a moment. Right now I wanted to know if Patty Kay's shoes had also tracked sticky remnants of the dessert.

I repeated my questions.

"How would I know?" He was perplexed.

"Haven't you been to the crime scene?"

He looked horrified. "God, no. That's for the police."

This man wouldn't win anybody's defense-lawyer-of-the-year award with that attitude.

"Mr. Marino, at this moment the police are looking solely for evidence to convict my nephew Craig. Nothing else interests them."

Anybody who thinks cops carefully peruse all evidence, keeping an open mind as to a suspect's guilt as they do so, probably believes politicians seek the greater good instead of snapping at the best deal for their constituency (i.e., themselves). Once an arrest is made, the cops are trying to build a case. All other evidence is extraneous.

"Mrs. Collins," Marino inquired briskly, "what does that have to do with Patty Kay's footprints?"

"Quite a bit. If her footprints are in that mess, obviously the cheesecake was thrown at the ceiling while she and her murderer were in the kitchen. If there are no footprints from Patty Kay, what does that tell us?"

It didn't come quickly enough to make him a star pupil, but it came. "She wasn't in the kitchen when the cheesecake splattered?"

I nodded encouragingly. "And?"

"If she wasn't in the kitchen . . ." His brow crinkled. "Was she already shot?"

"Yes."

"But why would anybody throw . . ." His face flattened out like a man who'd just taken a fist in the gut. "Oh, God."

Flashing neon couldn't have made it clearer that the lawyer had a story to tell about Patty Kay's famous dessert. "So what about the cheesecake?"

"It was bad enough—what I thought before. But now . . ." The bright eyes peered at me unhappily. "You see, I was afraid the police would hear about last week and—and think Patty Kay and Craig had a fight."

I waited.

Marino's face screwed up in concentration. "We play poker once a month." He looked up, down, away, but, finally, reluctantly, he continued. "A bunch of guys. We played last week and"—he eyed me doubtfully—"well, Craig drank a little too much. I mean, Craig's not really a big drinker, Mrs. Collins. But everybody overdoes it sometimes."

Everybody *doesn't* overdo it sometimes. But that wasn't the point here. "All right. Craig had too much to drink that night. What happened?"

"Last week the game was at my house. The wives do the desserts, but I'm a bachelor, so Patty Kay sends over her cheesecake. And Craig —oh, Christ—he got loud and obnoxious and started making up limericks about what he'd like to do with Patty Kay's cheesecake, how he hated the damn thing and how she always insisted he eat two damned pieces."

Cheesecake on the ceiling.

To the police, it would be one more indicator of Craig's guilt. The husband loathes his wife's cheesecakes. He comes home, they quarrel, he takes the despised dessert and hurls it around, then chases his wife to the playhouse. There he guns her down.

But there was another possibility, and it was this interpretation that was spooking Marino. Someone at last week's poker party—or someone who'd heard the story of Craig's indiscretion from a poker player there that night—set up the death scene to look exactly like the result of a domestic flap.

"Who played poker that night?"

Marino hunched over his desk. He picked up a letter opener, held it like a lifeline. But, grudgingly, he gave me the names.

I got out my notepad and wrote them down: Stuart Pierce, Willis Guthrie, David Forrest. And, of course, Marino and Craig.

One name I recalled from the news stories. "Stuart Pierce. Patty Kay's first husband?"

"Yes." Marino looked like a root canal would be more fun than my questions.

"So Husband One and Husband Two were in the same poker group. Chummy."

"Fair Haven's a small town, Mrs. Collins."

"I'd still say that was chummy. One of those so-called amicable divorces?" An oxymoron of the first order.

"Uh. No."

I waited.

The beautifully tailored suit barely moved when the lawyer shrugged. "Well, you know what Patty Kay was like."

That was the problem, of course. I had no idea—or at least only the dim beginnings of an idea—about the late Patty Kay Prentiss Pierce Matthews. But Craig's aunt couldn't admit that. Quite.

"I'd met her only a few times," I responded blandly.

"What you saw was what you got, Mrs. Collins." His face softened. "Patty Kay never did anything by halves. Ever. When we were little kids, she climbed highest in the tree or set off the most firecrackers. We got a little older and she danced the most dances. And that woman was crazy about Stuart. Nuts about him."

I couldn't quite identify the tone in his voice. Remembered anger? Wry dismay?

"Anyway, she came on too strong. She overwhelmed Stuart, never left him enough turf." Now he spoke briskly, telling a familiar tale. "Patty Kay was devastated when he walked out on her. And when he married Louise within a year, well, she took it hard. She couldn't stand being single. She was humiliated. She met Craig at a party at Cheekwood; three weeks later they got married."

"On the rebound."

He tugged at his collar, avoided looking at me. "I don't mean she didn't care about Craig. I think she did. But . . ."

Murky waters here. Had Craig realized he was a make-do replacement for an adored husband? How would that affect a man? Or had

Craig deliberately taken advantage of an emotionally distraught woman, picking up a very rich wife with little effort? Had Patty Kay decided that Craig married her for her money? Because it was quite clear who had the big bucks.

Some questions Craig's aunt couldn't ask.

Some I could.

"This quick marriage—is that the reason Patty Kay's lawyer"—I frowned, trying to remember the name—"doesn't like Craig?"

Marino looked embarrassed. "Mr. Fairlee's older. Very formal. He thought . . . well, Craig's younger than Patty Kay. And he quit teaching right after they got married and just worked at the bookstore. . . ."

I got it. Patty Kay's lawyer thought a younger man married an older woman—no matter how attractive—for her money.

I let Marino off the hook. "Who was Patty Kay's best friend?"

He thought about it. "Gina Abbott. She's an interior decorator here in town. They grew up together."

"Patty Kay's sister lives here too, doesn't she?"

"Right." There was no inflection at all.

"Mrs. Willis Guthrie." I recalled it from the news story. "The Willis Guthrie at the poker party. Is that her husband?"

"Yes. Willis is an accountant. Down the hall from me."

The little poker group got more interesting by the moment. "Were Patty Kay and her sister on good terms?"

Marino's gaze dropped. He studied the letter opener like an archeologist with a newfound artifact. "Patty Kay and Pamela were not close."

Hmm.

Finally he looked up at me. "Mrs. Collins, do you really think somebody knew about Craig's smarting off at poker and that somebody deliberately threw that stuff to make it look like Craig and Patty Kay had a fight?"

"Somebody" was such a nicely vague, undamning term. The lawyer didn't ask me if I thought a poker player had done it—or someone who'd heard the tale from that exclusive group.

There's more than one way to answer a question. I responded with one of my own. "You're Craig's lawyer. Do you believe he murdered his wife?"

"No, ma'am." His response was muted but definite. "No. Craig says he's innocent. I believe him."

"Why?"

He squinted pensively. "I've known Craig for five years. I've never seen him lose his temper. Not once. And that cheesecake—that sounds like a slambang, out-of-control fight happened there." He shook his head violently. "No. Not Craig. And besides, there isn't any motive. Oh, the cops probably think it's money. Patty Kay's money. There's a lot of it. Several million. And Craig probably gets a third. But he doesn't even think about money."

I eyed the lawyer carefully. Naiveté didn't become him. It's fairly easy not to think about money when married to pots of it. But the possibility of losing that status might have brought it sharply to Craig Matthews's mind.

And even easygoing people can go berserk—with enough provocation.

The problem was simply that I had no idea whether there was provocation.

I doodled a little on my notepad, a series of footsteps. "Either Craig lost his temper, threw the cake around, and then shot Patty Kay, or someone used guile and care and a great deal of thought to tangle him in a web of circumstantial evidence."

"That's a pretty sickening idea."

"Murderers generally are not very attractive people."

His mobile face scrunched up in distress. "Oh, God," he repeated. "What can we do?"

I told him.

5

A big city jail—the smell, the sights, the sounds —can make you want to cash in your card as a human being to spend your time with a higher order. Like snakes. Or weasels. Or maybe a convivial road crew of leprosy-carry-ing armadillos.

In comparison, the Fair Haven city jail was a palace. Three blocks from Main Street, it was a compact two-story redbrick colonial build-ing with a shining white front door. I stepped inside, noted a golden-oak bench with a stack of recent magazines on an end table, a clean tile floor (this alone was light-years distant from most jails), and a counter opening to the dispatcher's office.

". . . address is 1619 Willow Lane. The alarm went off five sec-onds ago. Check it out and call in."

By the time I reached the counter, the dispatcher was standing behind it, a helpful expression on her face. Fortyish. A fading blonde. Buxom. "Yes, ma'am?" Her greeting was very polite.

I could, after all, easily be one of Fair Haven's well-to-do matrons, reporting a lost dog or seeking a permit for a fund drive.

"I'm Mrs. Collins, Craig Matthews's aunt. I believe you're expecting me. Mr. Marino called."

She didn't have the blasé weariness of the big city. Her curious eyes swiftly took in every detail of my appearance. I'd make a good story to relate to her family and friends. "Oh, yes, ma'am. If you'll come this way." She moved to the gate beside the counter and held it open for me.

We walked down a short hall. It ended at a metal door. Yes, this was a jail.

She punched buttons on a shoulder-high panel.

Once past that door, the dispatcher led me through a metal detector into a small bare cubicle with two chairs. Here she left me.

I didn't have long to wait. A uniformed officer brought Craig in.

I've never discussed with a criminologist or sociologist the effect of jail uniforms. I suppose their purpose is to make it easy to identify a prisoner. Certainly the uniforms achieve that goal. Bright orange coveralls are distinctive, all right.

And demeaning.

As were the shackles on Craig's wrists and ankles.

He shuffled slowly through the doorway.

The coveralls were too big. He looked skinny and insubstantial. His narrow face was white and strained, his eyes dulled by despair.

It took him a moment to focus on me.

Then he simply stood there.

"Craig, I've talked to Desmond. He's trying to get you out on bail. But I wanted you to know I've come to town to help."

The officer, stocky, blond, and impassive, pointed at the chairs. "You can sit there, Matthews. Ma'am, you've got fifteen minutes."

The officer departed. I wondered if someone stood close to that open doorway to listen or if Craig and I were being taped.

It didn't matter.

I had no secrets. At least, none that I intended to mention here. Craig obediently shuffled to the first chair.

I sat down next to him.

"They think I killed Patty Kay. They think I shot her. They won't *listen* to me." His voice was inexpressibly weary and baffled.

"I know. But Desmond and I believe you. We intend to find out what really happened."

"You've talked to Desmond?"

"Yes. He's given me the keys to your house." Jails, of course, don't permit prisoners to retain personal possessions. The contents of Craig's pockets when he was jailed had been turned over to the lawyer.

"You're going to stay at the house? To help me? Why should—"

"Because Margaret and I are the only family you have. And because I wouldn't leave a maimed dog—even one I've never seen before —caught in a trap."

"A trap?"

"Exactly. A clever, carefully devised, potentially deadly trap."

The muscles in his face flattened. This was a new idea, and the shock devastated him.

"You mean—"

"If you didn't shoot Patty Kay—"

He shook his head violently. The movement made his chains jangle.

"—then you were set up. A diabolical little game of Gotcha. Because if you didn't kill Patty Kay, someone else did. And that person deliberately set out to make you take the blame for your wife's murder. Think about it. The two phone calls with no one on the other end. The message that brought you home. The cheesecake on the ceiling. Your gun. And why did the police arrive on the scene so conveniently? Because somebody called them. All of that tells us a lot."

There was a flash of life in that pale, frightened face. "Like what?"

"The murderer was either at last week's poker party or knows someone who was."

That brought him bolt upright in the chair. "The cheesecake—somebody threw the cheesecake because I—"

"Oh, yes. Of course. But that's not all. The murderer knew where you kept your gun. The murderer knew you well enough to be sure you'd come when Patty Kay called. And you know the murderer well enough to recognize his or her voice."

"Oh, my God." His face crumpled like newspaper left out in the rain.

I glanced at my watch. Twelve minutes left.

"Listen, Craig. We don't have much time."

He didn't look capable of thought. His face was ashen, his eyes blank. I had some urgent, sharp, hard questions for him. But it was better to start slowly.

I leaned close. "When did you leave the bookstore Saturday afternoon?"

He hesitated. His eyelids flickered. "About—about four o'clock."

"Did you go directly to the deli?"

"Yes." He sounded more assured.

"How long does that take?"

"Twenty-five minutes. It's in Green Hills."

The bookstore was on the outskirts of Fair Haven. I would time the drive to the deli in Green Hills, a Nashville shopping center.

"How long were you at the deli?"

"It took a while. Maybe ten, fifteen minutes. See, I was sure they had an order and lost it or something. Because Patty Kay"—he cleared his throat—"didn't make mistakes. At least, not very often."

"So you had them hunt for the order."

"And then, well, I decided I'd better get a fruit basket. I thought maybe it was going to be a gift for Brooke. Brooke Forrest. From the trustees."

"What trustees?"

"Walden School. Patty was president of the board. Brooke—she's a trustee too—headed up a fund drive for the school that brought in almost forty thousand dollars this year. Patty Kay was having the trustees to dinner that night."

My ears always prick up at the mention of money.

"Forty thousand dollars? Where is that money?"

"In the endowment fund, I suppose. They had a big party out at school last week, honoring Brooke."

"Could she have pinched some of it?"

"Brooke?" Astonishment lifted his voice. "No, look, Mrs.—"

"Henrie O," I murmured.

He cleared his throat. "Henrie O."

I hoped he managed not to sound quite so self-conscious when he spoke my name in the future.

"Brooke wasn't handling *cash*. She got pledges, checks, gifts. And besides, forty thousand dollars is peanuts to a Forrest. I mean, Patty Kay's murder couldn't have anything to do with the fund drive. But I thought that might be why Patty Kay wanted the fruit. I thought maybe it was going to be a surprise for Brooke, since the dinner party was a last-minute thing."

The timing of a dinner party hardly seemed a matter of cosmic importance. But nothing in Patty Kay's life that fateful Saturday could be overlooked.

"Really? When did Patty Kay plan it?"

"Friday, I guess. I didn't know about it until I got home from the bookstore Friday afternoon. Patty Kay said she'd changed our play-house tickets—we were supposed to go to *Charley's Aunt* Saturday night—and instead she was having the trustees over."

A spur-of-the-moment dinner party. Interesting. "Why?"

"She didn't say."

"You didn't ask her?"

He shot a glance toward the open doorway, then hunched closer to me. "She wasn't in a good mood Friday."

"What do you mean?"

"She'd been fighting with somebody. Her eyes—Patty Kay's eyes glinted when she was mad and her face turned red." He gave a small shrug. "I thought maybe she and Pamela had gotten into it again."

Pamela. The not-close sister. This, too, needed to be pursued. But time was slipping away. Eight minutes left. So little time. So much that I wanted to know. Like: *Did you love your wife?* But I thought I knew the answer. Craig was distraught, upset, shocked by violent death, but

I had no sense of soul-searing grief. In balance, I had no sense of smoldering anger either.

Right now the last-minute dinner party took precedence.

"Tell me about Walden School."

"Kindergarten through high school. Everybody sends their kids there."

"A private school?"

"Oh, sure."

So, not everybody.

"How many trustees on the board?"

"Six. Including Patty Kay."

I wrote down their names: Desmond Marino, Brooke Forrest, Stuart Pierce, Willis Guthrie, Cheryl Kraft.

Desmond Marino was Patty Kay's old friend.

Brooke Forrest was an active volunteer.

Stuart Pierce was Patty Kay's first husband.

Willis Guthrie was her brother-in-law.

"Cheryl Kraft?" I asked Craig.

"Oh, Cheryl's into everything. Just like Patty Kay and Brooke. She's president of AAUW right now, I think. And she's on the city council. Patty Kay liked Cheryl a lot."

"They were all invited, including husbands or wives?"

"Yes. And the headmaster, Chuck Selwyn."

Seven minutes.

"Okay, Craig. Back to Saturday. What time did you leave the deli?"

"Twenty to five. I noticed the clock on the wall behind the cash register." His face brightened. "I think the lady at the deli'll remember. I mean, I made her kind of mad because I thought they'd lost the order. I was in a hurry. I was afraid maybe I'd taken too long and Patty Kay would be mad. So I drove fast. It was right at five when I got home."

"Was there anything out of the ordinary when you pulled into the driveway?"

"I don't know." He lifted his hands and the manacles rattled. He glared down at the shiny steel peevishly. "Damn things hurt." His tone was plaintive.

"You got home," I reminded him.

"I jumped out of the car and hurried inside. With the basket. And you know the rest." He was suddenly weary.

"No, there's much I don't know. Don't quit now, Craig. Think about what you saw. *Think* about it. Picture it."

He moved restively, the steel shackles clinking, but to my relief he frowned in concentration.

Six minutes.

"Go back to it. You've just walked into the kitchen. Look at the floor. Remember the floor. What did you see?"

"The stuff was so dark against the wood. See, the kitchen's all light golden wood, the cabinets, the floor. There was liqueur splashed on the cabinets and all over the floor by the back door. The creme de cacao bottle was on the floor. The room smelled like a bar. I leaned over and picked up the bottle and put it on the table."

The fly had certainly made it easy for the spider. But there was no point in scolding him now.

"Did you step into the mess?"

"Not then. When you come into the kitchen, our breakfast room is to the right. Straight ahead is the back door, oh, maybe fifteen feet. There are cupboards and counters and the sinks and dishwasher to the left. There's a long built-up thing in the middle of the kitchen. Patty Kay called it a cooking island. It has cupboards above it. The ovens and the microwave are on the wall to the left as you first step inside."

The gourmet cook had apparently enjoyed a luxurious kitchen.

"The liqueurs and cooking stuff were spilled all around the island."

I didn't want to lead my witness, but I had to know. Four minutes to go.

"How many footprints did you see?"

"In the stuff on the floor?"

"Yes."

Abruptly, he shook his head. "There weren't any footprints. Just stuff, splattered."

No footprints at all.

"Okay, Craig. Quick. Where did you keep that gun?"

He flinched.

"Look, I know you found it there—somewhere—and that you took it with you when you ran. And didn't say anything about that little fact when we talked at the cabin. But that's behind us. For now. Where did you keep the gun?"

Two minutes.

He stared at the dull green floor. "In the car pocket."

"The pocket of your Porsche?"

"Yes."

"When did you last see it?"

He lifted bewildered eyes. "I don't know. I never paid any attention. This was a thing Patty Kay had. She said you couldn't tell what might happen out on the road and she wanted each car to have a gun in it."

"So you found the gun. Where?"

He stared down at his manacled hands. "In the grass. Near the playhouse. I picked it up. I didn't know what had happened. I just saw it. I knew it shouldn't be lying there."

One minute.

It wasn't going to be enough.

"Why did you try to hide it?"

His eyes shifted away from mine. His mouth folded in a stubborn line.

"What did you wrap it in?" I persisted.

He didn't answer.

Only seconds left now. I had one more vital question to ask.

"Craig, look at me."

He didn't want to, but slowly, reluctantly, he lifted his head.

The jailer's footsteps sounded in the hall.

"Who would want to kill Patty Kay?"

Something—uncertainty? fear? horror?—flickered in his eyes for just an instant. Then, violently, he shook his head. "It's crazy! I tell you, it's crazy. Nobody'd want to kill her. *Nobody!*"

•   •   •

I followed the dispatcher down the hall. Near the front entrance, I saw gold letters on a door to my right: CAPTAIN J. T. WALSH.

I stopped and knocked.

The dispatcher gave a little gasp. "You can't—"

"Of course I can."

"I'm supposed to—"

Guard the portal, obviously. But the door was already opening.

I held out my hand. "Captain Walsh, I'm Henrietta Collins. Craig Matthews's aunt."

Captain Walsh was tall, dark, lean, clean-shaven, and handsome, a 1950s moviemaker's dream of a policeman. Before Central Casting went in for real faces.

I recognized the type, not common among police. A politico, the kind of cat who would always jump the right way. Not quite smarmy, but close.

His handshake was just right, firm but not too firm.

"Hello, Mrs. Collins. I hope your meeting with your nephew was satisfactory." His voice was smooth and deep.

"Very. I'm confident Craig is innocent, Captain."

"Yes, ma'am." His tone remained polite, his strong-boned face impassive.

I could imagine Walsh's dilemma. He was accustomed to treating the well-to-do inhabitants of Fair Haven with deference. He certainly didn't want to be discourteous to a relative of a rich resident—just in case Matthews did turn out to be innocent. Obviously, the captain had agreed to permit my meeting with Craig in order to remain on good terms with Desmond Marino.

Perhaps I could take advantage of his ambivalence and also of his probable inexperience with murder. I doubted that Fair Haven was a hotbed of violence, either street or domestic.

I smiled up at him. "May I visit with you for a few minutes, Captain?"

His expression didn't change. "Of course, Mrs. Collins." He stepped aside for me to enter his office.

This office, too, was light-years distant from big-city realities. Instead of desks jammed corner to corner or a dingy cubicle that smelled like old cigarette butts, takeout hamburgers, and sweat, Walsh's office was bright and airy. There were framed diplomas on one wall, a large-scale map of Fair Haven on another. The thick scent of cherry pipe tobacco provided a fusty but distinctively masculine aroma. Walsh waited until I was seated in an unexpectedly comfortable chair, then he took his place behind a shiny gray metal desk.

"Captain, I would be very grateful if you would describe the course of your investigation. Beginning with the call that brought your officers to the Matthews home."

He fingered a bright orange manila folder. "The goal of the Fair Haven police is to serve our community, Mrs. Collins. I am happy to make available to you the final report provided to the news media."

With that he flipped open the folder, picked up a computer printout, and leaned across the desk to hand it to me.

I read it swiftly.

There were several interesting items:

A call reporting a homicide at 1903 King's Row Road was received at 5:06 P.M. Saturday by Dispatcher Harriet Keys. The caller spoke in a deep whisper and hung up when asked to repeat the information. Dispatcher Keys contacted car three on patrol in that area. Car three arrived at the Matthews residence at 5:09 P.M. Patrolman Wesley Adkins found the front door open. No one responded to Adkins's repeated calls. He searched the premises and at 5:12 P.M. discovered the body of a middle-aged white female (later identified as Mrs. Patty Kay Prentiss Pierce Matthews) in a structure behind the main house. Patrolman Adkins immediately notified . . .

The timing fit in with my theory that the murderer had watched the house then alerted the police as soon as Craig arrived.

The second interesting item concerned the murder weapon. Not the fragment of Craig's fingerprint found on the trigger rim, but the snag of beige cotton adhering to the gun barrel.

I skipped down the report and continued reading:

With a search warrant, Captain Walsh examined the 1994 Porsche belonging to Craig Matthews. Included in the materials found in the car was a plaid cotton shirt. Bloodstains on it later were identified as matching Mrs. Matthews's blood type. The shirt, which belonged to Mr. Matthews, was stained on the left sleeve from the wrist to the elbow. Fibers of the same composition as the snag of cotton found on the revolver were discovered beneath the driver's seat. Captain Walsh concluded that the suspect wrapped the weapon in a beige cotton article before fleeing the crime scene.

I scanned the rest of it. Not much I didn't know. Cause of death was a gunshot wound in the chest, rupturing the aorta. Wounds in the cheek and shoulder would not have been fatal but contributed to the massive blood loss. The bullets were from a .38 Smith and Wesson revolver identified as belonging to the suspect.

I folded the sheets, put them in my purse. "Chief, who made the call to the police reporting the murder?"

He leaned back in his chair. His face remained agreeable, but disdain flashed briefly in his eyes.

"If we knew who called, Mrs. Collins, it would not be listed as a call from an unidentified person."

"Have you made an effort to discover the caller's identity?"

He nodded amiably. "Of course. We have asked the news media to invite the caller to contact us."

"Has it occurred to you that the caller may have committed the murder after arranging for Craig to conveniently arrive on the scene?"

"In police work, it is extremely common to receive tips from people who don't want to be involved, Mrs. Collins. It seems quite probable that someone came to that house, discovered Mrs. Matthews's body, knew the police must be called, but chose not to get dragged into our investigation."

"Do you know that Craig received two uncompleted calls at the bookstore and that immediately after that a clerk received the message asking him to pick up a fruit basket and bring it home?"

His tone was patient. "There is no confirmation of the purported hangups. But even if they occurred, that kind of thing happens all the time. A wrong number. Caller hangs up. Redials. Makes the same mistake. Hangs up again. Those calls prove nothing. As for the fruit basket"—he shrugged—"there's no proof at all that the caller wasn't Mrs. Matthews." He picked up a silver pen, rolled it in his fingers. "Has it occurred to you, Mrs. Collins"—there was only a shadow of an edge to his tone—"that the mixup over that fruit basket may have set off the quarrel?"

"What quarrel?"

"The quarrel between Mr. Matthews and his wife. Obviously, he came home and a violent argument ensued. Maybe it made him mad that she called and treated him like an errand boy. Apparently, she was good at that. Or maybe there was a fruit basket somewhere else and she was furious he didn't go to the right store. We'll never know exactly what happened. But anybody can see that they had a real row and he went crazy. He threw the cooking stuff around, then stalked after her to the playhouse and shot her."

"When did he get the gun?"

"He was mad. He stormed outside. He kept his gun in the glove compartment. He got it, ran back through the house to the playhouse. Bang." His tone was impatient.

"Captain, do me a favor. Picture somebody tossing all that food around. Why didn't Patty Kay have sticky stuff all over her? At the very least, there should have been some on her shoes."

He shrugged. "Maybe she flounced out of the kitchen and he threw the stuff after she left because she'd made him mad. We don't know. We do know that he'd made it clear he was sick and tired of that cheesecake. It's one of those things that happens between couples where the object itself seems absurd to have caused trouble. It happens all the time."

I didn't try to argue. Walsh's mind was made up. But the fallacy— assuming you believed Craig's estimate of his time of arrival—was clear. If Craig arrived home at five o'clock and the anonymous call to the police was made at six minutes after five, there wasn't time for Craig and Patty Kay to have quarreled and for Craig to have shot her and left before this mysterious passerby happened to discover her body and made the call to the Fair Haven Police Department.

Proving the time Craig arrived home would be a strong argument for the defense.

But would a jury buy into it in the face of the bloodied shirt, his flight, and his clumsy attempt to dispose of the murder weapon?

Walsh glanced, not too obviously, at his watch.

"Captain, I don't wish to take up too much of your time. I just have a few more questions. . . ."

"Yes, ma'am."

"Has the article in which the revolver was wrapped been found?"

"No."

"Were any traces of that fiber found in Craig's car?"

"Yes. Beneath the driver's seat."

"Did the boys who saw him throw the gun away have any idea what it was wrapped in?"

"They said it was some kind of cloth."

I nodded and slipped my notebook into my purse. "I won't take up any more of your time, Captain. I'm certain your department conducts investigations in the most exemplary manner. So, if you would let me view the photographs made at the scene of the crime, I would be most grateful."

"I can do better than that." He rose, picking up the folder. "I'll provide you with a set—with the understanding, of course, that these are being made available to the family and may not be released to the news media."

And that's how I came out of the Fair Haven police station with a set of photographs of both the playhouse and the kitchen.

As I dropped them on the car seat next to me, I wondered if Lawyer Marino had made a similar request. If so, he hadn't mentioned it. Just how hard was he working to protect his client's interests?

6

ing's Row Road curved atop a ridge in Fair Haven's finest residential area. Limestone fences marked the boundaries of the half-acre and full-acre lots. Through the stands of huge chinkapin oaks and mossy-trunked hackberries on both sides of the street, I glimpsed elegant homes.

I drove past 1903 King's Row Road. The street curved. Around the curve, to my surprise, cars were parked bumper to bumper in front of a gray Cape Cod.

A navy Lincoln Town Car nosed close behind me.

I turned into the drive of the house across the street from the Cape Cod.

The Lincoln swept past. It parked in the turnaround where the street dead-ended.

As I was backing out of the drive, I saw a thirtyish woman in linen slacks and jacket get out of the car. She reached inside, bringing out a covered casserole dish.

The somber set of her face made clear the reason for the cars.

Cars gather for parties and for deaths.

King's Row Road was surely having more than its share of heartbreak and loss.

A time to be born, and a time to die.

As my MG made the curve, I hoped that the gathering at the Cape Cod was a celebration of a life well- and fully-lived. Death is always sad because it is final, but doubly hard when death strikes early, as it had with Patty Kay Matthews.

There were no cars parked in front of the Matthews house.

I couldn't help but mark the contrast.

Because Craig Matthews was in jail for the murder of his wife.

Anger flickered inside me. Craig was weak, yes, and foolish, but he deserved time to grieve and friends to grieve with him.

I slowed on the narrow blacktop. Across the street, a teenage boy on a riding mower turned his head to look sharply my way. Of course he was interested in anyone coming to the house of a murdered neighbor.

He watched as I turned into the drive to 1903. The entrance to the Matthews domain was marked by a pair of limestone pillars topped by crossed marble tennis rackets. Anybody for tennis? Obviously, yes. The house number was deeply carved into the granite lintel.

The drive led up to a magnificent Tudor house. It was a beautifully preserved example of the architecture favored by the wealthy in the 1920s. The sharply peaked gables would be a roofer's nightmare, and the half-timbering made me itch to quote Shakespeare. The vibrant English ivy was trimmed back to reveal the antique brickwork. An immense Tudor arch framed the front door. All the house lacked were turrets and Errol Flynn with a sword.

The main stem of the drive continued beyond the house to a more recent but similarly styled expanse of garages. It seemed a little like replicating Stratford-upon-Avon for use as a parking space.

I turned the MG into the circular terrazzo drive and parked by the front door.

Huge terra-cotta urns filled with brilliant purple and gold pansies stood on either side of the shallow front steps. They added a welcome touch of color to the dark swaths of ivy. It was almost balmy, but the air had a cool underside, reminding me that April weather in Tennessee can be treacherous. There was no wind. The sounds of life and movement in the neighborhood—the hum of the mower, the slam of another car door up the street, the yapping of an excited dog—seemed far away. I felt caught up in the somber quiet of spent violence.

As I walked toward the door, black wood in a purplish shadow, I was aware of being an intruder, an intruder intent upon pillage. Not, of course, in a literal sense. But I intended to wrest secrets from this house. Before I was done, I hoped to find out who Patty Kay Matthews was and why she died.

I turned the key Desmond Marino had given me in the lock. It stuck for an instant. I had a sudden fanciful feeling that the house was shuttered against me, loath to yield its grim knowledge.

"Nonsense."

I said it aloud, as much to dispel the brooding quiet as to reaffirm my rationality. I twisted the key hard. The lock clicked and the knob turned.

My discomfort was easy to understand. Violent death imbues its surroundings with dread and horror, forever casting a bloody shadow in our memory. Think of the stained passageway in Holyroodhouse in Edinburgh, or the chill when you pass the former Texas School Book Depository in Dallas.

The huge wooden door swung noiselessly on its gleaming bronze hinges. I stepped into a baronial entrance hall with hand-troweled stucco walls and a dark parquet floor. Dark wooden beams increased the gloom. Straight ahead rose the stairway. Massive arches opened on either side. It was as welcoming as a crypt.

I switched on a light.

And looked straight into huge, dull dark eyes.

The moosehead struck a jarring note, and not simply because

stuffed wildlife isn't politically correct these days. The nineties, after all, is the environmental decade. But this extraordinary—and huge—example of the taxidermist's big-game artistry was mounted eye level beside the arch to my right.

There was an odd scent I wouldn't care to identify. It was mixed with the sweet smell of ripening fruit in the pink-cellophaned wicker basket that sat on a butler's table to the left of the arch. Craig's dutifully delivered gift basket.

My eyes swung again to the mounted head. It was impossible to enter the living room of the house without engaging the forever-stilled glance of the moose. Casually snagged on the immense spatulate antlers was an eclectic variety of headgear, two billed caps, a gardener's straw with a chartreuse tie, a filmy wisp of patterned burnt-orange silk, a round yellow rainhat, a high-crowned silver-trimmed black sombrero, and a bright red swim cap.

The moose's bulbous nose was molting. One glass eye tilted, giving him a rakish air.

It was as impudent as an elegantly thumbed nose.

No decorator devised his positioning as a hat rack of first resort and an inanimate majordomo without peer.

No, this was Patty Kay speaking.

That Craig had a hand in decorating this house wasn't worth considering. I'd talked to him enough, even in his present distraught state, to know that Margaret's nephew was neither ironic nor clever. Nor especially self-confident.

Whoever chose this magnificent example of jubilant raffishness was most assuredly all three.

I was smiling as I set out on my survey of the house. It didn't seem half so gloomy now.

Unconventional touches were everywhere.

The living room, in addition to a white Steinway baby grand and a fabulous collection of Ming vases, contained a shiny bronze framework supporting a silk-cushioned swing. Shades of Stanford White's obsession.

The dining room was through the archway to the left of the main entrance hall. Past the stairs and down the hall, I saw a door that likely led to the kitchen. But that would come later. In the dining room, the mahogany Georgian-style table was still eerily set for a sumptuous dinner. Waterford crystal and Limoges china glittered in the diamond-bright light cast by the seven-tiered chandelier overhead. Utter elegance.

In saucy and deliberate contrast, one wall was covered with vivid but painfully amateurish paintings of fruits and vegetables and something that looked vaguely like a spotted cow. The initials PK were blazoned in electric pink in the lower right-hand corner of each painting.

I could almost hear a ripple of delighted laughter.

And I did hear, sharp and startling, the front doorbell. I hesitated for only an instant—the interloper with chutzpah to the max—then walked swiftly to the main hall. I opened the door.

"Cr—" A tall, anorexic-thin, metallic blonde stared at me in surprise. "Oh. Hello. I'm Cheryl Kraft from next door." She pointed vaguely to her right. "I saw the car. Knew it wasn't Jewel." She blinked. "My maid. Patty Kay's maid. Thought it was Craig." A shimmering ivory silk blouse was loosely tucked in burgundy linen trousers that sagged against her bony hips.

"Craig isn't home yet." I held open the screen. "Won't you come in? I'm Craig's aunt, Henrietta Collins."

That put her at ease. Aunts she could do. She stepped inside. "Good of you to come," Cheryl murmured. She clasped my hands in hers, but her eyes slipped swiftly past me toward the closed kitchen door. "I won't keep you. Actually, I'm doing a Paul Revere. Calling everyone to arms. I'm going house to house, inviting everyone in the neighborhood to come to my house. Tonight. At eight. Everyone but the poor Hollises, of course. We've got to find out what's happening, how we can help dear Craig. Of course, we all know the police position is *absurd*. We must take action. Murder! I can't believe it. Why, none of us even have alarm systems. We've never needed them. Not in Fair Haven. Half the time I don't even lock my doors! But two alarm companies called me this morning. Dreadful. Just like vultures. But my daughter Phoebe called from New York, insisting I order an alarm today." She gave my hands a swift, encouraging squeeze. "I'm so glad you've come," she gushed, then whirled and pushed through the screen, pausing just long enough on the top step to call out, "I'll look for you at eight—and please bring Craig. If he can come."

I watched her walk down the drive and cross the street. She waved at the boy on the mower and walked briskly toward the front steps of the colonial.

She hadn't given me time to answer. But I'd be there.

I closed the door. Toward the back of the house, a door opened to the outside. A telephone and answering machine sat atop another butler's table near a door to the kitchen. A woman's cotton madras patchwork purse, jaunty for spring, sat by the telephone.

The red message light blinked seven times in rapid succession, paused, blinked again.

I reached for the purse first. I lifted out a cream leather billfold. Inside, I found Patty Kay's driver's license, an astonishing array of credit cards, and sixty-three dollars in cash. A lemon lace handkerchief, a crystal vial of Mondi, Visine eyedrops, a sack of sugarless candies, loose coins, a used bridge tally, a column raggedly torn from a newspaper. I looked at the piece from the newspaper carefully, but it was merely a review of a new biography of Edith Wharton. A portion of an ad for swimsuits was on the other side. Lipstick, compact, makeup brush. An emery board. An address book. I flipped through it. So many names. Too many names. But the last page, entitled Useful Numbers, was useful indeed.

I opened my own purse and jotted down these names and numbers:

LAVERNE—9 a.m. Wednesdays—555-HAIR
JEWEL—Tuesdays, Fridays—555-7769
GINA—555-3781 Tennis 9 a.m. Thursday
BROOKE—555-4239 Tennis 9 a.m. Thursday
EDITH—555-1463 Tennis 9 a.m. Thursday
SCHOOL—555-5656

I returned the address book, unzipped a side pocket. A photo packet. Photos of Craig, of Craig and Patty Kay, of the two of them and a skinny teenage girl with sunlight glinting on her silver braces. Patty Kay's daughter Brigit, no doubt. I tucked the album back in the pocket. My fingers touched another slick surface. I pulled out a holder with a single picture, a man in swim trunks shading his eyes against the sun.

Not Craig.

Definitely not Craig.

Six feet tall. Built like a boxer, strong chest, powerful legs, sturdy shoulders and arms. A crop of thick, curly brown hair. An open, attractive face with a devil-may-care smile.

I turned the photo over. The inscription on the back read simply: *Hilton Head.*

I studied the man's face and smile for a moment more. I wouldn't forget this picture.

No woman would.

I returned it to the pocket, zipped it shut.

I held the purse beneath the rose lamp, opened it wide for a thorough check, then replaced all the belongings.

All that one would expect to find in a woman's purse—except for one thing.

I looked over the table.

No keys.

Hmm. Had she dropped them in the pocket of what she was wearing that afternoon?

I'd have to find out.

I put the purse down.

The message light on the recorder continued to blink.

I punched the Play button.

"Craig, this is Melissa Higgins from Patty Kay's guild, calling on Monday morning at nine. We'll plan on bringing food for luncheon after the services Wednesday, if that is agreeable to you. My number is 555-2094. We're so sorry. If there's anything else we can do, please call me."

The second call was in sharp, emotional contrast. *"Craig, I can't believe it! They can't keep you in jail. Oh, it's so awful! Call me."* The voice was young. Quite young. And terribly upset.

The next two calls were also from the girl. She didn't identify herself.

The fifth call was a woman's voice, hesitant and guarded. *"Craig, this is Stevie. Call me if you can."*

Melissa Higgins called a second time. Her voice was jerkily nervous. *"Uh, Craig, the guild—uh, one of our members talked to Pamela and we'll be serving the food at her house after the funeral. Thank you very much."* The disconnection was abrupt. Melissa obviously had learned of Craig's arrest.

The seventh call was the young voice, still fraught with unhappiness. *"Craig, I'll do everything I can, I promise. I won't let this happen!"*

I punched the Save button.

Hmm. Curiouser and curiouser. I wanted to know who the young caller was. And I intended to find out about Stevie. Her tone was so carefully uninflected.

But for now I still had much to explore. I opened the door on the left side of the hall. It was another entrance to the kitchen. To the right, an archway opened into a game room. I looked inside. Six carousel horses provided much of the seating.

I pulled myself up to sit sidesaddle on a wooden roan with its head tossing and mane ruffled. My weight apparently triggered a tape of tinny carousel music so faint that it seemed more a memory than a sound. If the carved mounts had begun to move, I wouldn't have been surprised. As the reedy tune tinkled, I surveyed the expensive assortment of entertainment devices, a huge television screen, VCR, pool table, Ping-Pong table, game tables. An unfinished game of checkers remained atop a table in front of the limestone fireplace. A box of marshmallows sat on the fireplace ledge.

When I dismounted, the music cut off instantly. I checked out the cabinets. They contained an astonishing array of board games, reams of photograph albums, and flamboyantly titled home movie cassettes. All were dated. Among the most recent were *Our Madcap Stay in Rio, Brigit's Sweet 16, To-and-Fro Aboard the World's Most Boring*

Yacht, Christmas with the Mudville Clan, Let's Have Another Round, and
Fair Haven Fives at the Tennis Spa.

I picked up the last one, dated only the month before. I turned
on the television and VCR and slipped in the cassette.

In living color with sound to match.

Scene: a semitropical tennis retreat.

I watched and was impressed with the tennis prowess of the four
women. I understood the tape's title. They obviously were all ranked
5.0 or better.

It didn't take me long to peg the players' names. Patty Kay, of
course, I recognized from the newspaper photo and the photos in her
purse. The redheaded pro at the tennis spa, Evan, was a flirty, sexy
Australian who always called his pupils by name, Gina, Edith, Brooke,
Patty Kay.

Gina's short dark hair fit her like a sleek fur cap. She danced
around the court and had an astonishingly strong serve for her size.
She talked incessantly. "Good shot. Good *shot.*" "Oh, damn!" "I've got
it, I've got it." "Did you drill that right in my face, Edith?" "Short,
Brooke, short!" This must be Gina Abbott, whom the lawyer described
as Patty Kay's best friend.

Edith's plump face was claret red by mid-match. She huffed and
puffed, but she had a wicked backhand and a corkscrew serve that
drove the others mad. She chattered brightly, but when she had a
chance to drill an opponent, her eyes glittered with undisguised satisfaction.

Brooke—Brooke Forrest, the trustee?—was the classic beauty of
the bunch. She had an elegant, patrician face, luxuriant jet-black hair,
aquamarine eyes, camellia-smooth skin. Somehow Brooke never
looked hurried or hot or frantic. Her timing was superb, and her
strokes smooth as spun glass.

Patty Kay was in charge. With great good humor, of course, but
there was no mistaking the leader. And she was the champion of the
doubles players, a booming serve, a slashing return of serve, put-away
volleys. She was always moving.

In life, Patty Kay Prentiss Pierce Matthews had a mischievous grin, sparkling green eyes, and a husky, almost breathy voice. Her laugh ranged from an infectious peal to an earthy whoop. She laughed a lot. She wasn't conventionally pretty. Her face was too angular, her mouth too wide. But she was compelling, fascinating, a woman who would always be noticed.

The laughter stopped when the tennis started. Patty Kay's eyes blazed with fierce determination and total concentration. She was the kind of player who would rather die than lose. But they all played hard, Gina making little cries of victory or despair, Edith's mouth a thin, straight line, Brooke's body arching gracefully for an overhead.

Patty Kay's iron will wasn't as apparent off the court. At night— the four women lounging in brief, expensive silk gowns as they played bridge and gossiped—Patty Kay was the life of the party. Her earthy laughter sounded again and again. She could outlaugh them all: Gina, thin and nervous, talking a mile a minute; Edith, smiling and agreeable on the surface, but eager to cut down her companions in a superficially nice way; Brooke, tall, dark-haired, serious, her beauty almost breathtaking.

Perhaps the four women took too long a holiday. It was toward the end of the tape, again during one of the nightly bridge games, that Brooke—Brooke Forrest?—and Patty Kay clashed.

"I wonder what David will think about you and Evan?"

Brooke was arranging her cards. Her beautiful eyes studied Patty Kay for a moment before she said, "What are you talking about?"

"Our tennis pro from heaven, my sweet. You can't tell me," Patty Kay said slyly, "that you aren't lusting for his body. I saw the way you leaned against him this afternoon. Mmm-mmm."

"Who wouldn't lean on him?" Gina gave a raucous whistle.

Edith simpered. "Brooke, your secret's out."

Brooke's exquisite face might have been chiseled out of stone. Her eyes flashed as she looked from Edith to Patty Kay. "You're not funny, either one of you. And don't you dare say anything like that to my husband."

"Tell the truth and shame the devil," Patty Kay crowed.

Brooke threw down her cards. "Patty Kay, stop it. You don't understand. David—" She shook her head and her lustrous black hair swirled around her narrow, elegantly boned face. "That would make David wild."

"Oh, ho. That's an almost irresistible temptation. Are you saying David Forrest, Mr. Perfect, can be roused to *passion?*" Patty Kay's eyes glittered with amusement. "Oh, dear. Now, that's another deep question. But one perhaps we'd better not pursue."

"Why not?" Edith asked, her laughter trilling.

Gina frowned, suddenly serious. Perhaps she had recognized the cruelty of their taunts. "Knock it off, you two."

Abruptly, Brooke shoved back her chair. "I've had enough. Sometimes you go too far, Patty Kay." The door slammed. The sharp crack almost drowned out Patty Kay's murmured "She's never had enough."

That was the end of the film. I punched Rewind. As the tape whirred, I kept hearing Patty Kay's final vibrant whoop of laughter.

I returned the cassette to the cabinet and checked my watch. Just after four. Plenty of time. The library came next. It appeared to be the least lived-in room in the big house. The books were so evenly aligned, I knew they'd not been moved in a long time except perhaps to be dusted and reshelved. But it wasn't the books, though many were beautifully bound, that attracted my interest.

The focal point of the room was the portrait of Patty Kay.

Portrait painters must despair of the unoriginal poses so often selected by their wealthy subjects. The most common, I suppose, are the demure hostess in a white organdy dress seated on a garden bench or the jodhpur-clad horsewoman standing next to an elegant Thoroughbred.

Instead, Patty Kay was forever captured in sweat-dampened tennis whites, her forehand curving into an overhead smash, her tanned face flushed, her green eyes intent and arrogantly triumphant, her curly dark hair bunched beneath a worn headband, her lips parted in effort, her tennis shoes smudged with dust from red clay. The portrait wasn't especially flattering. The tendons in her neck were distended, the muscles in her arm were bunched, the bones of her vivid face were predatory and implacable. But the artist without doubt captured her intensity, her vitality, her total and complete determination.

Here was a victor, a champion, fiercely proud of her strength, of her body, of her will.

Here was a woman who would never give up.

Or in.

I felt as though Patty Kay's ghost walked with me through the rest of her home. I imagined her grin as I surveyed the master bath.

It was Italian Renaissance–inspired: a vaulted ceiling, painted mirrors framed by blond onyx, a deep, golden marble bath. The space was generous enough for a bevy of nymphs to cavort in. Patty Kay could have practiced her serve in this sumptuous chamber—or whatever other physical pleasures she enjoyed.

The master bedroom, too, suggested physical delight as well as respite. A silk spread covered the king-size bed. The walls, too, were of silk, and the window hangings all in subtle shades of rich apricot. At the four corners of the massive bed hung delicate light golden muslin swaths that could be pulled shut. They and the spread were reflected in the mirrored ceiling.

I had no difficulty determining Patty Kay's closet from Craig's.

Hers contained rack after rack of designer dresses and suits with every possible matching accessory, all in vibrant, eye-catching primary colors. Gold. Emerald. Scarlet. There were dozens of equally brightly hued shoes and purses for every occasion and season. The drawers held elegant sports apparel for the seashore, the mountains, the courts, the riding trails.

It was easy to imagine her fresh from her bath, lithe and eager, ruffling through the sachet-scented drawers, hurriedly pulling one dress from a hanger, discarding it, picking another.

Craig's sparsely filled closet and a monogrammed silver hairbrush on the dresser were the only evidence he'd shared in the life of this luxurious room. A dozen suits for winter and summer. Ten conservative dress shirts. More sports clothes, mostly khaki slacks and patterned sports shirts. Two pairs of black dress shoes. Three pairs of loafers. Athletic clothes. Tennis shoes. Of course.

I would ask Craig. I felt confident he was a good player. But probably not quite good enough to beat Patty Kay.

The hallway walls were covered with framed photographs. I

scanned them quickly. The teenage girl, the same one in the album in her purse, had to be Brigit.

Definitely not a case of like mother, like daughter.

The girl's thin face was almost colorless, her wispy blondish hair mousy, her lips often tightly pressed together. Brigit seemed caught in a perpetual pout. Except in a number of photos in costume. Class plays, more than likely. The only photos in which she was smiling were a half dozen taken with Craig. These revealed a delicate, fawnlike beauty that her sullen demeanor had obscured in the other likenesses.

There were many photos of Patty Kay and a laughing, tanned, relaxed Craig. Playing tennis, as I'd expected. White-water rafting. Hiking. In European train stations. Skiing. Horseback riding.

I walked on down the hall and looked through an open door.

Into chaos.

7

aptain Walsh blocked the doorway to Patty Kay's office. He surveyed the dumped-out desk drawers, the shards of glass in the smashed bookcase fronts, the gouged surface of the once-elegant mahogany desk, the emptied file cabinets, and the cardboard files in untidy heaps.

I looked past him and shivered. There was a viciousness at work here that frightened me: Ink splattered against the cheerful daisy wallpaper, photos ripped from a bulletin board and scattered in pieces, papers ground beneath a heel, a lamp used like a baseball bat on the desktop, an upended aquarium and the limp bodies of the fish on the sodden rug.

Captain Walsh turned toward me and crossed his arms over his midriff. His expressionless eyes slowly moved to my face. "Interesting thing is, Mrs. Collins, this office was undisturbed when my men searched the house Saturday."

"So somebody broke in between Saturday night and this afternoon."

"Broke in?" Chief Walsh inquired. "Shall we check, Mrs. Collins?"

We made a survey of the ground floor together.

No broken windows. No smashed-in doors.

But the back door was unlocked.

Once again Captain Walsh stood, feet braced, arms crossed. "The house was secure when we left Saturday night." He pointed at the door. "That was definitely locked."

"Craig could have unlocked it on Sunday and, with a good many other things to think about, not locked it when he left."

"He could have." Chief Walsh's voice was flat. He turned and pointed at the madras patchwork purse on the butler's table. "There's Mrs. Matthews's handbag. And there are a great many valuable articles in this house. Silver, right out on the dining room table. VCR. Can you describe any missing items?"

He knew I couldn't. "We'll have to wait until Craig gets home to answer that."

"Yes."

"Patty Kay's office is a mess," I said sharply.

"Yes. I'll agree to that."

We glared at each other.

I got the picture.

Captain Walsh believed I'd planned a diversion.

Now I crossed my arms. "I didn't touch that office, Captain."

"No, ma'am."

"Are you going to investigate this?"

"Of course, ma'am. I'll make a full report."

As the captain's black unmarked pulled away—and I have to hand it to the Fair Haven police, it arrived four minutes after I phoned —I marched down the drive and crossed the street. As I waited by the white rail fence for the riding mower to come toward me, I admired the two-story colonial overlooking the sloping lawn. A cream Mercedes turned into the next driveway. A cocker spaniel bounded into a tangle of underbrush, his high, excited bark announcing pursuit of a squirrel or cat. Toward the end of the curving street, Cheryl Kraft strode briskly up another manicured drive.

This was the kind of neighborhood where people noticed strangers. Most assuredly every eye on King's Row Road would have been turned toward the Matthews house since the murder story broke in the Sunday papers. The young man on the riding mower certainly noticed my arrival this afternoon.

The mower turned, heading back to me.

When it was no more than a dozen feet away, I lifted my hand.

The driver of the mower was a handsome youth. He had thick, lustrous black hair, strong, even features, intelligent, dark blue eyes. At my summons, he looked surprised. But he promptly switched off the motor and jumped down. He hurried toward the fence.

"Yes, ma'am?" He was slim and athletic in a blue polo and white tennis shorts.

"I'm Henrietta Collins. I'm staying at the Matthews house. I'm Craig Matthews's aunt."

I held out my hand.

He yanked off brown gardening gloves, swiped his right hand against his shorts before holding it out to shake mine. "Yes, ma'am. I'm Dan Forrest." His grasp was firm.

I looked at the boy more closely. He was truly extraordinarily handsome—and the masculine image of Patty Kay's beautiful tennis partner, Brooke. Brooke, the tennis player. Brooke Forrest, the trustee.

"Did your mother and Patty Kay play tennis together?"

"Yes, ma'am. Mom loves to play. Mrs. Matthews was one of her best friends." Dan waited politely, tucking the gloves in a back pocket.

I did some quick figuring. Craig must have returned to the house at some time on Sunday to change clothes before he was questioned by the police. I didn't know what time he was arrested. The newspaper article had indicated the arrest was made Sunday evening. So—

"Dan, between late yesterday and about four this afternoon, Mrs.

Matthews's study was burglarized. Have you seen anyone near the house?"

"My gosh." His eyes widened. "I guess I should've called somebody. Gosh, I'm sorry." He sounded uncomfortable and embarrassed. "But I thought it could be the wind."

I scarcely dared to breathe. "What happened?"

"Well, it was just a little while before you came." His eyes slid away from me. "I mean, I couldn't help but notice when you turned in. Your car's neat."

I abruptly understood. The teenager was embarrassed that he had indeed been curious and couldn't keep his eyes off the Matthews house. He didn't want to admit to poor manners. Interest in sports cars was acceptable, however.

I hastened to give him an out. "I imagine a riding mower gets pretty boring. You can probably tell me how many squirrels have crossed the road this afternoon. And certainly I'm glad you were here and happened to be looking around."

"Yeah. That's funny too. Usually I'd still be at school. But they canceled sports today. I guess they thought it wouldn't seem right. Not until the funeral."

I tried to sort that out. I thought Patty Kay's funeral was Wednesday. Why no sports on Monday? But that didn't matter. What mattered was what this boy saw.

"So you were home this afternoon?"

"I got home about three-fifteen. I started mowing about three-thirty. Anyway, I happened"—his tone was painfully casual—"to look across the street and I saw the Jessops' little white poodle dashing up your driveway. And Mitzi's not supposed to be out. She gets lost. So I ran over, but by the time I got there, she'd run around back. I went back there and I heard Mrs. Jessop calling and then I realized Mitzi'd gone home. So I was turning around and that's when I saw the back door was open."

His face wrinkled in remembered indecision. "I looked around the drive and Mr. Matthews's car wasn't there, just hers. And so nobody was home. I mean, there weren't any cars but hers. But the door was open. I just stood there and looked at it and then I thought that was odd, so I went up to the screen and opened it and poked my head in. I called out for Brigit, but I didn't think she'd be there. I mean, not" —Dan Forrest paused, then said awkwardly, "with what had happened. So I stepped into the hall." He stopped and jammed his hands in the pockets of his shorts. "And I thought I heard something—like a bump, maybe?—upstairs. So I called out real loud this time for Brigit. It was quiet. Real quiet." He looked sheepish, a different kind of embarrassment this time. "It was—I don't know. I just felt funny. So I decided to leave. I closed the door and came back home and started mowing again."

I didn't say anything. I looked at his handsome, uncomfortable face and wondered if maybe Dan Forrest had been luckier than he would ever know. If Patty Kay's murderer had waited upstairs, listening—

Dan mistook my silence.

"I'm sorry," the boy said miserably. "I guess I should have called somebody."

"No, you did fine. You couldn't have known. And everything downstairs looked all right?"

He nodded eagerly. "Yeah. Everything looked okay."

"You didn't see anyone leave?"

"No, ma'am."

But I hadn't expected that. Obviously, the searcher would have heard Dan call, heard the door close. It would be easy to go down the alley or to slip through the thick woods behind the Matthews house and gain the street—or a nearby yard?—without being seen.

"Thank you, Dan."

"Yes, ma'am."

I heard the mower start up again as I walked swiftly back to the house. I went by my car and retrieved my .35mm camera.

All the way upstairs, I thought about Dan Forrest—and luck. But maybe it was also my lucky day—and by extension Craig Matthews's. Because the trashed study had to mean something.

Captain Walsh thought it meant I'd do anything necessary to help my "nephew."

I knew better.

I took careful photos that would overlap and show the precise condition of the room.

The more I looked at the destruction, the more somber I felt.

The rampage that had turned this room into a shambles reflected enormous anger. And frustration?

Surely the search was made to find something the murderer feared anyone else seeing.

It had to be something so shocking, so revealing that the search was made despite Craig's arrest.

The desk was littered with papers. It would take hours to sort through them. And, more than likely, they would mean nothing to me.

The same was true of the emptied files.

It looked very much as though the searcher had taken whatever came to hand and dumped it out, then mixed the papers into untidy heaps.

Searching for something specific?

Or angrily destroying order.

Behind the desk, a ring-binder notebook lay spread-eagled on the floor. Gold letters on the navy vinyl cover read: *Walden School, Special Projects*. In a corner of the room was a cracked Rolodex. Jammed against the wall was an appointment book.

I used a pencil to edge the appointment book over. I opened it to Friday, April 2.

Patty Kay's handwriting was as distinctive as her laugh. Oversize looping letters were scrawled in vivid scarlet ink.

She evidently used the daybook simply to jot down appointments and reminders. That didn't surprise me. It takes a more reclusive, inwardly turned personality for journal keeping. So I didn't expect to find a diary entry relating the latest upheavals in what had surely been a life filled with controversy and confrontation.

Nor did I.

I found, instead, these unrevealing notes:

FRIDAY - 9 a.m. Class
<u>Chuck</u>

Brooke
<u>Call Stuart——Brigit</u>
Noon——singles/ Craig
7 p.m. Symphony
SATURDAY - 9 a.m. tennis
8 p.m.——Charley's A.

I flipped back a page.

THURSDAY - 9 a.m. tennis 9–7 Gina/ 5–7 Brooke/ 6–2 Edith
Alterations
Walden Files

I described the notes as unrevealing. Yes. But they did raise some questions.

The Friday tennis game with Craig was marked out. On Saturday Patty Kay had marked through the theater date and written "*trustees.*" She had double-underlined two Friday entries, Chuck and Call Stuart ——Brigit. A slash was marked through the Saturday morning tennis notation.

Why these changes in her plans?

Why were two entries double underlined?

I quickly made a copy of the three pages in my notebook. Though I had to wonder if anything in the appointment book mattered. Because surely the pages could have been torn out or the book removed if there had been anything remotely incriminating in them. Still, I had to start somewhere. At the very least, those notations were clues to Patty Kay's thoughts and actions on the last days of her life.

The quartz clock—lying on the floor, its delicate face smashed—chimed the hour. Five o'clock. It was time.

I hurried down the main staircase.

Craig said he had arrived home at just after five on Saturday. He came in through the front door to the main hall. He called out for Patty Kay.

I stood in the main hall.

Yes, anyone coming in the front door—if he called out—should be heard in the kitchen.

I imagined his shout. *"Patty Kay? Patty Kay?"*

No answer.

Craig made the natural assumption that his wife wasn't in the kitchen. It made sense that he didn't check the kitchen first.

When his call wasn't answered, he went into the main part of the house, seeking her. Having no luck, he hurried upstairs.

Then he returned downstairs and went to the kitchen.

I pretended to be Craig, timing it, upstairs and back down.

Two minutes forty-two seconds.

I pushed in the kitchen door. A faint odor of burned chocolate lingered, overlain by a deeper, ranker smell. It was dim and shadowy. I was sure lights blazed when Craig arrived. I flipped the switches.

The sticky, smelly mess was shocking. I was surprised. The police were finished there. No yellow crime scene tape declared this room off limits. The police had their damning photographs and drawings and video film. Why hadn't Craig arranged for the kitchen to be cleaned?

It was, I suddenly felt certain, just like Craig. He was waiting for someone to take charge, to tell him what to do. Although, to be fair, he'd had very little time for such practical concerns.

But I was glad. I was seeing the kitchen as the police had found it.

Three doors opened into the room, one from the dining room, one from the back hall, where I stood, and one from outside.

Dark, gooey bits adhered to the high ceiling.

Congealed pools of green and brown formed an irregular, alcohol-scented mass between the cooking island and the door to the backyard. It was easy to spot the smears where Craig had skidded across the spilled liqueurs.

I didn't see either liqueur bottle. Or the cake tin.

I got my pad out of my purse. My fingers brushed the packet of photos Chief Walsh had given me. I pulled it out, found the kitchen shots, and compared them to the scene.

I studied the ceiling again. I estimated the trajectory of the cake tin when it was hurled.

It placed the tosser squarely in the middle of the spilled liqueur.

Unless, of course, the tin was thrown first, and the liqueur spilled after that.

Craig admittedly had a long smear of liqueur on one trouser leg.

That wasn't nearly enough.

As I understood it, the police believed that Craig came home, he and Patty Kay quarreled, and, enraged, he lost control, crazily flinging the liqueur bottles to the floor, then heaving the cake tin at the ceiling. Or he tossed the cake tin, then knocked over the bottles. Meanwhile, presumably his wife ran from his mad attack out the back door and into the playhouse.

I ran through the possibilities in my mind.

And shook my head.

Both Craig and Patty Kay would have been splashed with liqueur in the first version.

In the second, crumbs from the cake tin that didn't stick to the ceiling would have fallen on them.

But the clincher—to me—was the series of skid marks Craig left through the spilled liqueur. They ran in a straight line from where I stood, just inside the hall kitchen door, to the back door.

Not a single mark disturbed the sticky goo congealed near the cooking station, the point where the action should have occurred, because that's where the cooking stuffs were. But there were no foot-prints, no streaks, just an unbroken sheet of dried syrupy liqueur.

That undisturbed residue told me Patty Kay wasn't standing there when the cooking stuffs were spilled, that the liqueur bottles had been removed from the cooking island to a point near the back door, that the cake tin was heaved first and the tosser darted out of the way, then the liqueur was splashed against the cabinets and the bottles thrown—

I looked for the bottles (physical evidence that would have been removed by the police) in the official photos. One bottle sat on the kitchen table (courtesy of Craig, as I recalled) and the second lay unbroken on the floor near the cooking island.

If Craig had left that second bottle by the island, his footprints would necessarily have led away from the area.

They didn't.

So the second bottle must have been tossed there.

Captain Walsh might discount my interpretation, but to me the lack of footprints proved without a shadow of a doubt Craig's innocence.

Assuming, of course, Craig hadn't mounted a dangerous double bluff to incriminate himself.

I considered that coolly. I didn't think he was smart enough or had the guts. But I could be wrong. He might have a surprising streak of wiliness. Or would it be so surprising? Craig was obviously wily enough to use his undeniable charm to manipulate those around him, especially women. That kind of indirectness would fit in perfectly with a double bluff. So, yes, he was wily enough. Was he gutsy enough?

Of course, there was another overpowering, unarguable reason the police version couldn't be true.

Not physical evidence this time, but an instinct as convincing and unalterable as any smear of blood or shred of cloth or fragment of hair.

I already felt I knew Patty Kay well enough to be sure that she never ran from any man.

And certainly not from Craig.

Patty Kay was a fighter.

If she had run, realizing her peril, it would have been to her car for a weapon.

No, Patty Kay hadn't run.

She'd walked out to her death in the playhouse with someone she didn't fear.

This carefully arranged scene, this deadly snare, was created after she lay dead or dying in the playhouse.

I checked the time. I'd taken two minutes there. It seemed reasonable Craig would have looked at this frightening scene at least that long. So now five minutes were gone.

I skirted the irregular stain and opened the back door.

Daffodils bordered the path to the playhouse. If Craig left a sticky trail from his skid across the kitchen, I couldn't spot it on the dark flagstones.

The glass-walled playhouse had been built perpendicular to the house, facing a twenty-five-yard pool. A stand of huge chinkapin oaks framed the playhouse and the pool. To the right were the garages and the drive. I guessed the bright blue Lexus near the back door belonged to Patty Kay.

I took the time to walk—it must have been a hundred yards—from the house to circle behind the garages. I wasn't surprised to find an old-fashioned alley there. Otherwise, Craig would have passed the police coming into the grounds as he sped away.

An owl hooted.

I had Craig's keys in my pocket, but the playhouse door was unlocked.

Sticky stains from spilled liqueur are one thing.

Massive, congealed pools of blood are decidedly another.

This was beyond the scope of a cleaning crew. These rugs would have to be destroyed and replaced.

The rank smell sickened.

The playhouse was created for sunny times, for happy days. Golden white wood, glass walls, orange linen sofas and easy chairs—and white shag rugs.

Anger flickered within me.

Until now, I'd focused primarily upon Craig's plight.

Now I was seeing where a vibrant woman had lain in her own blood, dying—and not by the hand of a stranger.

. . . *a time to die.*

It should not have been her time to die.

"I'm sorry, Patty Kay." Yes, I said it aloud in that sunny, violence-marked playroom. Mark me a sentimental fool, if you will, but age grants some definite rights, and one is the willingness to be open about your feelings. I was sad and angry because life is so fragile, so fleeting, its loss so final.

I looked at those dark stains and I knew I was determined to find out the truth. Not solely for Craig now, but for Patty Kay too.

From the position of the stains, I figured Patty Kay and her murderer were facing each other when the shots were fired. Patty Kay was close to the north entrance. I stood by the west door that opened onto the deck. She'd staggered backward a few steps and fallen. The ballistics department and the forensics laboratory would have determined how far away her assailant stood from her when he fired. My guess was that the killer gunned her down, then left the playhouse through the west door.

In the police photos, Patty Kay lay on her left side curled in the fetal position. The door was wedged against her where Craig had pushed his way in. The stain on Craig's left sleeve was consistent with his having knelt beside her and lifted her head.

Actually, the fact that his shirt was stained at all was another compelling argument for his innocence. It had happened only because he tried to help her. If he had shot Patty Kay down, why would he have touched her, gone near that spurting blood?

But, as is so often true in life, there was always an answer that could be made. The prosecution could effectively argue that once the deed was done, Craig had reacted in horror to his own lethal act. He had knelt, they would say, in a futile, mad attempt to help her. But there was no undoing Patty Kay's deadly injury. (In that event, wouldn't his right sleeve have been stained? He would have come to her from the front, not the back.) The police rationale would fit in nicely with Craig's running away, which could also be seen as a demonstration of his chronic unwillingness to face reality.

I'm not much for glib answers.

I felt certain there was more to Craig's running than terror that he would be accused.

I didn't see it as a confession of guilt.

But he was not an unsophisticated man.

He'd told me he ran because husbands are so often suspected when a wife is murdered.

True.

But he and Patty Kay were not on bad terms. So far as I knew.

There had to be another, stronger, more damning reason.

I tried to imagine Craig's thoughts at that moment.

The shock, of course, would have been enormous. Murder is not a staple companion to small-town life, certainly not this rarefied kind of small-town life.

So Craig was stunned, shaken, overwhelmed.

Then sirens shrilled.

He decided to flee. To me it seemed evident his actions fit exactly the amount of time he had.

He took the gun with him.

Where was the weapon at that moment? Craig told me he'd picked it up out of the grass before he went into the playhouse and found Patty Kay there. Had he kept it in his hand when he lifted her head? It was possible, if he was carrying it in his right hand. He could have turned back to the open door, holding the gun, when he heard the sirens.

Actually, he could have run, not even realizing he had the gun in his hand—

No, no, no. He'd wrapped the gun in something.

That bothered me. Why? And with what? And where was it?

It mattered. It had to matter, because Craig was in the biggest trouble of his life, and he wouldn't answer that simple question. Or what seemed to me to be a simple question.

Why wrap the gun, dammit?

Because he wanted to clean off his fingerprints?

Maybe.

What did he wrap it in?

Captain Walsh said they hadn't found anything to match the snag of cloth on the pistol.

Cloth. Beige cotton.

I looked around. Webbed plastic bins sat on either side of this exit. One held a tall stack of vividly hued towels, orange and green and raspberry, purple, red, and navy. The other held soiled towels.

If Craig wanted to wrap the gun, hide it from view, wipe it clean, he had an ample supply of towels right at hand.

But the cotton snag was beige.

Not a Patty Kay color.

Beige cotton.

It didn't take long for me to satisfy myself. There wasn't a single piece of beige cotton of any sort in the playhouse.

Okay. Craig was standing there in a desperate panic, listening to the sirens come closer and closer. I'd think he'd run to his car, gun in hand, frantic to escape.

Why would he even start to think about wrapping the gun in anything at that moment?

I didn't think he would.

So how to account for the snag of material on the weapon? And it definitely was wrapped in something when the two boys spotted Craig getting out of his car on the country road.

Maybe the answer was super simple. Maybe there was something in Craig's car that he wrapped the gun in.

No. If it were that easy, he'd have had no reason to get rid of the material. And the police hadn't found it in the car or in the area with the gun though there were matching fibers beneath the driver's seat.

So Craig had hidden it somewhere between that country road and his arrival at the cabin.

There had to be a reason.

I recalled our talk at the jail.

Craig refused to answer when I asked why he'd gotten rid of the gun and what he'd wrapped it in.

And when I asked who might have reason to kill Patty Kay, I'd swear there'd been a flash of uncertainty—and fear—in his eyes before he cried out that it was ". . . crazy. Nobody'd want to kill her."

But what if there were someone he feared might have done it— because of something he found in the playhouse by his wife's body? Something made of beige cotton, something he recognized.

That made sense. Craig would scoop up that article along with the gun and there would be a reason to run, the frantic, terrible necessity to get the damning cloth out of there, away from the police.

I left the playhouse. Back in the main hallway, I found the telephone directory. Again I dialed the police station.

I had to wait only a moment.

"Walsh here."

"Captain Walsh, this is Mrs. Collins."

"Yes, ma'am." If they gave awards for lack of inflection, he'd be a cinch to win. "Glad you called. I talked to Mr. Matthews. According to him, the house was locked tighter than a drum when he left it Sunday." Uninflected, yes, but puffed with smugness.

I love to deflate smugness. "A teenage neighbor, Dan Forrest, found that back door unlocked earlier this afternoon. I'm sure you'll want to talk to him. The boy may have heard the intruder."

Walsh agreed. Grudgingly.

"Captain, you said there were fibers in Craig's Porsche of the beige material snagged on the murder weapon."

"That's correct."

"If I were you, Captain, I'd request the help of the highway patrol and the county officers in a search of roadside trash cans between Snell and Monteagle. Obviously, they should look for something made of beige cotton. It will be bloodstained."

he phone rang as I rinsed out the mop one last time.

The kitchen sparkled. My back ached. And I was ravenous. I'd already checked out the refrigerator and freezer. There was plenty of food. Patty Kay not only enjoyed cooking, she was an orderly and saving homemaker. I'd picked out my supper, a frozen package of homemade beef Stroganoff, neatly labeled in her looping crimson script and ready for the microwave.

I didn't reach for the receiver with any great expectations, but I've learned that you can't predict who may call or where the call may lead. In my years of reporting, I'd circled the world twice, visiting every continent, and many of those journeys grew out of a telephone summons. Right now I was standing in the kitchen of a murdered woman.

So I got it on the second peal.

I didn't even have time to say hello.

"Craig, Craig?" The now-familiar young voice trembled with eagerness. It was astonishing how much emotion she'd packed into saying his name. I was glad Captain Walsh wasn't on the line to hear it.

"No. This is Henrietta Collins."

"Who are *you*?" It was the direct, unvarnished question of a mind obsessed with its own quest.

"His aunt."

"Oh. The aunt he went to see after he found Mother?"

"Yes." So this was Brigit. I heard no reflection of Patty Kay's husky, distinctive voice in her daughter's.

"Oh." Brigit accepted it without question, almost without interest. "Is Craig there? Is he home?"

"No. Not yet."

"I can't *believe* they've put him in jail. And Daddy won't let me talk to the police. I could tell them. I know him better than anybody, better than Mother even. Craig wouldn't hurt anybody. Ever." She choked off in sobs.

"Brigit, do you want to help Craig get out of jail?" I will admit I felt a qualm. Taking advantage of children has not been a customary ploy of mine.

There was no hesitation. "Oh, yes, yes, yes."

"Could I see you tonight? Or sometime tomorrow? I need to know more about your mother and who might have been angry with her."

"I can tell you a lot." The switch from tears to venom was startling. "I can . . ." Abruptly the sound was muffled, but I could hear some of what she said. ". . . Paulie . . . she's got my copy of the play . . . home early, I promise."

Then swift and short: "Sure, Paulie. I'll meet you at the library. At seven. Don't forget the play."

The line went dead.

Slowly, I replaced the receiver. Seven o'clock. That would give me plenty of time to get back to King's Row Road for the neighborhood meeting Cheryl had mentioned. But I was just as interested in meeting Brigit. *"Don't forget the play."* An artful touch. Apparently Brigit, too, was a glib liar. Like her stepfather. But many teenagers have secret lives.

Sometimes the secrets are innocent.

Sometimes they are not.

I checked the phone book. One Fair Haven library. I called for directions. I had time for a quick supper and a shower.

It's sweaty work, cleaning up after a murderer.

Clean and freshly dressed, I carried the plate of Stroganoff and some iced tea into the game room. It wasn't that I was trying to make myself completely at home. I intended to work while I ate.

I slipped in the video entitled *Brigit's Sweet 16*.

I immediately had to turn down the sound. The band played music I always make it a point to avoid on my radio at a decibel level which must have made the neighborhood dogs howl.

A patio party: The girls and women in pretty summer frocks, the boys and men in slacks and sport coats, Japanese lanterns in pink and yellow, carnation-laden bowers, table centerpieces of hurricane lamps wreathed with pink organdy bows, and loud, loud music.

"My God." I said it out loud, the shock was so great—Patty Kay with a bulging face, double chins, and a bored, peevish expression. Then I blinked and realized my mistake as slim, dark-haired, vivacious Patty Kay greeted the woman who was her heavy doppelgänger. The resemblance was striking. The same angular face, mobile mouth, green eyes. What a difference forty pounds and an attitude made.

"Hi, sis." Pamela Guthrie offered a carmined cheek.

The sisters lightly embraced, turned away to talk to others.

Body language is just that. It was evident in the faces of the sisters, in their lack of animation, in their barely concealed indifference. These siblings weren't remotely interested in each other. I didn't sense hostility so much as disengagement.

It was their only contact on the birthday video.

Patty Kay was a gracious hostess, warm, welcoming, good-humored. She smoothly moved from person to person with real interest. She was never perfunctory. Craig was a better host than I would have expected, quick to refresh a drink or make an introduction.

It was easy to spot the tennis chums and their husbands. Brooke Forrest was gorgeous in a hibiscus-patterned sarong, but one very modestly cut. I noticed that she danced only with her husband. David, wasn't that his name? I could see why Patty Kay teased. David Forrest had a Mr. Rochester–harsh face, and his smile never reached his cold gray eyes.

I recognized another tennis player, chunky Edith. She kept pushing back her reddish curls as if she were hot. As always, she smiled. But her smile seemed automatic. I had the distinct feeling Edith wasn't enjoying herself. Occasionally, she danced with a stocky, balding man, but he spent most of the evening buttonholing other men to talk earnestly. He never seemed to notice how quickly they moved away. Except for Craig, a good host. At one point, he clapped Edith's husband on the back and asked, "How's your golf game, Ed?"

Small, feisty Gina Abbott didn't appear to have an escort. She was all over the party, refilling a punch bowl, urging young people to dance, holding a discarded beach towel like a matador's cape as she recounted a story that evoked peals of laughter. At one point, Gina shooed young Dan Forrest to the dance floor with an eager blond girl who looked up at Dan with adoring eyes despite his scarcely masked boredom.

Cameras film without prejudice. This video caught so many unguarded moments: Brooke's proud smile as she watched her son on the dance floor, David Forrest's downturned mouth as he observed them both, the immobility of Patty Kay's face as Craig whirled by with a deliriously happy Brigit—no braces here, so why didn't her mother have a more recent picture in her purse?—Edith's irritation as she shrugged away a stocky teenage girl tugging on her sleeve, Gina's almost frantic pursuit of laughter.

I felt I was seeing the merest surface of many tangled relationships.

I reran it and saw more than I'd noticed the first time:

A cheerful red-haired boy kept trying to interest the blond girl who looked so adoringly at Dan, but he didn't have any luck.

At his father's nod, Dan was quick to bring a plate to his mother and to help gather up discarded wrapping paper from the presents.

The red-haired, freckled girl, whom Edith had shrugged away, bubbled with happiness throughout the party. The girl's broad, freckled face was ecstatic when Brigit managed to blow out a final stubborn candle.

The blond girl who'd danced so happily with Dan was always at his elbow despite his indifference.

Near the party's end, Gina, her shoulders drooping, stared bleakly toward the woods, then, whirling about at Brooke's call, once again slipped into her frenetic party personality.

In the final frame, Patty Kay swept her daughter into a tight embrace.

But Brigit was looking over her mother's shoulder into the eyes of her mother's second husband. It wasn't a look her mother would have liked.

And Craig's face?

It gave no inkling that he realized his attraction for the teenager.

How could he have missed it?

The public library reflected the prosperity of Fair Haven, sprawling and beautifully maintained, lots of glass, an adjacent playground, and a small pond rimmed with benches.

I arrived early. Of course. Is there any reporter who isn't compulsive about being on time?

This library had on-line capabilities. I checked the local media, calling up the file on Patty Kay Prentiss Pierce Matthews. Lots of entries. It was clear that Patty Kay had been a power in Fair Haven's social and civic life. It was interesting that only rarely was her sister, Pamela Prentiss Guthrie, mentioned. In fact, I came upon Pamela's name only when she married and when she was listed as a survivor in her grandparents' and parents' obituaries. Two sisters who didn't sing the same song.

I had two stories on Patty Kay printed out. The second was pay dirt all the way. I scanned it, but it was nearing seven o'clock, so I tucked it in my purse for later study.

I watched the main entrance. I knew, of course, what Brigit looked like from the video, but I kept a sharp eye. The library was full of teenagers coming and going, some studying, some pursuing other interests. They appeared practically interchangeable, and it wasn't the big-city grunge look. Not in Fair Haven. These teens looked—as they were—like young replicas of the country club set. All wore button-down shirts and slacks, cotton wraparound skirts or floral print cotton pants and cotton pullover polos. The only common link to everyday USA teen culture were the odd hairstyles so popular now, many of the boys with their hair cut in layers, the girls with hair that looked as though it had undergone an unfortunate confrontation with an electric circuit.

Brigit's costume was de rigueur. The dazed look in the teen's reddened eyes was not.

I walked toward her and softly called her name.

She had a new hairstyle since the video. Her unremarkable blondish hair now frizzed around her face like coiled wires, making her narrow features seem even more waiflike. Her skin was so fair, the red-rimmed eyes jumped out at you.

"Mrs. Collins?" Her voice had more resonance in person than on the telephone. At my nod, she glanced warily around. Then she said swiftly, "Let's go outside. I see Mrs. Galloway. European history."

I took that as an elliptical identification of a teacher.

Privacy suited me too.

We walked halfway around the pond to a wooden bench that faced the library entrance. The lights from the library were reflected in the pond. It was cool enough outside to make my sweater welcome.

"Just in case Louise comes." Her voice oozed disdain.

I had sense enough not to ask who Louise was. After all, as Craig's aunt I could be expected to be familiar with most family names. I guessed Louise must be Brigit's stepmother.

"Does she do that a lot? Follow you around?"

She looked at me sharply, but I'd kept my voice nonjudgmental.

"Craig says I imagine it. He says it's a small town, for chrissakes, and not to take everything personally."

I could hear the echo of his voice in hers.

She began to cry, tears rolling down her thin cheeks.

"Crying won't help Craig."

At that, she rubbed the sleeve of her sporty jacket across her face. She took a deep breath. "I know. But I can't *stand* it if anything happens to him. I love him so much."

And not, obviously from her tone, in a way appropriate for a stepfather. This was what I'd feared. If the police cottoned onto this little family complication . . .

I might as well know the worst.

"How does Craig feel about you?" What had he seen? A cute little girl with a crush on him? Or a sexy nymphet? And, more important, how had he responded?

Brigit lifted her hands to her cheeks. Her whole face was transformed, and I had a brief, tantalizing glimpse of the woman she would be. "He kissed me. Just on my cheek. But if Mother hadn't been there, I know—" She broke off. She hugged her arms tightly to her slender body.

Was this her dream alone? Or had she aroused him too? Perhaps the truth of it didn't matter. What mattered was the girl's perception.

"Did your mother know how you feel about Craig?"

She trembled. Her light blue eyes blazed with an unchildlike fury. "She laughed at me. She *laughed* at me."

I remembered that mocking whoop of laughter in the video. Yes, I could believe it. Patty Kay made a joke of almost everything.

But there's nothing funny about first love. Requited or unrequited. Appropriate or silly. There is an elemental starkness to a first passion that later, more experienced loves will never possess.

Remembered anger—God, still vivid, living anger—thickened Brigit's young voice. "She wanted to send me away. She said I was making a fool of myself and embarrassing Craig. She said"—the girl swallowed miserably—"she said Craig thought I should go away too. I could have *killed* her!"

I said nothing.

The passionate, heartbreaking words pulsed in the dusky silence.

Blues eyes brimmed over with sudden tears. "But I *didn't*. You don't think . . . you can't think . . ."

I avoided that. "You're upset," I said soothingly.

Brigit's face was abruptly so young, so stricken. She pressed her hands hard against her eyes, but the tears streamed down her cheeks.

I found a tissue in my purse, handed it to her.

"Mother . . . oh, Mother . . ."

"I'm sorry, Brigit. So sorry."

She scrubbed at her face, tried to stifle the little sobbing hiccups.

But I wondered about Brigit. Yes, she was crying for her mother, but perhaps crying for more than her loss. In fact, Brigit might have the best of all possible reasons to believe in Craig's innocence.

Brigit would know where Craig's gun was kept. She would know how to call the bookstore and arrange for him to come home.

Why would she involve him?

She loved Craig, didn't she?

Had she believed Patty Kay's taunt? Did Brigit think that Craig, too, wanted to send her away? Had scorned love turned ugly?

But now she was sobbing because her mother was dead and distraught because Craig had been jailed.

No one ever said human desires and emotions could be totted up like arithmetic sums. Any kind of mix was possible.

"No." Her head jerked up. "No. I didn't do it. I wouldn't hurt Mother. I *wouldn't*. And I know Craig didn't. Listen." She reached out, her fingers clamped on my arm. Her words tumbled out feverishly. "I can help you find out what happened. I know that Mother and Aunt Pam were mad at each other. Really mad. And something must have happened at school Friday, because Mother was frosted with Mr. Selwyn." Her face fell. " 'Course, that's probably not anything."

Mr. Selwyn? Then I remembered. "That's the headmaster at Walden School? You go there?"

"Of course."

Of course. Everybody did.

I was very interested in Walden School and anyone connected with it. Because Patty Kay had suddenly decided to throw a party for the trustees of Walden School. And before the chosen guests could arrive, she was dead.

Cause and effect?

I couldn't know, but I sure intended to look hard at Walden School.

Friday, Brigit said.

"Why do you peg it to Friday?"

"Because I saw Mother talking to Mr. Selwyn Thursday afternoon —down at the track—and she was flirting with him. Of course." Scorn sharpened her voice. "But on Friday—"

I interrupted. "Of course?"

"Oh, Mother couldn't see anything in pants and not turn it on. I don't know why Craig put up with it. I'll bet Daddy never did."

If this child didn't hang her stepfather one way, it looked like she'd manage another.

But Brigit was oblivious of my thoughtful gaze. She continued without prodding. "On Friday he was stalking down the hall—"

"Who?"

"Mr. Selwyn. And he was really ticked off. Mother was glaring at him. She had a certain look when she totally despised somebody, and that's how she was looking at Mr. Selwyn. Not mad exactly. But really icy. Like he was some kind of scum. Maybe she came on to him and he turned her down."

Her eyes glinted with malice. The child looked a little like a white rat when she was being spiteful. That would become more pronounced with age.

She was obviously obsessed with sexuality. Not, of course, an unusual condition at her age.

I doubted very much that she'd correctly read the situation between Patty Kay and Mr. Selwyn. Nobody becomes headmaster of a posh school without learning exactly how to handle women of all ages, whether budding or fully bloomed, whether eager to be picked or prickly.

No. It must be something else entirely. The headmaster would never have intentionally offended Patty Kay. He would know how to flatter her sexually without going over the bounds. That was part of his job.

I was looking forward to meeting Mr. Selwyn.

I wondered, too, if there was a Mrs. Selwyn.

Just in case he *had* forgotten the boundaries.

"Oh, damn." Brigit jumped to her feet. "There's Louise's car. Checking on me. I know she is. I'll have to go."

She darted up the path toward the library. I wondered if this was an often-reenacted ritual.

I didn't try to follow her. I could find her again if I needed to.

I looked after her running figure soberly.

Yes, Brigit could be the one.

Vertical slabs of limestone glistened in the wash of lights illuminating the shadowy garden. The huge front door—carved teak—was swinging shut as I pushed aside a sweep of ferns to reach the steps.

Everywhere there was the sound of water, slipping, sloshing, splashing. I spotted at least three waterfalls, artfully lighted. Massive granite boulders formed pools and water eddied and swirled beneath overhanging banks of vines and potted flowers, bright peonies and masses of scarlet phlox. I suspected Cheryl Kraft had a full-time gardener with waders.

I pulled a bellrope. The low, reverberating gong sounded like that of a temple in Tibet.

The door opened immediately—or as immediately as a huge slab of teak could move.

Cheryl Kraft welcomed me. Tonight she was dramatic in gold hostess pajamas. Diamond dolphins dangled from an enormous gold chain that looked too heavy for her razor-sharp shoulders.

She reached out to take my hands, and I felt the heat of too-thin, feverish fingers. She glanced swiftly past me. No Craig. I saw the flicker in her eyes, but she jumped right in. "You're the last to come, Mrs. Collins. I'm so pleased you're here." She held the door wide and made no mention of Craig. No doubt she felt it would be tactless.

Women like Cheryl Kraft excel in tact. "We were hoping you'd make it. Everyone's down in the atrium."

She led the way across a bridge. The foliage flowed into the house, as did a stream of water inhabited by foot-long red and orange carp.

I followed her down a winding stone stair into an astonishing lair, three separate levels fashioned of redwood. Ferns, vines, several banana trees, more water, and iridescent fish thrived on every level. I'd last felt this immersed in sticky humidity in a Costa Rica rain forest.

She was now quite at ease. "Almost everyone's here. Except the Neals. They're in Egypt. A trip on the Nile. I do hope they don't get shot. Or bombed. The world's such an unsafe place now. Especially when you go where people have these religious persuasions. So unpredictable. And horribly, horribly hostile. And the poor dear Hollises. That's where all the cars are tonight. You know, that darling Cape Cod on the other side of the Jessops. Family from away, of course. So terribly sad. But they probably couldn't have helped us anyway. Too far from Patty Kay. And Edith isn't much of a gardener. I do wish Gina had come, but she felt she had to go over to Edith's."

The Cape Cod. I'd been right when I judged that heartbreak wasn't confined to Patty Kay's house. The poor Hollises, dealing with grief, unable to be a part of a neighborhood aroused by murder.

I felt awash in a swirl of names and circumstances that I didn't understand. But I would learn.

We reached the base of the staircase. Cheryl gripped my arm as if I were a prize. "Here she is. Dear Craig's aunt, Mrs. Collins. She's come to help. Now, let me introduce everybody."

In that first quick survey, a half dozen or more faces turned toward me. Shuttered faces. Wary faces.

Because I was Craig's aunt?

Or because violent death had come so close to them?

It was odd to pretend total ignorance when I did indeed know some of them. At least, I felt I knew them after viewing the videos.

But the first introduction fascinated me.

He pushed away from a redwood pillar to gaze at me somberly—the man whose photograph Patty Kay had carried with only the notation *Hilton Head*. The same thick curly brown hair and strong, bold features. He wasn't quite as trim now and there was a touch of gray in his hair. But the striking difference was in his face. In the photograph he was young and happy. It was summer with no hint that winter would ever come. Tonight he didn't look as though he'd ever smile again.

"Stuart Pierce." Cheryl shot me a swift glance.

But I knew. "Brigit's father," I said easily. I held out my hand. "I'm so pleased to meet you."

It wasn't awkward. After all, the American family in the nineties is often a hodge-podge. To put it gracefully.

"Of course, Stuart and Louise"—Cheryl smiled at Patty Kay's somber ex-husband—"don't really live right here on King's Row Road. But they're close, right around the corner on Pennington Way, behind Gina's house. I'm sorry Louise couldn't come this evening, but I know she will try to help."

So Stuart Pierce's second wife had declined to attend this neighborhood gathering. How had she felt about Stuart responding to Cheryl Kraft's summons?

Cheryl swept ahead. "And here are Pamela and Willis. But, of course, you know them."

Thank God for the videos. It was still an awkward moment for me. Had Margaret visited here, met Patty Kay's sister and husband? I could always pretend to be another aunt. . . .

But Pamela Prentiss Guthrie's protuberant eyes slid over me with neither recognition nor interest. She murmured insincerely, "So good to see you again. Very good of you to come. Under the circumstances."

The little flash of venom was intended. It caught me by surprise. She looked like such a boring blob. But the blob wasn't stupid—and she didn't like Craig.

Pamela's husband Willis was tall and bony with a concave chest, thinning ginger hair, and a scraggly, light mustache. His pale blue eyes looked at me coldly. His hand felt moist. "Yes, yes, good of you to come."

Cheryl swiftly shepherded me past them.

A distinguished-looking older man with crisp white hair and aristocratic features stood behind the wet bar. He had that air of confidence that only power and money provide. He was used to chairing meetings in boardrooms. Genial. Unless crossed.

"My husband, Bob." Cheryl favored him with a bright, surprisingly sweet smile.

Bob Kraft reached across the bar to shake my hand in a painful grip. "I'm so glad you could come, Mrs. Collins. What would you like to drink?"

"Gin and tonic, thanks."

The final couple I didn't know at all. They had the lean bodies and leathery faces of the horsey set. It was all too easy to picture them in a paddock. I suppressed a smile.

"Carl and Mindy Jessop. They live on the other side of Patty Kay." Cheryl clapped her thin hands together. "Everyone, come gather round the pool table."

Bob Kraft flicked a switch. Light flooded yet another level and a pool table.

Cheryl led the way down five stone steps.

Her guests obediently followed, though I saw Pamela Guthrie's heavy shoulders move in a shrug of disdain.

Cheryl waved us around the table and she took her place at one end. "I've been giving all of this a lot of thought." With the air of a conjuror, she pointed at nine upended whiskey tumblers on the table. "See, I have them arranged. On this side"—she touched the bottom of each glass in turn—"we have the Neals, the Jessops, Patty Kay, our house, and Gina's. On the other side of the street are"—*plink, plink, plink*—"the Hollises, the Forrests, and the Guthries. Over here on Pennington"—one glass sat by itself—"is Stuart's house." *Plink.* "Now, King's Row Road is a dead end." She glanced at me. "You remember, the street ends just past the Hollises' house."

I nodded. The Cape Cod with too many cars and women bringing food.

Cheryl's bright eyes moved restlessly from face to face. "It's very important for us to put our heads together. This police idea that poor, dear Craig hurt Patty Kay is absurd. We all know it."

It was my turn to glance swiftly about.

Brooke Forrest crossed her arms tightly across her chest. She stared at the glasses in sick fascination.

Brooke's husband watched Cheryl. David's cold gray eyes were skeptical.

Bob Kraft's face was thoughtful and not at all genial.

Pamela Guthrie sipped greedily at her drink, then plunged pudgy fingers into the amber liquid to lift out a maraschino cherry. She popped it into her mouth. She gave no attention to the table or the glasses.

Her husband's lips curved into a tiny, unpleasant smile, then he lifted one hand to stroke his limp mustache.

Stuart Pierce gripped the edge of the pool table. A muscle twitched in his jaw.

Not one of them jumped to Craig's defense.

Only the Jessops were nodding eagerly.

"Damn right." Carl Jessop pounded a fist on the green felt. The whiskey tumblers quivered. "Got to get busy, find out what the hell happened, who came in here, did such a thing. Not Craig. Couldn't have been Craig."

Mindy Jessop pushed back a lock of short-cropped gray hair. "So sorry I wasn't home. I was out at the stables. Sweet Delight's due any day now."

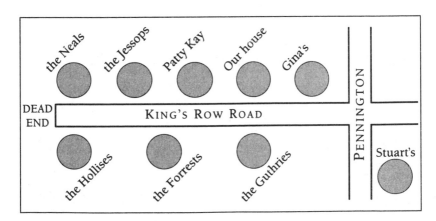

"How about you, Carl?" Cheryl asked, pointing at "their" glass.

"God, I wish I could help. I was at the club. Playing a round with Buddy Fisher."

It didn't take long. Only Brooke Forrest, her son Dan, and Pamela Guthrie appeared to have been at home on Saturday afternoon between four and five o'clock.

Cheryl looked at them eagerly. "Oh, good, good. You see, I was in the front yard from four o'clock until the police car came screaming up —except for just a few minutes right around five! And I know that not a single car turned in while I was outside." She turned toward Brooke. "So, if you or Pamela were outside, did either of you see a car come to Patty Kay's?"

Pamela shook her head. Her high voice was mildly surprised. "Why would I be outside?"

Brooke turned her slender hands over helplessly. "I was planting sweet Williams in the backyard. I couldn't see the street at all."

Cheryl tapped her fingers on the rim of the pool table. "I can't believe this. Someone must have seen *something*." She sounded slightly petulant.

"Maybe there wasn't anything to see." Pamela Guthrie's tone was bland.

I didn't let it pass. "No one but Craig may have driven into King's Row Road. But let's not forget the alley."

It was a fairly nice counterpoint.

But Cheryl Kraft's damning testimony that not a single car came into King's Row Road during most of that critical period on Saturday afternoon would certainly delight Captain Walsh.

9

I woke to rain. I'd not slept well. It isn't pleasant to dream of murder. Again and again I saw the same scene in my mind, Patty Kay backing away from her killer, one reluctant step after another. In those last desperate seconds—seconds that were forever too long and too brief—Patty Kay's expressive mouth would have opened in shock, her vivid green eyes flared in surprised disbelief. That's how she would have reacted— incredulous that anyone she knew intended to kill her, robbing the vigorous minutes and hours and days of her life.

In my dream I saw gloved hands aiming the pistol.

Yes, they would have been gloved because the murderer came prepared.

Sometimes the gloved hands belonged to Brigit.

Surely it wasn't her young mind that had connived so murder-ously and cleverly. But it could be. I knew it could be. The young are so often underestimated, their pain and passions ignored.

I quickly fixed my breakfast, pushing away thoughts of Brigit. There were other roads to go down. And, irritably, I admitted to my-self that I didn't want it to be Brigit. The pain of that betrayal would have been deeper for Patty Kay than the burn of any bullet.

Rain splashed against the kitchen windows. I turned on all the lights. As I drank my coffee, I read the article from the *Fair Haven Gazette* that I'd printed out at the library. It was accompanied by a picture of a smiling Patty Kay, her face crinkled in exuberant delight.

A three-column head:

FAIR HAVEN'S
PATTY KAY MATTHEWS
LEADS WITH LAUGHTER

She's arrived atop a circus elephant, climbed a fire ladder to plant a flag, led a Dixieland band in a mock funeral march, shouted down protesters, and engaged in a public "strip-tease" (of sorts).

She is Patty Kay Prentiss Matthews, a civic and social leader in Fair Haven, who laughs as she says, "I'll do any-thing for the arts. And I'm determined to prove you don't have to be stuffy to support the art museum or the library or the playhouse."

Mrs. Matthews certainly could never be considered stuffy. Interviewed at her home recently, she was in a rare state of relaxation. "The community fund drive is done—and we earned twenty thousand dollars more than our goal! —so for me it's downtime until we [Fair Haven Women's Society] put on the May charity auction."

It was for the community fund drive that she climbed a fire truck ladder to place the Fair Haven flag on the flagpole at the Fair Haven Mall.

Even a modest assessment of Mrs. Matthews's many accomplishments reveals that her efforts on all fronts have earned Fair Haven's charities and social agencies more than a half million dollars over the past decade.

Mrs. Matthews's late parents, Merriwether and Cornelia Prentiss, were also active in civic affairs. "Mother and Dad made giving fun. They loved to host ice cream socials and picnics for worthy causes. So I learned to have a good time while raising money. But appetites are jaded today, so I decided the best way to get everybody out is to offer irresistible bait. That's why I came up with Catch a Ride with Dumbo for the drive for underprivileged children."

Three years ago Mrs. Matthews hired the lead elephant from a circus appearing in Nashville. She staged a community-wide picnic at Hickory Park and sold rides on the elephant for five hundred dollars each, earning the largest amount ever—$46,000—for the summer camp program.

Mrs. Matthews's efforts aren't restricted to fund-raising. She is willing to ruffle some feathers in this conservative community by the causes she passionately espouses. The mock funeral march was in protest against the *Gazette*'s decision not to carry a comic strip with political overtones. Mrs. Matthews rallied support from enough advertisers to change the *Gazette*'s policy.

One of Mrs. Matthews's principal detractors is the Reverend James Holman. Pastor of Mt. Zion Revival Church, Reverend Holman opposes abortion, gay rights, and feminism. Reverend Holman and Mrs. Matthews are both members of the board of directors for the Fair Haven Public Library.

Supporters of the minister shouted in opposition to a recent library board decision, proposed by Mrs. Matthews, to add materials on prevention of AIDS to the library's Saturday morning reading programs for children.

Mrs. Matthews yanked the microphone from Reverend Holman, then challenged the protesters to admit that their opposition to the dissemination of information on safe sex would result in needless suffering and deaths. "You people will do anything to prevent abortions because you want to save lives, but you are willing to see young people die rather than permit them to discuss sexual activities. For shame," she cried.

Mrs. Matthews has mounted an active campaign to see Reverend Holman defeated in the next library board election.

The much-ballyhooed "striptease" was the highlight of the Revelry Dance Club's annual Christmas ball last year. Mrs. Matthews's "performance" was offered at an auction to raise money for Walden School and was the item bringing in the highest bid, 1,400 dollars. As promised in the auction offer, Mrs. Matthews divested to a skintone body suit at the dance to the accompaniment of drumrolls. She explained, with a laugh, that she had on more than most of her friends wore to aerobics and that raising money might as well be fun.

Last October, Mayor Jane French presented Mrs. Matthews with an Honored Citizens Award for her fund-raising efforts over the years. "I wish we had more dedicated citizens like Patty Kay," the mayor said.

Oh, my, yes. Patty Kay loved to have fun—and to hell with anybody who didn't like it—or her.

It took only a few minutes to do the dishes and leave the newly cleaned kitchen immaculate. I had no intention of tackling the playhouse. Scrubbing would never clear away the dreadful remnants of bloody death.

Twenty minutes later I was showered and dressed for the day. I chose a navy knit with gold buttons. I was in the main hall, walking toward the telephone desk, when I heard a key in the back door. The lock clicked, and the door swung in.

"Mr. Matthews? It's me. Jewel." A small black woman in a neat gray maid's uniform bustled inside. She ducked out of a plastic rain cap and propped a wet umbrella in the corner, then looked up and saw me.

Jewel. Of course, the maid employed by both Patty Kay and Cheryl Kraft.

I smiled in welcome. "Good morning, Jewel. I'm so glad to see you. I'm Henrietta Collins, Mr. Matthews's aunt." The lie came easily.

She shifted a crocheted bag from one arm to another. "Oh, yes, ma'am. I did hear you was here."

It's a small town, for chrissakes.

She hesitated, then added softly, "I'm real sorry, ma'am. About the trouble." She cleared her throat and moved toward the door into the kitchen. "I guess I'll do my regular."

I followed her into the kitchen. "That will be fine. I'm going to be in and out today. I expect Mr. Matthews will be home sometime this afternoon."

Dark eyes slid quickly toward me, then as quickly away. She opened a broom closet, placed her bag inside.

"Jewel, you know the police have arrested Mr. Matthews?"

"Yes, ma'am." She continued to avoid looking at me as she closed the closet door.

The rain was heavier now, drumming against the panes.

"What do you think about that?"

She walked toward the sink. "I reckon it's harder to get out of jail than get in jail. Least, that's true for black people. Jail is a bad place to be."

"Mr. Matthews is innocent."

Jewel bent down, opened a cabinet, began to lift out cleaning materials.

She didn't say a word.

"How long had you worked for Patty Kay?"

She picked up a pair of rubber gloves, then turned to face me, crumpling the gloves in her hand. "I worked for her mama. I was with Mrs. Patty Kay when she and Mr. Stuart lived here. I was with her when Miss Brigit was born." Her mournful eyes glistened with tears. "No one had ought to have hurt her like that. No one."

"Craig didn't do it, Jewel."

"You have to be for your kin," she said quietly. "But I tell you, even nice men sometimes they goes after a pretty face and they do things they shouldn't have."

She yanked on the gloves, grabbed up a plastic pail, and walked swiftly toward the hall door.

She paused only long enough to say, "I don't know nothing but that Mrs. Patty Kay she was upset as she could be all day Friday and if I was you I'd ask Mr. Craig about that apartment he goes to so much. My grandson Matt works the yard over there at those Sandalwood apartments, and he's seen him there. Plenty."

It was at that moment, of course, as I listened to the tattoo of the rain and grappled with a new and chilling consideration of Craig that the telephone rang. I reached for it.

"Hello."

"Henrie O, you're there."

And, for God's sake, it was Margaret.

I gave her a crisp factual report of everything—except the disturbing encounter with Jewel.

"Henrie O, you're wonderful. Of course that stuff was thrown after she was dead!"

"I'm making progress." But not all of it positive. "How are you feeling?"

She was, she said firmly, doing well.

But her voice was very weak.

"You concentrate on getting well. And don't worry about things here. I'll take care of everything." Oh, Henrie O, such brave words. "I'll keep in close touch."

But I wasn't feeling cheerful when I hung up.

If Craig had a lady love . . .

Distantly I heard the growl of a vacuum.

The grandfather clock boomed nine.

I settled at the telephone table and found in my purse my copy of Patty Kay's useful numbers.

My first call was to Laverne. I was lucky. She'd had a cancellation for her ten o'clock. She could take me for a shampoo and set.

My second call was answered promptly. "Mt. Zion Revival Church."

"May I speak to Reverend Holman, please?"

"Our assistant pastor, Mr. Wickey, is taking Reverend Holman's calls."

"I'm sorry. I can speak only to Reverend Holman."

"Reverend Holman won't be back in the office for at least four more weeks."

"Where is he?"

Her voice quivered. "In Vanderbilt hospital. He had open heart surgery last Friday."

"I see. The matter will wait. Thank you."

I checked with Vanderbilt Medical Center. The Reverend James Holman was still in intensive care.

That answered that. I was sorry. I'd thought it might be quite interesting to talk to the reverend about Patty Kay Matthews. A pleasure I would have to forego.

My last call was to Desmond Marino. I'd left him with a list of things to do when we'd parted yesterday.

"Yes, ma'am," the lawyer said briskly. "I've got what you wanted." His voice oozed satisfaction. "An old friend from law school's in the D.A.'s office. Now, in answer to your specific question, the lab didn't find any trace of the stuff in the kitchen on Patty Kay's clothes. Ditto her shoes."

"That makes an enormous difference."

"It does?" He sounded skeptical.

"Look, Desmond, the police theory is that Craig arrived home, he and Patty Kay squabbled about the fruit basket, she was cooking, he lost his temper and started flinging stuff around, and she ran out to the playhouse to get away from him."

"Right."

"So picture it. If Craig and Patty Kay quarreled and Craig started throwing liquids around, surely at least a bit of it would have splashed on her. Even if not, how could she have been standing there cooking and not have had to walk through the stuff to run out to the playhouse?

"The fact that her shoes have no trace of chocolate or cream cheese or liqueurs has to mean that when she left the kitchen, *nothing had yet been thrown.*

"And the only reason to throw it *after* she'd been killed had to be to incriminate Craig. Besides, the timing doesn't work. I'm going to check that out later today. If we get definite testimony about when he left that deli and when the police arrived on the scene, it won't leave enough time for a quarrel, the mess in the kitchen, and her murder."

"You should have been a lawyer." The highest praise any attorney ever gives. "I can use this today with the judge."

"Good."

"Oh, one thing more. The state police found a sweater in a road-side garbage bin that matches the snagged thread on the murder weapon. The sweater's stained with Patty Kay's blood." He sounded queasy. "The police think it belonged to Patty Kay and Craig tried to dump it because he'd used it to try to stop the flow of blood after he shot her. You know, remorse. Then he just took it with him in a panic."

A sweater. Patty Kay's sweater? If this were so, why on earth was Craig stubbornly refusing to admit it?

"Do you have a description of the sweater?"

A pause, a rattle of paper. "Here it is. One hundred percent cotton cardigan, beige, size large. Label from Lands' End."

I recalled Patty Kay's closet. Crammed with gorgeous, vivid clothes. Lots of natural fibers, of course. All designer label and extremely expensive.

I didn't recall a single item that looked like Lands' End.

I'd not checked all the labels. I could do that. But I was certain what I would find.

Nothing from Lands' End.

I'm not knocking the clothes from that giant catalogue company. I'm very fond of them myself. There was a black Lands' End cardigan upstairs in my suitcase.

But it wasn't Patty Kay's kind of sweater.

"Desmond, are the police sure the cloth fragment on the murder weapon came from this sweater?"

"Yep. Absolutely. They've got details about microscopic evaluation of fibers in here." The papers rustled again.

"All right," I said slowly. "We're on to something here. And the police have it all wrong. Craig may have grabbed that sweater up in a panic, that's true enough. But the rest of their theory's wrong. Either the sweater belonged to the murderer or the murderer brought it to the scene and deliberately sopped it in Patty's blood, then left it."

"Jesus, why?"

"Because, Desmond, the police will discover ultimately that the sweater didn't belong to Patty Kay."

"Why not? It's a woman's sweater. It must be the right size—"

"It isn't the size that matters. It's its modest provenance. And its color."

"Huh?"

"Desmond, Patty Kay never owned a beige sweater ordered from a catalogue in her life."

"But why would somebody leave some other woman's sweater there and why would Craig—" He stopped short. "Oh, Christ. You mean it belonged to some other woman and Craig recognized it?"

"I'm afraid so."

He groaned. "God, that'll make it worse for Craig."

"Not if we can prove that sweater was a plant and Craig ran away because of panic over the presence of the sweater and not because he shot Patty Kay."

"Oh, sure. Walsh is really going to believe that."

"Don't sound so glum, Desmond. Panic is better than guilt."

"But I can't go to the police and say there was another woman— you know damn well how that's going to sound—and Craig was trying to protect her. Hell, Mrs. Collins, that's all he needs."

"Don't do it, then. Let's keep poking around." I had one final question. "Obviously, someone who knew Patty Kay well murdered her. Who do you think it might be?" My tone was encouraging.

I expected the usual lawyer's spate of words ending in a firm refusal to do anything as outrageous as make an accusation against anyone.

Instead, after a somber, lengthy silence, Marino surprised me.

"She made enemies. You'll find that out. The problem was that Patty Kay never took anything too seriously and she didn't have the imagination to see how other people could be so, well, so *deadly* serious. I'm thinking about a preacher here in town—"

"The Reverend James Holman?"

"So you've already dug that up?"

"It didn't take genius," I said dryly. "And I've not only dug it up, I've reburied it," and I told him why.

"Oh."

"Is there anyone else Patty Kay had infuriated?"

"No. No, I don't think so."

Craig had said to Brigit, *It's a small town, for chrissakes.*

But not small enough, apparently, for Desmond to offer any other suspects. The Reverend Holman was the only candidate Desmond was ready to propose. His lawyerly instincts hadn't deserted him. Far be it from him to focus on anyone in his own poker group.

"In any event, we need to check on the whereabouts of the poker players when Patty Kay was shot. Will you do that?"

He didn't sound overwhelmed with joy at the task, but he gruffly acquiesced.

"What are you going to do?" he demanded.

"Talk to people. Lots of them."

The funeral procession was a long one. I pulled over to await its passage. The heavier rain had eased, but a steady sprinkle spattered against the windshield. The trees along the street looked sodden, their spring glory dimmed. It was a fitting day for grief. Patty Kay's funeral would be tomorrow. Surely Desmond would be able to get Craig out of jail by then.

Finally, the long cortege was past. I drove out to the Fair Haven Mall. There were plenty of parking spaces in front of Books, Books, Books.

I shook my umbrella and left it dripping in the entryway. Books, Books, Books was a booklover's dream. Perhaps twenty thousand square feet, islands and islands of books face out (book business lingo for the cover showing instead of the spine), and a coffee and surprisingly lavish dessert bar.

It took only a moment for me to find Amy shelving new books in the history and politics section. The clerk Craig had mentioned was small, dark, and very thin. She wore her hair in two lengthy braids. Oversize glasses magnified her eyes. She wore a name badge: AMY FOSS.

"Pardon me."

"Yes, ma'am?"

"Amy, I'm Mrs. Collins, Craig Matthews's aunt."

Amy got that look of dumb anguish that afflicts people confronted with a situation they haven't the faintest notion how to handle. I couldn't fault her. Even Miss Manners might find it hard to know what to say to a relative of a man accused of brutally murdering his wife. "Nice day" doesn't cut it.

I flashed a reassuring smile. "Don't be upset. Mr. Matthews will soon be out of jail." This was a rumor I didn't mind starting. Who knew what effect it might have. "We both know he's innocent."

"Oh, yes, ma'am." Behind the glasses, her eyes remained wide and anxious.

I glanced around. "So if we could find a quiet spot—"

She gulped nervously, then led the way to a bench in the deserted poetry section. She perched at the far end of the bench, her hands twisted tightly in her lap.

"How long have you worked here, Amy?"

"Two weeks. I'm part-time during the week because of school. All day on Saturdays and Sundays."

There's a feeling when you draw a straight flush. It's the way I felt at her answer. Amy was new. She wouldn't recognize voices, not even that of Patty Kay Matthews, the store's owner. Certainly not those of longtime customers.

An essential element of the murderer's scheme.

"College student?"

"Yes, ma'am."

"Now, tell me about Saturday afternoon—and the phone calls."

She peered at me uneasily. "I can't say about the calls Mr. Matthews got. I mean, I wasn't watching him or anything. He may have answered the phone just like he says, but I didn't see it." Defensiveness threaded her high voice.

"No reason you should have," I agreed easily. "Whose job is it to answer the phone?"

"Whoever's standing there."

"Where?"

She stood to point. "There are phones at the information desk and the coffee bar and the office and the main desk. Some are different lines. For example, in the office. Anyway, whoever's closest to the phone that rings, they answer it." She shrugged.

"Where were you?"

"I was working the main register."

"Tell me about the call where you took the message for Mr. Matthews."

She sank back onto the bench, misery in her eyes. "Everybody keeps asking me and asking me. But I didn't pay a lot of attention. It was just a message—he was to go to this shop over by Green Hills and pick up a basket of fruit—but I don't exactly remember what she said."

"She?"

"Yes. A woman. I think. I mean, it *sounded* like a woman. She spoke fast, like she was in a rush. She said something like"—the clerk's face tightened as she strove to remember—" 'Tell Craig to go by Finedorff's and pick up a fruit basket and bring it home pronto. Thanks.' That's all there was to it. And people keep asking me and asking me about it. They ask if it was Mrs. Matthews. I don't know. How should I know? I met her only once and I don't even remember if she said anything. She smiled. She had a nice smile."

"You're doing fine, Amy. No one could expect more. So, you took the call. Then, when Mr. Matthews had finished with his customer, you told him about it. What did you say?"

"I told him his wife wanted him to pick up a fruit basket at this shop and bring it home right now."

"So he would have thought the call came from Mrs. Matthews."

She clasped her hands together and stared down at them. "Yes. I guess. But I didn't know. I mean, I just gave him the message."

"Yes, of course. Did he leave immediately?"

For an instant laughter touched her eyes. "Yes, ma'am. He was out of here in a flash."

"And that was around . . ."

"A quarter to four."

She spoke with utter confidence.

And Craig had just as definitely and strongly told me he'd left the store at four o'clock.

An extra fifteen minutes could put Craig in prison, possibly on death row.

"I thought it was closer to four."

"No, ma'am. It was exactly a quarter to four. I know because I'd just looked at my watch."

"Why?"

A tiny flush of pink edged her cheeks. "I break at four. I was going to go into the coffee bar and have a caramel brownie. And then I couldn't when he left. I had to stay on the floor."

"I see. Mr. Matthews thought it was a few minutes later than that."

"No." Her voice was sharp. "It was exactly a quarter to four."

And she'd swear it today and tomorrow and forever. She might be young and uncomfortable. She was also stubborn.

I changed course. "How do you like working here?"

"Oh." She was surprised. Understandably. After all, what did her appraisal of the store have to do with anything? But, the customer is always right. She brightened. "I like it a lot. At least, until all this happened. I wasn't sure I would. They're all so rich, but they're nice."

They?

"Who?" It was my turn to be surprised.

"The ladies who work here. I mean, in addition to us. Me and Jackie and Paul and Todd and Candy. Oh, and Stevie, the assistant manager. She does most of the work. We're all just regular people. But all these rich ladies who work one day a week. I thought they'd be snotty. But they're not, they're real nice. At least, most of them are. I handle the scheduling." She grinned, and I caught a glimpse of a likable, fun girl when she wasn't under pressure. "It's like musical chairs. You'd think anybody could always be sure of one day a week, but they have Conflicts." Her voice capitalized it, making me smile too. "Like going to Atlanta to shop. Or they need to sub at tennis for a friend. Or their rottweiler's having pups. So Mrs. Forrest switches with Mrs. Hollis, who switches with Mrs. Pierce. But they're mostly nice. And they know everybody who comes in." She looked suddenly shrewd. "That's a big plus in a retail store."

Yes, it was smart marketing.

And now I had the funny little tingle you get with a full house.

This was Patty Kay's store. The rich women who worked here would be her friends. Were some her enemies?

I asked for the list of part-time employees.

Amy hesitated. "I don't know—Stevie's not here. She'll be in at noon and she probably—"

I headed off a declaration I wouldn't like. "Mr. Matthews knows I'm here," I said firmly.

That was enough to satisfy her.

She led me back to the office and quickly found the right file on a computer. As the file was being printed out, I said loudly, "A wonderful convenience, but noisy, isn't it?"

She nodded.

"I wonder—when you took that message Saturday, was there any noise behind the voice? Music? Traffic? Phones ringing? Anything like that?"

She was relaxed now. She didn't feel badgered. I wasn't pressuring her to identify a voice—or not identify it. "No, ma'am. It was real quiet."

The printer clattered to a stop, and she ripped off the sheet and handed it to me: Edith Hollis. Brooke Forrest. Louise Pierce. Pamela Guthrie. Cheryl Kraft.

Two names surprised me.

"Louise Pierce. Is that Mrs. Stuart Pierce?"

"Yes, ma'am." Amy's face was placid. Old marital history meant nothing to her.

"And Mrs. Guthrie. Is that Mrs. Matthews's sister?"

Amy frowned. "She's the only one who's rude. I called Mrs. Guthrie last week to see if she'd be in on her day and I woke her up. At ten o'clock in the morning. She was real hateful."

I folded the printout, put it in my purse. "Amy, thanks for talking to me." I took a step, then turned back. "If you remember anything else about that call, the one about the deli, please give me a ring. I'm staying at the Matthews house."

"Oh, yes, ma'am. I will. I promise."

10

L averne kneaded my scalp with practiced fingers and the hot, soapy water tingled against my head. She rinsed my hair, wound a towel expertly around my head turban-style, and we walked back to her chair.

"You visiting here in town?"

"Yes. I'm doing some historical research in the area. My great-grandfather was killed in the Battle of Franklin."

That satisfied her. Genealogy is a passion in the South.

I sat down and Laverne covered me with a peach gown. As she set to work, I looked around the mostly empty salon. "Pretty slow today."

"Everybody's at the Hollis girl's funeral. It's really too bad. Sure makes you realize money isn't everything."

The stylist at the next station was buffing her nails. "That's for sure," she chimed in. "So they all went to Walden School. So what? At least my kid didn't walk into a lake. And I've heard there's something really odd going on. Judy Holzer—she works over at the Braidwood Florist—she says she heard it was suicide. Isn't that awful? A kid fifteen years old."

I must have jerked, made a movement or a sound.

Laverne paused. "Oh, I'm sorry. Did I comb too hard?"

"No." My voice sounded thin even to me. "No. I'm fine."

But I wasn't fine. She hadn't combed too hard. I concentrated on relaxing, and suppressing, as best I could, the emotion that always threatens to engulf me when I see a child's obituary. Bobby was twelve, only twelve . . .

Laverne picked up a handful of curlers. "Well, I think that girl was a little slow, Tammy. Maybe it was an accident. That's what the family's saying. I do Mrs. Hollis's sister's hair and she said it was some kind of kid dare and poor little Franci didn't know any better than to try and swim across that lake."

"Franci Hollis," I repeated. "Is that—" I broke off. I'd almost revealed myself, almost asked if this was the family on King's Row Road. But I knew the answer. *"The poor Hollises,"* Cheryl Kraft had said. Oh, God, yes. The poor Hollises with friends and family gathering in the wake of a family's bitter tragedy.

The beauticians were waiting politely.

And I shouldn't know anything about King's Row Road and its heartbreaks.

I cleared my throat. "What a lovely name. I'm so sorry. Children so often don't think when someone makes a dare."

"I used to see her at soccer games," Tammy continued. "My Jack and the Hollis girl's brother were on the Y team together." She shook her head, her thick blond hair swaying. "Sure makes you think."

I willed my muscles to relax. Forced them to relax. And managed, despite the pain, to focus on my task. "Bad things seem to happen all at once. Isn't this the town where that young woman was murdered out in her pool cabana?" I felt Laverne's fingers slacken for an instant.

Tammy sat up straight. "I tell you, I don't know what the world's coming to! Patty Kay Matthews, the richest woman in town."

"Was it a robbery?" I asked innocently.

Laverne tilted my head to work on the back curls. "No. God, it's worse than that. They've arrested her husband—but I can't believe he did it. My Billy worked on his car. Billy says no way did Craig Matthews shoot somebody. One time Matthews was going to leave his Porsche and Billy saw the gun in his glove compartment and he asked Matthews to take it with him. Billy said he's never seen a man act so silly. Matthews didn't even want to put his hand on it."

"I know somebody who didn't have any use at all for Patty Kay." The blond stylist wriggled with excitement. "I saw Patty Kay at Kroger's just last week and she came around one of the aisles and there she was face-to-face with Louise Pierce, her first husband's wife, and you know what?"

Laverne and I both looked at her expectantly.

"Well, if *looks* could kill! Louise Pierce gave Patty Kay the meanest, hardest glare and she stalked right by without saying a word. Not a word. And the funny thing is, see, it was always Patty Kay who was mad because Louise got Stuart and Louise always went around looking like a cat with cream on her whiskers. But last week it's *Louise* who's furious. Now, I just have to wonder why."

I wondered too.

"And after Louise stomped by, Patty Kay turned and looked after her. And she looked real funny—almost like she was scared."

The sign hung a little crooked on the doorknob, a pasteboard clock face with movable hands. They registered eleven A.M. The legend informed: OUT OF THE OFFICE. BACK SOON.

I used my umbrella to fend off the light drizzle and strolled the length of Fair Haven's Main Street. The restored brickfront buildings offered a charming assortment of shops. I admired patchwork quilts, wooden carvings, hand-wrought jewelry, and antique furniture and silver.

I walked back to Gina Abbott's shop. Her display included a long swath of Manuel Canovas fabric with a floral design—bright pink peonies and stylized jade-green leaves—draped over an eighteenth-century gilt wood backless seat patterned after a Roman camp stool.

Gilt letters in the lower left pane of the window read simply: GINA ABBOTT, DECORATOR.

The light rain, persistent, elegiac, misted against the windows. I stepped into the recessed entryway. I tried the doorknob and was startled when it moved. Was it an oversight or was this indeed such a law-abiding small town that Gina Abbott didn't bother to lock up? More likely, she'd forgotten. Whatever, I propped my umbrella against the wall and went in.

Her taste ran to earth tones—mauve, coral, sand, peach. The showroom was fairly small, but it afforded several enclaves for customers, comfortable chintz sofas and chairs grouped around coffee tables at a good height for studying catalogues and swatches and wallpaper samples.

I wandered toward the back. A door stood ajar. I pushed it wider.

Gina Abbott's office was a jam-packed mess, but cheerful. Bolts of cloth, swatches of fabric, photographs, house plans, and stacked catalogues were everywhere.

The walls were bare except for a snapshot-laden bulletin-board. I walked closer. I recognized four faces immediately. The tennis quartet was obviously of long duration. Lots of tennis pictures with Patty Kay, Gina, Edith, and Brooke when they were in their late twenties and early thirties. Sometimes their children were there. It didn't take long to figure out which belonged to whom.

Brigit didn't smile very often. But as a little girl, she was always stylishly dressed. Trust Patty Kay for that.

Elegant Brooke apparently had only the one child. Even when he was a little boy, Dan was as spectacularly handsome as his mother was beautiful, perfect bone structure, glossy black hair, wide-spaced blue eyes, even white teeth in a confident smile.

I recognized the freckle-faced, stocky girl who'd tried to get Edith's attention at Brigit's birthday party. And the red-haired boy who'd admired Dan's dancing partner was obviously her brother. The little girl had an especially sweet smile, the boy a steady, inquiring gaze. Edith Hollis was usually the model of brightness, but every so often the camera caught that edge of surliness. Was it jealousy? Lack of confidence?

Most of the snapshots, of course, were of elfin Gina's children. Gina's daughter was the chubby blond girl who'd danced so adoringly with Dan Forrest. Gina's two sons were wiry, short, dark, and exceptionally athletic. There were lots of photos of wrestling matches, swim meets, tennis tournaments. In contrast, her daughter was fair and plump and usually carrying a book.

"Who the hell are you?"

I hadn't heard a sound.

I turned around calmly.

She'd come in through the back door. She stood just inside, water dripping from her apricot silk raincoat, her bony face drawn into a furious scowl, her sleek black hair damp against her head.

She reminded me of a very small cat I'd once had. Sophie didn't weigh four pounds dripping wet. But let anything or anyone invade her domain, from a six-foot-six television repairman to a boxer dog, and she'd gather herself for combat. And mean it, all the way to her marrow.

"Mrs. Abbott?"

"You got it. This is my office. Who the hell are you and how did you get in?"

"The front door was unlocked. I didn't mean to trespass. I'm Henrietta Collins, Craig Matthews's aunt. I'm in town to try to help him. His lawyer, Desmond Marino, told me you were Patty Kay's best friend."

She yanked off her rain cap, tossed it toward a green jardiniere on a small rosewood stand.

"Oh, God. I'm sorry." She shrugged out of the raincoat. "This has been a fucking awful day." She flung the coat toward a coat tree and walked past me. Her face crumpled into lines of misery as she began to cry. She reached blindly for her chair, sank into it.

"I'm sorry. I'll come back another time . . ."

"No. Wait. I'm sorry." Gina snatched a handful of Kleenex, scrubbed at her face. Mascara streaked her cheekbones. "I keep saying I'm sorry. I sure am. I'm sorry as hell. For everybody. You ever been to a funeral for a fifteen-year-old?"

I felt as though I'd been carved out of ice, without a heartbeat, without a breath.

Not quite fifteen. Bobby was twelve years and four months and sixteen days old.

Some wounds never heal. Never. So yes, I understood Gina's tears, and I understood, too, the fear, the soul-deep fear, that spurred her outburst.

Because if it can happen to a friend, it can happen to you.

As it did to me.

I could see Bobby's face so clearly, even after all these years, sandy hair and laughing green eyes and a generous mouth, so much like his father's.

I couldn't answer Gina.

But she didn't give me a chance.

The words came in an anguished torrent. "Why the hell can't they tell you when something's that bad? I told my kids, 'Jesus Christ, come to me if you've got a problem. I don't care what it is—a baby, cocaine, you're gay, just for Jesus Christ's sake, *tell* me!' " The tears trickled down her grief-ravaged face. "It doesn't matter what it is. That's what I tell them. We can handle it. But when you die, you die." She clenched her small fists, pounded them against the desktop. "I'm so mad. So mad! I could shake Franci until her head pops off. But I can't. Because she rode her bike to the other side of the lake on Friday and walked out into the water and never came back. And do you know why?"

My heart ached at the agony in her cry.

"Because of some stupid fucking *letters*, that's why. That's all it was, anonymous letters telling her she was ugly, a lesbo, and everybody knew it, that she was too stupid to go to college and she had a funny smell and was a four-eyed loser. Most of it was just stupid, silly childish crap, but it got nastier and nastier. Some of it was sickening.

Stuff Franci couldn't even start to understand. But she knew it was bad. And Franci was this uncertain, self-conscious, pudgy kid—and yes, dammit, she was slow—with thick braces and an awkward way of walking, up one day and down the next like most kids, and she couldn't handle it and she couldn't tell her folks because they didn't talk about things like lesbians and maybe they'd believe it since everybody else did. That's what she told Chloe. My Chloe. And Chloe, the idiot child, didn't tell me because she promised Franci that she'd never say anything to anybody."

Franci Hollis, the girl they'd talked about at the beauty salon. The daughter of Patty Kay's tennis friend, Edith Hollis. The sweet-faced girl in the film of Brigit's birthday party.

Gina struggled to breathe.

I walked over to a water cooler, pulled down a paper cup, and filled it.

Gina took it gratefully. Gradually, her sobs eased.

"They're going to have counseling for all the kids who ask. Out at school. But it won't bring Franci back." Gina downed the rest of the water, crumpled the cup, and reached for the phone. She swiftly punched the numbers.

No, nothing ever brings anyone back. And there are the long, agonizing hours in the night when the refrain goes on and on in your mind. "If we hadn't driven to Cuernavaca that night on the twisting, narrow mountain road . . ." A rusted pickup out of control, smashing into us, and Richard and Emily and I were all right. But not Bobby. And I'd been the one who'd insisted we go. I didn't want to miss the fiesta. Oh, Christ, a fiesta. I'd insisted. . . .

Gina kneaded her temple. "Chloe? Just thought I'd check. Are you going back to school? Look, I can close up and come home—You're sure?" The decorator's eyes looked bruised. "Honey, honey, you couldn't have known. There was no way you could've known." Her fingers closed tightly on the silver necklace at her throat. "That's right. Go on back to school. Yes. I'll see you tonight."

Replacing the receiver, she blearily focused on me. "I still can't take it in. First Franci. Then Patti Kay. And I know Craig didn't—God,

I can't even say it, it's so sick. God, I feel like I'm choking." Abruptly, she reached behind, unsnapped the necklace. The metal clinked against the desk as she flung it down. "Okay, Mrs. Collins, I'll get myself together. What do you want to talk to me about?"

It took a moment to push away the questions I'd never been able to answer—or escape—and plunge myself into the present. "Patty Kay."

"All in one week," she muttered. "Nothing like this's ever happened in Fair Haven. Never."

I understood. Patty Kay's shocking murder and a teen's tragic suicide would have the same devastating impact as the kidnapping of the Exxon executive from the driveway of his home in another exclusive suburb. A well-ordered universe was abruptly revealed as inimical, incalculable. Fair Haven had no place in its cosmology for cruel malevolence.

Gina yanked open her desk drawer, began to root around. "Oh, crap." She looked at me desperately. "You have any cigarettes?"

I'd quit more than thirty years ago. Thank God.

She answered her own question. "No, no. Damn, I know I hid some somewhere. The last time I quit." She jumped up, tugged her chair up to the shelving behind the desk. She climbed on the chair, poked her hand behind a stack of wallpaper rolls, then heaved a sigh of relief.

Her hands were trembling when she returned to her chair, clutching a crumpled pack of Winstons. She pulled out a worn cigarette. "It'll taste awful." She lit it, pulled the smoke deep in her lungs, made a face. "All right. Where were we? Oh. Patty Kay. What can I say? It's insane. Now I'm afraid for Chloe to be home by herself after school. Maybe I ought to stay home. I never worried when the boys were home. They'd take care of their sister. God, that's sexist, isn't it? Chloe's as capable as anybody. But she's a girl and girls aren't strong. But it wasn't strength that mattered for Patty Kay, was it? Somebody had a damn gun. Jesus, Craig's gun! But the idea that Craig did it is stupid. Craig hates guns. It really upset him when Patty Kay got onto the gun kick. He acted like a nun at a nudist colony." She flashed me a quick, contrite look. "I'm sorry. That's my theme song with you, isn't it? I don't mean to make fun of Craig. But I grew up with guns. My dad hunted. My husband—when I had one—he hunted. My sons hunt. I just thought Craig was a wimp. But I *know* he couldn't shoot anybody. But somebody did it. The thing is, how did some stranger get Craig's gun? And why would Patty Kay be in the playhouse with a stranger? I mean, she definitely wasn't born yesterday. I tell you, I'm confused as hell."

There had been no description of the kitchen in the newspaper accounts.

I described to Gina what Craig had found, what the police had seen, what I had cleaned up.

"God, that's weird. Just last week—" Her mouth snapped shut.

"Last week?"

"Nothing, nothing." She stared down at the desk.

"The limericks? At the poker party?"

She looked relieved. "Then you already know. But Craig just had too much to drink. It didn't mean a thing."

"How did you happen to hear about it?"

"Brooke told me. David's in the poker group."

I knew that. And, as I had thought, the cheesecake story had obviously had wide currency.

Gina's relief at not having to tell me about Craig's transgression faded. "But if Craig didn't shoot Patty Kay—and I *know* he didn't—then somebody knew about those stupid limericks and threw the cake to make it look like him." She took a last greedy puff from the cigarette, dropped it into a Coke can. "Oh, Christ. That's awful. That means . . ."

She wrapped her arms tightly around her body. Her tear-streaked face suddenly looked old, the bones harsh against tight skin.

"You were her best friend."

The only response was a spasm of pain on that haggard face. Her lips trembled.

"Desmond Marino *said* you were her best friend."

She pushed up from her chair, bent across the desk to grab the cigarette pack. She began to pace, head down, smoking, before she replied, in a staccato burst. "Yeah. He got it right. I *was*. I mean, I still was—even though we weren't speaking to each other. I was so damn mad at Patty Kay." She stopped, flung her head up. "Christ, she was so *rich*. She couldn't even begin to understand about not having money, or having to worry about money. I mean"—she whirled—"she couldn't see any side to things but *her* side. I've been working a deal that could mean almost a hundred thousand dollars to me. It all hinges on getting some property I own rezoned for commercial instead of residential. It's right on the edge of the historic district. This property was home to historic flophouses and, a long time ago, to Fair Haven's fancy ladies. The buildings sure as hell aren't worth saving. But Patty Kay wanted a buffer area between the historic houses and commercial development. And it's the only thing I've got that could bring in some real money and I truly need it for the kids' college expenses. My ex, the sorry asshole, is too busy with his new little brood to help the kids go to school. So it's all up to me."

She dropped into her chair again, stubbed out the cigarette, and yanked out the center desk drawer. She found a cream-colored envelope and held it out to me. "I swear to God, I could have *killed* her!"

I pulled out the enclosure, embossed with Patty Kay's initials, and saw that familiar, flowing, crimson script:

Dear Gina,

I wish I could support you in your efforts to have the Brewster property rezoned. But I can't. We have to stop the encroachment of commercial building within the historic district. Fair Haven must not lose its most precious heritage.

I'm surprised and disappointed by your defection. I thought we were *both* committed to historic preservation. Obviously, we can't be supporters one day and opponents the next. I didn't think you would succumb to financial considerations.

I hope you'll see the necessity for consistency and drop your request for rezoning.

Love,
Patty Kay

"Did you tell her how much you needed the money?"

"Tell her! I *begged*. So she offered to pay for the kids to go to college, and that was the last straw. Dammit, I don't want charity—I want to be able to pay my way."

"But you were still playing tennis with her?"

She flung her hands up. "Oh, yes. We just weren't speaking. Brooke was irritated with us and Edith kept trying to patch it up—and now Patty Kay's dead." Tears sparkled in her eyes. "And I can't even tell her I wasn't really mad at her. I was *nuts* with everything! Trying to get by on too little money, trying to get my ex to cough some up, trying to keep up appearances—God, the guttering's bad on the house and I can't afford to replace it, but you don't ever want anybody to know you're down and out. They'd avoid you like the plague."

"Okay," I said mildly. "You and Patty Kay had a quarrel. But you still knew her better than anybody else."

"Oh, yeah. I've known her forever. Since we were little kids. Even then, she bossed me around. Patty Kay was always in charge. But she was so much fun. So damned much fun. And now you're telling me somebody she knew—somebody *I* know—shot her down." Again, compulsively, she reached for the cigarette pack.

"When was the last time you actually talked to her?"

Gina lit another cigarette, stared at its flaming tip.

A billboard announcement couldn't have made it clearer that she didn't want to answer.

"Recently?" I persisted. "After your quarrel over the property?"

"Well, something else came up. And I did talk to her. And it made her madder than hell."

"About?"

"Nothing that could have anything to do with—with her murder." She chose her words with enormous care. "So the last time we talked—even when we weren't talking—was pretty harsh. And I hate it." Her voice quivered. "Because no matter what, I loved her."

"Someone didn't."

She snatched another Kleenex, wiped her eyes. She didn't look at me. "I know of one person. There's this preacher—"

"The Reverend James Holman. But—"

"Yeah. I know it sounds crazy, but Holman's one of those far-right nuts. He and Patty Kay despised each other. Somebody told me he preached one Sunday and told his congregation she was visited by the devil. I think maybe it's DEVIL in capital letters." She smoothed the crumpled cellophane on the cigarette box and shook her head. "But I can't imagine how Holman could know about the cheesecake. Sure, this is a small town, but believe me, he didn't move in the same circles as Patty Kay. Not socially."

"Unless he's a remarkable specimen, he's not in the running. He had open heart surgery Friday. He's still in intensive care."

"Oh."

I understood her disappointment. Wouldn't it be lovely to fasten the blame on someone who wasn't a part of Patty Kay's social scene?

She blew out a spurt of smoke. "Okay. The cheesecake So you figure either one of the poker players shot Patty Kay or told somebody about the limericks and that person did it. Who are the poker players?"

"Desmond Marino, Stuart Pierce, Willis Guthrie, David Forrest, and Craig Matthews."

"Well, Desmond has a mouth like Niagara Falls." A tiny smile. "Guess I'm a great one to talk. God, yes, that's true, both ways. But Desmond tells everybody everything. Patty Kay always said the only way Desmond kept from spilling client secrets was by keeping his big mouth busy with everything else." She shrugged. "Of course, knowing how people are, all the others came home and told their wives. It's too good a story not to. We were all sick of that wretched cheesecake. But you couldn't say so because Patty Kay was so damned proud of it."

Gina's eyes closed for just an instant. Then she looked at me. I knew she'd steeled herself not to cry. "Okay. The poker party. I guess we're trying to figure out who might have had a motive. Not Desmond. There's no possible reason. He wasn't Patty Kay's lawyer. Braden Fairlee took care of her legal affairs and always has. And Desmond and Patty Kay have been friends since they were little kids. So, let's see. Stuart . . ."

She glared at me through the swirl of smoke. "Dammit, I don't like this."

"I know."

"Patty Kay's going to be buried tomorrow." She smoked and rubbed her temple, her face puckered in thought and misery. She stubbed out the cigarette.

A minute ticked by.

Finally, grimly, Gina looked straight at me. "Okay. Last week I was in Atlanta. A home decorator show. I stayed at the downtown Marriott. Convenient to the convention center. Had a damned tiring day. So about four I went to the bar. It sits up a level in the middle of the lobby. You know, kind of like an island. So you can look down and see the lobby and the elevators. I saw Stuart first. He was standing by an elevator. Then, damned if Patty Kay didn't walk up. They were standing side by side, ignoring each other. Like they'd never met. They got on the elevator. Just happened it was only the two of them. The car went up to the sixteenth floor, stopped, came down again. I'd had to be brain-dead not to figure that one out quick. They were shacking up. I know it. I know it as well as I can tell you where the scar is—was —on Patty Kay's right elbow. And what the hell that means with all of this, I don't know. If anything."

It would be one more bar in Craig's prison cell if it checked out. At least as far as the police were concerned.

"I mean, I know how I read it. They couldn't live together, but they still—" She paused and looked at me doubtfully.

Why do younger people get so uncomfortable talking about sex to anyone over sixty? It's part of the American youth cult. If they should live so long, they'll discover that, as with most aspects of life, the more you've done it, the better you get—and give. Trust me.

"Oh, hell, the truth of it is, Patty Kay and Stuart were meant for each other, but they were both take-charge types so they could never live together without killing each other. . . ." She clapped a hand to her mouth, then violently shook her head. "I didn't mean that. I didn't."

Perhaps not. But she'd said it.

"What I'm getting at," she continued hurriedly, "is they couldn't keep away from each other. That's why I called Patty Kay even though we weren't speaking. She was mad as hell because I didn't mince words. I told her it was wrong, told her she was playing with dynamite."

"What did she say?"

"She told me to take my platitudes about love and marriage and go straight to hell. And if I knew so damn much about marriage, what happened to mine? We yelled at each other." Gina buried her face in her hands.

I wondered. It was an effective story. It saddled Craig with the additional motive of his wife's infidelity. It also set up Stuart Pierce, her ex-husband, in the background as a solid suspect. And, if true, Patty Kay's extramarital fling certainly was a lot more flamboyant than an argument over rezoning.

Gina lifted her face. Her eyes were swollen. "I remember when we were girls, the first time Patty Kay saw Stuart. It was like watching Fourth of July fireworks."

"A grand passion."

"A grand passion." She rubbed the balled-up tissues on her face, smearing what remained of her makeup. "Yes. That's what it was."

"For Stuart too?"

She sagged back in her chair, drained. "Hell, I don't know. Who's to say, with a man. She had a gorgeous body. Maybe that's what he wanted. Maybe he didn't really care otherwise. I know that whenever she walked into a room, Stuart had a damned hard time keeping his eyes off of her. Even after they were divorced. Even after he remarried. It must have driven Louise crazy."

Louise Pierce. Stuart's second wife. Brigit's stepmother. The one who snooped. How far did she snoop? How much did she know? Was this why she'd glared at Patty Kay at the supermarket?

But these weren't the only questions that needed answers.

Was the rendezvous between Patty Kay and Stuart a regular occurrence? If so, were both satisfied with the status quo?

Or was Patty Kay hoping and planning and counting on having Stuart back again as her husband?

That would mean a divorce for her from Craig. Craig would lose his extremely comfortable life as the husband of a very rich woman. The public humiliation would be profound. Even a mild-mannered man could be moved to fury by adultery. And a lazy, comfort-seeking man might be desperately determined to preserve his cushy existence.

What about Stuart?

What if he wanted Patty Kay, desired her, lusted for her, but had no interest at all in destroying the fabric of his present life?

What if Patty Kay were pressuring him? What if Patty Kay had threatened to tell Louise?

Or turn it around, what if Patty Kay wanted dalliance and Stuart wanted permanence?

What if Stuart threatened to tell Craig?

"I suppose I shouldn't say it . . . but Louise really hated Patty Kay. She always did." Gina frowned. "This is like lifting up a garbage can and finding all those squirming white slugs. And the horrible part of this is, I know you're thinking Patty Kay was cheap and trashy. But that's absolutely not true. Okay, she slept with Stuart and she shouldn't have, but anybody can have a blind spot." Gina's reddened eyes entreated me. "She was good and decent and—and honorable. I know that sounds funny, but it's like with that preacher and the AIDS thing, Patty Kay just wouldn't let it go. She knew it was wrong not to try to save people just because society is so stupid about sex. And she despised cruelty. One time when we were teenagers there was a workman kicking a dog, and she took a broom and lit into him. She was never afraid to do what she thought was right."

"She made fun of Brigit's crush on Craig. That was cruel."

"She didn't mean it that way. She just liked to make a joke of things. Sometimes she didn't realize that she shouldn't. She really believed people should be open about things. Good and bad. But she wasn't cruel. She hated for people to take advantage of those who couldn't protect themselves. In a funny way, I think she thought Brigit was trying to take advantage of Craig, that she was going after him just to provoke her mother."

A serpentine approach surely. But possible. You can't underestimate the young. Remember Joan of Arc and Billy the Kid.

And I had to believe Brigit was self-absorbed. She'd shed tears for her mother, but her first thought was for Craig because of her own passion for him. And she hadn't even mentioned the schoolmate who'd recently taken her own life. All those cars at the gray Cape Cod. I knew about the kind of pain behind those closed doors.

I clenched my hands, but kept my voice even. "How about Willis Guthrie?"

Gina thought about it. And rubbed her temple again. "I hate looking at people I know and trying them out in my mind as killers. The odd thing is, I've known Willis and Pamela all my life and I don't have any idea at all what goes on in his mind. I doubt if Pamela does. Maybe it's all numbers. He's an accountant. He's the kind of person who doesn't even seem to be there when you're around him. Boring. Hardly ever says anything. Never gets excited. Never saw him lose his temper." She wriggled uneasily. "But he likes things. Collects old silver. And rare books. And Chinese pottery. And Pamela's nuts about porcelain dolls and seventeenth-century snuffboxes and antique toys. Their house looks like a museum. They're damn lucky they never had any kids. Of course, if they'd had kids, maybe they'd have thought about something besides *things* all the time."

I was, I realized abruptly, liking Gina much too much. Her heartbreak over Franci, the empathy she had for people who had nothing in their lives but things, moved me. I needed to keep my distance. Because she'd shared a great deal with me—much of it damaging to others—and that could be very deliberate indeed.

I gave her more room to maneuver. "So Pamela and Willis are greedy?"

"Greedy. Avaricious. Grasping. But maybe I'm wrong. I mean, maybe it's just that they don't have anything else to care about. Things make some people feel good. Sometimes it isn't just that my clients want their homes to be beautiful, they want to be surrounded by expensive objects. It's beyond aesthetics. The more it costs, the better it makes them feel." She shrugged.

"Will Pamela gain financially from Patty Kay's death?"

"Look, everybody in town knows—Pamela and Patty Kay'd been

feuding for months over some of the estate property their parents had left them. Pamela's all for selling out to some condo developers. Patty Kay refused to agree. Kind of like my deal but on a much grander scale. Patty Kay wanted to keep the land undeveloped. She wanted to cede it to Walden School for a wilderness area. The land adjoins the school property. They were furious with each other."

Money.

Such a good, old-fashioned, solid motive for murder.

"Did they—either Willis or Pamela—dislike Craig?"

"I guess not. Why would Willis play poker with him? 'Course, you can end up doing things with people you don't like in a small town and there's no way to avoid it unless you're willing to be rude. But I don't have any reason to think so. Except Craig's not their kind of guy." She looked suddenly embarrassed.

My supposed relationship to Craig was gaining me entrée; it could also shade responses. I spoke up quickly. "Don't hesitate to say what you think. I don't care about anything but finding out who shot Patty Kay."

"Well." Gina cleared her throat. "Craig's the nicest guy in the world, but he isn't a hard charger. I mean, he's not very ambitious. In the eyes of somebody like Willis. You know what kind of hours accountants work."

I smiled. "You mean Craig's a charming young man who married a rich wife and was perfectly content to work—not very hard—at a bookstore she owned for pleasure."

She didn't meet my eyes. "Uh, yes."

"That's Craig. That doesn't offend me. But it could offend others." An envious person might take great pleasure in stripping my "nephew" of his life of ease.

She hurried to change the subject. "David Forrest would be too uptight to stage the mess in the kitchen. I mean, this guy's Major Dad without a glimmer of a smile. He's still in the marine reserves. Marine boot camp was probably the highlight of David's life."

"You don't like him."

"No." It was crisp and unequivocal. "If I had to point to somebody who could shoot in cold blood, he'd be the guy. He gives me the creeps. Everything has to be just right for Mr. David Forrest. I don't see how Brooke stands it."

"Stands it?"

"Living with him. It would be like having sex with a robot."

Her face flamed. For a moment, she'd forgotten her audience.

"How did David Forrest and Patty Kay get along?"

"Polite to each other. Of course, David's always polite. Patty Kay thought he was boring, but so far as I know, he'd have absolutely no reason to kill her. Except maybe to rid the world of an uppity female."

"Antifeminist?"

"Oh, honey, you'd better believe it."

"How does he treat his wife?"

"David treats Brooke like he treats everybody else, as an underling. Of course, he was bred to it. There have always been two top families in this town, the Prentisses and the Forrests. And maybe the Forrests are even a little richer and a little more proud of themselves. Fuck them all," she said cheerfully. "My dad ran a grocery store. Brooke and I grew up across the street from each other. Brooke knew what she wanted from the time she was tiny. She wanted to be 'important' and she set out to catch David Forrest when she was in junior high." Her grin flashed. "Brooke was always the prettiest girl in town. And she prepared to be a rich man's wife the way some girls set their heart on med or law school. And she made it."

"I'm surprised Forrest didn't—to use an odious phrase—marry a girl from his own class."

Now the grin was a little wicked. "I guess I was wrong. I guess he's not really a robot."

"But the bottom line is you don't know of any reason why David Forrest would have murdered Patty Kay?"

The malicious light in her eyes died. "No. None." She slumped back in her chair.

I knew she was weary, too weary for much more.

"Just one more thing. Brigit thought her mother might be angry with the headmaster at Walden School. Would you have any idea why?"

"With Chuck?" Gina rolled her eyes. "Who could get tired of Mr.

Eternal Youth? That man makes all grown-ups feel like they're eighty. Christ, if he believes half the stuff he spouts! According to Chuck, Walden School is right up there with Eden, the garden spot of the world." The good humor fled her face, leaving it sharp and angry. "Well, there's a goddamn snake in Eden, all right, and Chuck's going to have to root it out. He's got to find out who wrote those notes to Franci. He's got to!" She grabbed the cigarette box and stuck it in her purse. "In fact, I'm going to go talk to him now."

I wished her well. I wished I could help in the quest for Franci's tormentor. But this was a task that had to be done by an insider. Craig's aunt had no entrée here.

But I could be sure of one thing.

The headmaster of Walden School was going to be under siege.

Which could be quite helpful to me.

I always loved the rough-and-tumble of news conferences. The pressure of answering sharp, sometimes loaded questions with no prep time can reveal a man's or woman's character fast. I didn't want to miss the session between Gina Abbott and the headmaster. And Chuck Selwyn was definitely on my list. Thanks to Brigit.

"I'm on my way to see Mr. Selwyn too."

She shrugged impatiently. "Mrs. Collins, I know you're going the extra mile for Craig, but I have to tell you Chuck's not a candidate for first murderer. I mean, this guy's a certified eagle scout. Mom and apple pie are absolutely sacred to Chuck. Patty Kay absolutely terrified him."

"Brigit said her mother was very angry at him. I want to know why."

Gina was slipping on her raincoat, digging out her car keys. "Who knows?" she replied absently. "Maybe Chuck finally had the guts to stand up to Patty Kay over something. Sure, you can ask him. But I get first crack. . . ."

11

"I'm looking forward to seeing the school." And I was. I'd heard enough about Walden School to pique my interest. I reached down and grabbed my umbrella. "I'm parked in the public lot."

Gina slipped into her raincoat. "I'm there too."

At the front door, she rattled the knob to be sure it was locked. She didn't look at me.

As we crossed the street, she said briskly, "Walden School's on land near the river that was donated by the Prentiss family. The old Prentiss house, built in the early 1800s, is the school administration building."

The air was damp, but it had stopped raining. I tucked my umbrella under my arm. "I suppose Patty Kay felt rather proprietary about Walden School since her family donated the land. Is that why she was on the board of trustees?"

Gina nodded. We walked briskly down the side street and into the parking lot. She stopped beside a silver BMW. "That, and she loved to teach."

"Teach?"

She shot me a quick glance as she leaned down to unlock her car. "Surprised. I can see why. I mean, it was dilettante, sure. Three mornings a week. Comparative lit. Spanish. Patty Kay had a thing about Latin writers. Said they saw death in life better than anybody. Greek to me."

"So she was often at the school." I should have looked Patty Kay's daybook over more thoroughly. Yes, I'd read the notation "Class" at nine A.M. Friday. Read right over it, actually. Class literally had meant *class*. I'd assumed she was often on the campus in her capacity as a trustee. I'd better be careful about making assumptions.

"Sure. She was out there a lot." Gina slid behind the wheel.

I walked quickly to my MG.

The silver BMW roared down the street. Gina Abbott drove the way she talked, fast and jerky.

I had to slip through on the tail end of two yellow stoplights to keep up. I had plenty to think about. Brigit had seen her mother in cheerful conversation with the headmaster late Thursday afternoon. The next morning Patty Kay was icily cold to Selwyn. According to Brigit.

Whatever had affected Patty Kay's behavior must have occurred between late afternoon Thursday and her encounter with the headmaster Friday morning.

At the edge of town the BMW careened onto a black asphalt road. Puddles geysered beneath the sports car's wheels.

The BMW was gaining on a black Jaguar moving at a much slower pace. The cars shot up a hill, just short of the solid stripe warning not to pass.

Gina leaned on the horn and jerked the wheel left. The BMW surged past the Jaguar. Gina lifted a hand in a choppy wave.

I waited until we crested the hill, then accelerated and passed the Jaguar too. Far ahead, almost at the top of another hill, the BMW shot right. I followed, turning in beneath the ornate iron grillwork. Walden School's massive gates stood open wide.

A half dozen or more buildings were scattered among the oaks, magnolias, and hackberries. The buildings were Greek Revival in style.

The silver BMW swung into a parking area close to a lovely old house that served as Walden School's administration building. I pulled in beside it.

"That was Brooke. In the Jaguar. She's probably been at Edith's. Brooke always does all the right things. Always. I went over last night, but I just couldn't stand it today. Edith's practically a zombie. She's popping Valium like peanuts. She was loaded to the gills last night."

"Yes."

Gina looked toward the administration building. She didn't have to say a word for me to understand. The snake in Eden.

She walked so fast I had trouble keeping up. And she talked fast. "Over there"—her arm swept to the right—"that's the lower school. See, with the playground next to it. The middle school's through those pines. The upper school buildings are closest to the lake. These buildings house mathematics, art, music, languages, and computers. And that's the theater."

Weeping willows rimmed the placid lake. Geese and ducks waddled near the shore and paddled in the water. And Franci died in those quiet green waters.

"The gyms and the field hockey, soccer, baseball, and football fields are on down the road, just around the bend. You can see the tennis courts from here."

And hear the *thock* of balls. The players, in gray shorts and white shirts, looked to be middle-school age. They were quite good.

As we neared the house, bells rang and students poured from the buildings. The boys wore khaki slacks, white shirts, ties, and blue blazers. The girls wore navy uniform skirts and white blouses.

"It's all very impressive."

And there, running and laughing, was a group of little boys, boys about twelve . . .

"But not Eden," Gina said sharply. She hurried up the shallow steps to the front porch. She grabbed the bronze doorknob and pulled the heavy door. "Or maybe it's just like Eden. Like everything in life. Lots of beauty and underneath horror waiting to happen."

"Horror doesn't always happen."

Gina didn't answer. Young Franci's suicide and Patty Kay's brutal murder had made the skull beneath the skin too vivid for her.

We stepped into a cool, spacious hall. A gorgeous cream and blue Persian rug covered the pegged wooden floor. A middle-aged woman sat behind a well-ordered walnut desk. She looked up from her computer as we approached and gave a solemn nod.

"Hello, Mrs. Abbott." She smiled at me politely.

"Hello, Alice. I need to see Mr. Selwyn."

"Oh, Mrs. Abbott, I'm not sure. He's having such a hard day. So many parents have called. Everyone's so upset about Franci." Her voice was suitably grave, but her eyes gave no hint of distress.

"That's why I need to see him." Gina turned to her left toward closed double doors. An eye-level nameplate proclaimed in gold letters:

CHARLES EDWARD SELWYN
Headmaster

The secretary's eyes flashed. She started to rise, ready to do battle to protect her boss. "Mrs. Abbott, please—"

The main door opened and Brooke Forrest stepped inside. She gave us a tremulous smile.

Gina took a deep breath. She didn't even say hello. Instead, she asked gruffly, "How's Edith?"

Brooke's kind of beauty is rare—classic bone structure, cameo-smooth skin, huge aquamarine eyes beneath perfect brows, sleek raven-dark hair. But today even her ageless loveliness reflected intense stress. Dark shadows curved beneath haunted eyes. Deep lines bracketed her mouth.

"Dreadful . . . Oh, Gina, it's so awful, so *awful*."

The two friends came together, embraced.

Belatedly, Gina remembered me. "Brooke, I want you to meet Henrietta Collins, Craig's aunt."

"We met last night, Gina. At Cheryl's." Solemn aquamarine eyes turned toward me. "How are you, Mrs. Collins?" But she looked faintly surprised at my presence.

"She wants to talk to Chuck. Patty Kay was mad at him. Mrs. Collins is looking into everything. She and Desmond think somebody framed Craig."

"Framed him? Why, that's dreadful." Brooke stared at me in horrified concern.

"Yes," I said crisply, "it's quite dreadful."

"Certainly, yes, you must see about it." Brooke nodded. "But there's so much that needs to be done. We have to decide what kind of memorial the board will make for Patty Kay. It's so important to do the right thing. . . ."

"The right thing," Gina repeated emphatically. "Yes. I want to see the right thing done." She grabbed the handle of one of the double doors to the headmaster's office and yanked it open, ignoring the secretary's startled protest.

Originally a drawing room, the headmaster's office was remarkable for its high, coved ceiling with an elaborate cornice. The desk, an antique French dining table, faced the double doors. It sat between two ceiling-tall windows in the west wall. Equally tall windows opened onto the front porch. Elegant rose silk hangings framed all the windows. A half dozen Chippendale chairs were scattered about on the flowered Brussels tapestry carpet. On the north wall, trophy cases were mounted on either side of a black marble fireplace. Inscribed silver trophies glittered in the light from the multitiered chandelier.

Charles (Chuck) Selwyn, headmaster of Walden School, halted in mid-stride as we entered his office unannounced. He held a cordless telephone receiver in his hand. His navy blazer was beautifully tailored, his Oxford button-down blue cotton shirt crisp, his rep tie predictable, his khaki slacks perfectly creased.

I wondered for a moment if I'd wandered into a 1950s Peter Lawford movie. Selwyn had that kind of boyish good looks, complete to a lock of dark hair that fell across his manly brow. He raised a hand in greeting, and continued to talk into the phone. ". . . certainly understand your concern, Mrs. Wherry. We're doing our very best to protect the younger students from this sad event. Of course, it does give all of us, parents and faculty, an opportunity to reach out to our students, a growth experience, if you will, and—" The handsome face winced. He held the receiver a little way from his ear.

We could all hear ". . . *don't* send children to an *expensive* school to have them involved in this kind of *upsetting* situation. I want some *assurances* that there won't be *any* more talk about this. Susan's *cried* out in her sleep every night since we heard about it. And how could a student *do* that kind of thing on school property without *anyone* seeing it? Even if it did happen on the other side of the lake. I *certainly* feel—"

Gina darted across the room.

Selwyn never had a chance.

She snatched the receiver from his hand. "Listen, lady, you get to tuck Susan in tonight, don't you? How do you suppose Franci's mother feels? Talk about feelings—don't you have any, for Christ's sake?" She jabbed the Off button.

Selwyn looked like somebody'd spit on the American flag. "Mrs. Abbott, we may lose that family. We can't talk to people like that. They're *upset!*"

Gina's face bunched into a furious scowl. "I'm upset too. Edith's daughter is dead. Dead!" For a moment I feared she would lose control again. "The important thing is to find out who wrote those damn notes. We've got to do everything we can do to find out who's responsible and—"

Brooke frowned. "Responsible? Responsible for what?"

"—kick whoever it is out—"

The phone buzzed.

Selwyn stepped toward Gina, trying to retrieve his phone.

She continued to grip the receiver tightly. "No. We're going to talk. Brooke, go tell Alice to hold the calls. *All* the calls."

Brooke, with a small shake of her head, obediently turned and opened the hall door. "Alice, no calls for the headmaster, please."

"Mrs. Abbott." Selwyn's voice was sharp. It had lost some of its boy-hero quality. Maybe there was a real man hidden in those preppy clothes. "I'd like to remind you that this is *my* office. I have my responsibilities. It's my duty to reassure parents in a time of crisis and this is—"

Brooke shut the hall door.

Gina was trembling with barely-suppressed rage. "Yes, this is a time of crisis," she snapped. "This is going to be the event that marks whether Walden School can deal with reality, the reality of cruelty—and do something about it."

"Of course death is cruel when it takes one so young, Mrs. Abbott, and we're definitely dealing with all aspects of the problem. Counselors have arranged group sessions throughout today and tomorrow, and there will be an upper school assembly Thursday morning. I assure you it will be—"

"Shouldn't school close tomorrow?" Brooke interrupted softly. "In Patty Kay's honor? Her funeral's at ten."

Selwyn began to look like a man with a bad headache. Still, he managed to keep his voice pleasant. "I understand the sentiment, Mrs. Forrest, but in view of the other tragedy we're confronting, I strongly believe it's imperative to maintain as nearly normal a schedule as possible, all the while encouraging our students to communicate their grief and fears and to understand that a disturbed person cannot be held responsible for his or her acts." He brushed back that lock of hair. "And we didn't have sports yesterday. We've got to get back to normal."

Gina stalked toward him, stood a few scant inches from him. "Chuck, for Christ's sake, stop talking like a Woody Allen movie." She confronted him, her hands balled into angry fists, her face fierce with disgust. "Let's put it on the table, Chuck. Stop blaming the victim. Somebody—a real person—a *student*—was responsible for a little girl killing herself. Another Walden School student wrote those hideous notes to Franci. Degrading, sickening, nasty notes. That student must be held accountable. So how about letting *all* of our students grapple with moral responsibility? Okay?"

"Notes? What notes? Gina, what are you *talking* about?" Brooke's soft voice was bewildered.

Gina swung toward her. "You don't know?"

Brooke shook her head, and her silky black hair swayed.

Gina's eyes glittered. "Someone's been sending Franci notes full of filth, saying she was stupid, describing really sick sex, asking her how she'd like to have some, slipping porno pictures into the letters. Oh, God, Edith found a whole shoebox of this crap under Franci's bed."

Brooke stepped back in a vain attempt to escape the furious diatribe. Her lovely face creased in horror. "Oh, that's dreadful," she cried. "I can't imagine it. Oh, we mustn't let anyone know—"

"Not let anyone know?" Gina's raging stare was incredulous. "Do we live on the same planet? Of course we *have* to let people know. And someone will have seen something, someone will know enough to lead us to whoever wrote them."

Brooke's long, graceful hands rose in dismay. Her nails were perfect, a pale pink this morning. Selected, I was certain, for Franci's funeral. Brooke would have thought about that. Nothing too bright. She was that kind of woman. Her black silk suit, the V-necked jacket cut short and square with subdued silver buttons and a moderate straight skirt, was perfect too. The jewelry was tasteful. Small silver studs in her ears, a single-strand pearl necklace, a fine-linked silver bracelet. Only the distress in her lovely face marred her modeling-ramp appearance. "How awful for Franci, to have it all come out. All those things . . . Oh, no. We can't. The scandal. It would be so awful for Franci."

"Brooke, Franci's *dead!*" Gina shouted it. "What would be awful would be to let the person who drove that child to her death get away with it. We've got to find out who wrote that nasty stuff." Her bony face scrunched into an ugly mask of revulsion.

The headmaster lifted his hands as if quieting an unruly class. "Mrs. Abbott, I must insist that I know the proper role for us to play in this tragic drama. This, after all, is my domain. I'm an expert in dealing with the emotional traumas of young people. Mounting a witch-hunt among our students would surely be the most counterproductive act possible. I do fully understand your concern with responsibility, and I assure you that I will bend my efforts—*quiet* ones—to seek out the perpetrator. But"—he spoke firmly—"I must stress that the proper approach will not be vengeance or retribution but a sorrowful confrontation and appropriate counseling." Mournfully, he shook his head. "Can you not imagine, Mrs. Abbott, the sorrow and despair in some youthful heart even as we speak? A childish prank has resulted in a terrible tragedy that is certain to scar the young person responsible. Perhaps forever . . ."

"Forever would be too short." Gina's voice cut through his banalities. "This was not a childish prank, Chuck. This was a vicious, thoroughly nasty, depraved attempt to deliberately destroy a vulnerable child."

"Those are strong words." Another sorrowful headshake. "I must urge you, too, to seek counseling, Mrs. Abbott. Our counselors are available to our patrons. You must work through your anger."

"Yes," Brooke murmured. "We've got to put it all behind us." She smoothed back her silky hair. "We can't let it destroy Walden School. And we can't let poor Franci's name be dragged in the mud."

Gina jammed her hands in her raincoat pockets, scowling at Selwyn and Brooke. "I see. Least said, soonest mended, that sort of thing?" Her voice was even, uninflected, her eyes opaque with anger.

The headmaster beamed at her as if she were a difficult pupil making unexpected progress. "Exactly, Mrs. Abbott. I knew you'd understand."

But Brooke knew her better. She said carefully, "I know it isn't perfect, Gina. But we have to take everything into account. We must think how it would make Edith feel. It would be so humiliating for the family to have all that come out. And it would be dreadful for Walden School."

Gina stared at Brooke in disbelief. "All *what?*"

Brooke looked faintly bewildered. "Well, you said it—all those awful things in those notes. Why, it would just kill Edith."

"Brooke, the notes were filthy lies—"

"That doesn't matter. If people say things, then there are whispers and everything could get so ugly, and you can't fight that kind of thing. And what if it got in the newspapers? It would be a dreadful scandal. It could ruin Walden School." Brooke nodded decisively. "I know Patty Kay would want us to do everything possible to protect the school."

"So you and Chuck want to hush this all up?"

Brooke glanced at the headmaster.

Selwyn smoothed back that lock of hair. "Mrs. Abbott, the board is meeting here tomorrow night. My strong recommendation will be to keep matters as calm as possible. We must realize that our acts have repercussions." He looked hard and long at Gina. "I certainly can envision a loss of scholarships resulting if this unfortunate incident became public. And we would hate to have to withdraw scholarships that have already been awarded. Don't you agree, Mrs. Abbott?" His eyes challenged Gina.

It was like watching a balloon deflate.

"Oh." Gina's shoulders slumped. "I see."

No one had to tell me that her daughter was attending Walden School on a scholarship.

I almost jumped into it. God knows I wanted to. A little girl driven to suicide . . . But Craig was alive and in jail and in desperate need of help. Young Franci Hollis was beyond any help I could give. Poor little lost lamb, walking out into cold water, the muddy bottom sucking at her shoes, tendrils of reeds clinging to her body . . .

Selwyn clasped his hands together prayerfully. "We shall weather this storm. I've scheduled an upper school assembly Thursday morning. It will be a wonderful opportunity to bring us all together as a family."

Brooke nodded eagerly. "That might be a good time to announce a memorial for Patty Kay."

The memorial was clearly Brooke's agenda. She intended to address it no matter what the others had in mind.

"I believe," the headmaster interjected carefully, "that it would be better to delay that announcement. Perhaps on Founders Day next month . . . That's when we traditionally recall our debt to the Prentiss family—"

But I, too, had an agenda. "Mr. Selwyn, I'm Henrietta Collins—"

Gina looked embarrassed. "I'm sorry. I forgot to introduce you. Chuck, Mrs. Collins is Craig's aunt."

It didn't take a calculator to add up the headmaster's thoughts in swift sequence: *Craig Matthews's aunt, Craig Matthews might inherit a good portion of Patty Kay's fortune, Craig's aunt must be treated with deference.* Selwyn looked toward me. His smooth, attractive smile was dutifully in place.

"I'm sorry to intrude when I know you have so much to attend to, but I wanted to find out about your disagreement with Patty Kay."

The charming smile congealed.

Brooke gave me a startled glance, then her eyes jerked toward Selwyn.

Hands jammed into the pockets of her raincoat, Gina stared moodily at the floor.

It was so quiet for a moment that the *bong* of the grandfather clock announcing the noon hour sounded obscenely loud. Faintly, we could hear, too, the boisterous shouts of students from the athletic fields and the roar of a passing car.

The headmaster's handsome face creased in lines of sorrow, but anger flickered in his eyes. "If we could but recall words spoken in anger, especially over so trivial a matter." Now his smile turned rueful —and, of course, so boyishly appealing. Except for those angry eyes.

Brooke's face softened. She nodded encouragingly at him.

Selwyn sighed. "I've not even had time to come to grips with Mrs. Matthews's passing." He gestured mournfully.

I almost interrupted to remind him that hers was scarcely the natural departure implied by his words. I restrained myself.

He continued: "And to think we parted in anger. Over nothing, really."

"What was it?"

His eyes flicked irritably toward me.

I wasn't winning any popularity contests with Headmaster Selwyn.

"A matter of policy," he replied smoothly. "As you know, Mrs. Matthews was a person of such enthusiasm. Whenever she became involved in an activity, she felt very strongly that the world should also participate."

"What did Patty Kay want you to do?"

"To offer our students flying instruction."

"Flying?" Brooke swiftly shook her head. "Oh, no. That's too dangerous."

Gina explained, "Patty Kay'd just learned how to fly. I don't know if Craig'd told you. She loved it."

The headmaster turned his hands up. "Her enthusiasm was un-bounded. She was furious when I told her that it was out of the question. The insurance alone would be insurmountable." He looked at me earnestly, the fund seeker's eagerness seeping into his voice. "I'm sure you appreciate, Mrs. Collins, that no matter how prosperous a school may appear, our budgetary concerns are always pressing. There is the new technology to provide. It's astonishing how quickly com-puter labs become obsolete and new machines must be purchased. And upkeep for this magnificent physical plant requires an enor-mous—"

"Was that why she treated you with such cold contempt on Fri-day?" I waited attentively.

His eyes blazed now, but still he managed to keep his voice pleasant. "I would not characterize her attitude in that fashion—"

"*Contempt* is not the right word?" I looked at him inquiringly.

Brooke was staring at me, her eyes troubled.

"Certainly not, Mrs. Collins." His smooth façade cracked. Finally, he spoke sharply. "That is a gross misinterpretation. As these ladies know, Mrs. Matthews was quite open about her feelings and I will certainly be the first to admit that she was deeply—*deeply*—disap-pointed at my response. And I'm sure I would have heard much more about it. In fact, I believe she intended to proselytize for her plans at her dinner party Saturday evening." His voice dropped lugubriously. "The dinner party that never was. Ah, we must always be aware of our mortality and strive to do our very best at all times."

I didn't have a chance to answer. There was a sudden flurry at the door, the murmur of voices, all suitably hushed.

But perhaps it was just as well. It wouldn't have been seemly in those civilized confines to inform Headmaster Chuck Selwyn that I thought he was phonier than George Bush in calling for a kinder, gentler America while authorizing inflammatory Willie Horton ads.

I contented myself with a sardonic glance.

Selwyn's face didn't change from its suitably somber mold; his eyes glistened with smug satisfaction.

The secretary's voice announced: "Mr. Selwyn, I'm so sorry to interrupt. But the student council officers are here for their appointment."

The headmaster moved toward the door. "Come in, young people. Come in." He waved the three students to seats. There was one familiar face, Brooke's son, Dan. "These ladies are just leaving." Selwyn was trying to shepherd us toward the door. "I hope I've addressed everyone's concerns adequately."

Gina gave a tiny shrug and turned to go. Her lips were set in a grim, tight line.

To my surprise, socially obedient Brooke didn't move. She was looking at her son. Her face was open and vulnerable. The passion of a mother's love was as loud as if she'd shouted it to the world.

I suspected a great many parents of Walden School students were looking at their children today with equal emotion. No parent who cared would be untouched by Franci's tragic suicide.

Dan Forrest gave us a subdued smile. His handsome face was pale. "Hi, Mother. Mrs. Abbott." He nodded politely to me. He wore the uniform of an upper school student, blue blazer, white button-down Oxford shirt, and khaki slacks. They looked better on him than on Selwyn.

The headmaster's greeting was brisk. "Hello, Dan. Appreciate your stepping in and taking charge since Walt can't be here today."

An awkward silence followed this greeting. Gina reached out and took Brooke's hand, then told me soberly, "Walt is Franci's brother."

The teenager took a deep breath, then, obviously impressed with the seriousness of his task, addressed the headmaster. "Thank you for making time to see us, sir. I'm here as student council vice president and acting president to represent the student body"—was there just the slightest lift of self-importance?—"in the matter of a memorial for Franci Hollis. I met this morning with my fellow officers"—he nodded toward the tall, willowy brunette and stocky, athletic blond who accompanied him—"Secretary Laurie Adams and Treasurer Mark Kennedy. We voted to ask the board of trustees to plant a rose garden near the lake and name it in honor of Franci."

Selwyn stepped forward and shook the boy's hand vigorously. "I'm impressed with the thoughtfulness and delicacy of feeling this request represents. Out of this tragedy can grow a greater understanding of the needs of all students. Franci's rose garden can be an ever-present reminder of the beauty of each individual and the need to take time for reflection and communication of our care for one another."

Gina pressed her lips together.

Brooke smudged away a tear.

Dan's stiff shoulders eased slightly. "I thought—*we* thought maybe we could get it planted, then have Walt lead the dedication."

"A splendid proposal, Dan, Laurie, Mark. I'll present your plan to the board. I feel confident it will be adopted."

Another flurry of handshakes. Then the students were gone.

As the door closed on them, Selwyn seemed to realize we were still with him. Pointedly, he glanced at his watch. "Ladies, I do have another appointment in a few minutes. . . ."

"Oh, yes, of course." Brooke moved toward the door. "We understand. There is so much to be done. I'll see you at the board meeting tomorrow night."

Gina wasn't saying a word. She moved toward the door.

I held up my hand. "Just one thing more."

Gina and Brooke paused.

Selwyn eyed me with the enthusiasm of a zookeeper spotting an escaped viper. I could almost hear the calculations running through his mind—*a meddlesome old bitch, but the Prentiss money, the Prentiss money, the Prentiss money . . .*

"Yes, Mrs. Collins?"

"I'd like to ask where each of you were between four and five o'clock on last Saturday afternoon."

Gina looked at me sharply, but her reply was icy and swift. "At my office. Working on a bid. *Alone*."

Brooke stared at me as if she couldn't believe her ears. "You're asking *me* where I was when—isn't that about the time Cr—" She broke off, clapped a hand to her mouth. "—the time someone shot Patty Kay?" she finished in a rush.

"Yes."

Her eyes searched our faces. I'm not sure what she sought. Outrage on her behalf, perhaps. When she finally spoke, her voice was indignant and beautifully controlled. "I was working in my garden."

"Alone?"

"Why, yes. Of course. David doesn't like to garden. Besides, he was at his office. But Dan was in the clubroom. I could hear his music."

That left Mr. Eternal Youth.

In Selwyn's eyes I could read it as sharp as three lemons in a slot machine window: *meddlesome old bitch*. Yet he replied.

"I was hiking. At Lake Radnor."

Lake Radnor is one of the great joys of Nashville, a patch of wilderness in an urban area, a lake that on placid days reflects the trees on its banks in shimmering shades of ghostly green. And it is so safe that solitary women can walk its trails and roads. That in itself makes it special.

"Alone?"

"Of course."

"Thank you." I nodded. "It's good to know where we stand." I opened the door and walked out.

Three hostile pairs of eyes watched me go.

12

I knocked on the partially open door.

"Come in."

I stepped into a tiny office. It was one of a pair tucked between the rest rooms and the elevator on the first floor at the back of the bookstore.

The young woman slowly looked up from the catalogue on her desk. She forced a smile. It didn't reach blue eyes loaded with distress. "Yes?"

Stevie Costello, the manager of Books, Books, Books, was trying for a business-as-usual demeanor. I could have told her she wasn't making it. She looked like she hadn't slept, and her orange cardigan didn't go with her burgundy skirt. She was in her early thirties, slender, with masses of soft curly brown hair. Stevie Costello had that kind of fragile, china-shepherdess prettiness that age or hardship can so easily destroy.

"Miss Costello, I'm Craig Matthews's aunt. Henrietta Collins." I shut the door behind me.

"Craig's aunt?" One hand touched the coral beads around her slender throat. "Did Craig send you?" Her eyes remained uneasy, but eagerness lifted her voice.

A purist might contend my answer should have been *no*.

In my view, Craig's acceptance of my aid gave me carte blanche to claim Craig did send me.

"Yes." I took the single straight chair facing the cluttered desk.

"In the paper it said he'd been arrested—I can't believe it. He's such a gentle person. To think he—I can't believe it."

"Arrest is no proof of guilt."

Her fingers tightened on the beads at her throat. I feared she would snap the necklace. But she didn't answer.

"Craig should be out on bail later today."

"On bail? That means the police still think he shot her. He didn't do it. I know he didn't. Craig would never hurt anyone." She said the last so forcefully, I knew she was battling a lingering wisp of fear that Craig, gentle though he might be, had indeed shot his wife.

"You're preaching to the choir, Stevie. I've good reason to believe Craig had nothing to do with his wife's death."

But qualifications buzzed in my mind: Craig lied about the time he left the bookstore—if I believed the clerk's stubborn assertion. And I couldn't forget the maid's enigmatic remarks about Craig's visits to the Sandalwood apartments.

I was still confident.

But not positive.

"But the police arrested him."

"Craig's lawyer and I hope to persuade the police that they've made a mistake." I told her how I figured the crime had occurred. "And you can help us."

"I can? How?" She stared at me, her face eager and dubious and a little bit frightened.

"Tell me about Craig. How he acted this past week. What you

know about Mrs. Matthews. If you know of anyone who'd quarreled with her."

The necklace broke in her hand. Beads scattered. She ignored them. "Craig was just as usual. Just as usual." She spoke with utter surety. I wished Captain Walsh were hearing this.

"Everything was fine. And the idea that he'd get mad enough to throw things around—why, that's silly. He's not like that. Ask anyone who knows him."

"Stevie, how well do you know Craig?"

The comfort zone swiftly eroded. She was abruptly wary, her pretty, wan face taut. "I've worked here for two and a half years." She picked the words carefully, like a cat seeking dry grass. "I've always found him to be an extremely considerate and thoughtful employer."

"How about Patty Kay?"

"I've dealt mostly with Craig. Patty Kay was here a lot, but she was busy with ordering. She was really into carrying a wonderful stock. And she had a lot of charity commitments. He was the person you always went to with problems or questions."

"When you did work with Patty Kay, did you like her?"

"She was very nice."

Four bland words. Damningly bland.

"Come now. Obviously somebody didn't like her."

The manager shivered. "It's so awful. So awful. She was—she had a very strong personality. She laughed a lot. You always felt excitement when she was in the room. Like something grand could happen at any time. . . ." Her voice faltered.

"What do you suppose it would be like to live with someone like that?"

"I suppose it would be exciting." Stevie's tone was noncommittal.

"Do you know of anyone who didn't like her?"

"It seems ugly to talk about people."

"We're going to have to talk about a lot of people if Craig is to go free."

She moved uncomfortably in her chair. "Mrs. Guthrie works here one day a week. She always had something snide to say about her sister. It made us—the staff—uncomfortable. I mean, Mrs. Matthews is the owner and here's her sister bad-mouthing her. What were we supposed to say?"

"What kind of things did Mrs. Guthrie say?"

"Oh. Like Patty Kay was so politically correct it was nauseating. That she was selfish. Impossible. A showoff."

"How did Mrs. Guthrie act around Patty Kay?"

"Snippy. But it never seemed to bother Patty Kay. Once I remember she just rolled her eyes. She said, 'Pamela, you are *so* boring.' "

"No love lost between the sisters."

"That's right." She nodded eagerly.

"Why do you suppose Mrs. Guthrie worked here if she felt that way about her sister?"

"Oh, she didn't do it to please Mrs. Matthews. Mrs. Guthrie didn't want to miss out on anything. And this is the place to be in Fair Haven. Everybody drops in here for coffee. Businessmen. Lawyers. Everybody." She spoke with pride, forgetting for a moment the reason for our conversation.

"Do you know of any disagreement Mrs. Matthews had recently with anyone?"

"I don't know." Her tone was thoughtful. "But Friday afternoon she was in her office—it's right next to this one—and I opened the door and she was on the phone. Actually, she was just finishing a conversation. She said—I think her exact words were—'That's the way it's going to be. Like it or not.' And she hung up. She sounded absolutely determined. I didn't think much about it. I mean, Patty Kay could really handle people like suppliers or it could even have had to do with, say, a charity drive. But this time there was something awfully grim in her voice. When she looked up at me, I could tell she wasn't even seeing me. Her mind was a million miles away. Then she came to and asked me what I wanted. But she didn't smile the way she usually would when you approached her."

Friday afternoon—*"That's the way it's going to be. Like it or not."*

"You don't know to whom she was talking?"

"No. I've no idea."

"Is there anything else different or unusual, anything that strikes you now as odd?"

I saw a flash in her eyes.

Her lips opened. She seemed about to speak. Then, abruptly, she shook her head. "No, ma'am."

I held her gaze for a moment. "Give it some thought. It could be the difference between life and death for Craig."

That shook her.

I stooped and picked up one of the pretty coral beads.

She shifted again in her chair. "Look, it couldn't have anything to do with it. Not really. But Patty Kay'd been calling around lately, talking to boarding schools. For her daughter. Brigit wasn't happy about it. But—"

She didn't want to say it. She didn't want to put it into words.

I wasn't so squeamish.

"Brigit could have shot Patty Kay."

Stevie drew her breath in sharply.

I stood. "After all, someone did." I paused in the doorway. "You weren't at the store that Saturday afternoon."

"Saturday's my day off . . . I was out shopping in the afternoon. In Green Hills."

"Did you buy anything?"

Many charge card transactions record the time.

"No. No. I was just looking."

"Alone?"

"Yes. But you can't think I would have done it. Why would I?" Her voice grew sharp with fear.

"I don't know," I said agreeably. "But if you had a reason, Stevie, I'll find it."

Handing her the bead, I left.

Twenty minutes later I stood in front of Stevie Costello's second-floor-apartment door at Sandalwood Courts. After knocking briskly, I gave the surroundings a quick survey. A UPS delivery man was trotting across the newly mown grassy rectangle toward the opposite side of the complex. In a bed of iris, a gardener worked with his back to me. I wondered if he was Jewel's grandson. He didn't glance my way.

I used my Frequent Flier card to jiggle the lock loose. There was, fortunately, no deadbolt.

It took about thirty-five seconds. Lock-picking is a skill I picked up over the years.

It didn't take much longer to examine Stevie's bedroom closet. More than a dozen items, including skirts and sweaters, were from Lands' End. I saw what was probably the matching skirt to the beige cotton sweater that was now in police custody.

Interesting that Craig had apparently recognized the sweater.

Even more interesting that it prompted him to run away, taking both the sweater and the murder weapon with him.

I took a few more minutes to check out the apartment.

I didn't find any photos of Craig. No letters from him. No traces of masculine occupancy.

But what I had found was certainly thought-provoking.

I could imagine Richard's headshake and a murmured "Careful, sweetheart."

Every minute might turn out to matter for Craig Matthews. I drove back to the Fair Haven Mall, pulled into the Books, Books, Books parking lot, glanced at my watch, and headed back across town to Hillsboro Pike. Twenty-five minutes later I turned into the parking lot of Finedorff's, across from Green Hills.

If Craig left the bookstore on Saturday at four o'clock—but Amy insisted it was a quarter to four—he would have arrived at Finedorff's around four twenty-five. That would have given time for the fruit basket to be discussed and prepared, say by four-forty. Then Craig would have headed home. I'd clock that next.

Finedorff's smelled like a rich mix of pickles, pastrami, and sauerkraut. The first and the last from barrels near the meat counter, the second from the sandwich I was buying for my lunch. I also bought a

Dr Pepper and two Baby Ruths, one for dessert, one for emergency rations.

The small, intense woman behind the cash register, her dyed red hair piled in heavy ringlets atop her head, rapidly checked my purchases, including the latest newspaper.

The headline below Craig's indistinct photo read:

HUSBAND'S ARREST SHOCKS
FAIR HAVEN NEIGHBORS

I pointed to his picture. "Were you here on Saturday when this man came in?"

The red-haired woman finished sacking my stuff. Then she looked down at the photo. Her glance was shrewd, birdlike. "So why do you ask?"

"He's my nephew. I'd really appreciate it if I could visit with you for just a moment. . . ."

"Oh, so. You got trouble, bad trouble." She looked across the rows of foodstuffs. "Eric!"

A weedy young man with acne poked his head around a corner.

She ordered him to take over for a minute. We sat in an oak booth. I unpacked my sandwich, pulled the tab on my Dr Pepper. I realized I was very hungry and I started eating in earnest. Excellent pastrami.

She pulled out a gold case, selected a long cigarette, and stuck it in a mother-of-pearl holder. "So he made me mad, that young man." She stabbed the holder at Craig's picture. "I told him, we don't miss orders. We don't lose orders. We don't throw away orders. Orders, they are our bread and butter. But this one, he was in a real panic. Said his wife told him to pick up this basket. Said there'd be hell to pay if he came home without it. I wanted to tell him a man in the family should wear the pants, but, like I say, orders are our bread and butter. Maybe I'd get an order, so I don't say it. He tried to call her; there wasn't any answer. He left a message. 'Patty Kay, I'm at the store and they don't have an order, but I'll get them to fix up a basket anyway and I'll be there as soon as I can.' So I fixed him up a basket, real nice.

Pineapple, kiwi, golden delicious apples, everything the best. And I wrapped it in pink cellophane, pretty, with a red velvet bow."

I finished half the sandwich. And took a bite of the other. "He was here quite a while?"

A shrug. "We got other orders ahead of his. So maybe fifteen minutes. I say fifteen max." She said this with assurance.

"Do you happen to know when he arrived?"

Another shrug. "Afternoon. My feet hurt by then, I can tell you."

"He said he left here about twenty to five."

A swift frown. "Maybe so, maybe no. Me, I can't say. It was busy, busy. Because we are the best. If you have a party, you come to Finedorff's. We fix the meats, the cheeses, the vegetables, the dips. Everything. So, he came, he fussed, he got his basket. That's all I know." Her shrug was eloquent.

I clocked the drive from Finedorff's to 1903 King's Row Road. I drove quickly, but I didn't speed. I ate my dessert, the Baby Ruth, and thought about Craig Matthews. And time.

If he left the bookstore at a quarter to four, arrived at Finedorff's at five after four, spent fifteen minutes there, departing at four-twenty, he certainly would have arrived home in plenty of time to have quarreled with Patty Kay, then to have murdered her.

The drive from the deli to the Matthews house took twenty minutes.

And Craig pointedly said he left the deli at twenty to five.

Did he?

I unlocked the door. Inside, I called out Patty Kay's name, then I walked quickly through the lower part of the house. I came back to the front hall. The fruit basket still sat on the butler's table. I smelled the sweet scent of too-ripe fruit.

Surely Craig had hesitated, called out again, then started upstairs.

I hurried up the steps.

The bedroom. Patty Kay's study. The bathroom.

And back downstairs.

Four minutes. It would have been four minutes past five on Saturday.

Out to the kitchen.

Shock would surely have held Craig motionless for a moment.

Out the back door. Skidding on the sticky floor.

The gun on the grass—

Gina's words echoed in my mind: *Craig hates guns.*

I took time—just an instant—to wonder if that was another lie that Craig had told.

Oh, yes, without question, he had found the gun, taken it, tried to throw it away.

But I'd bet my little MG he didn't find it on his lawn between the kitchen and the playhouse.

The interesting thing about lies is that the smart liar clings to the truth as much as possible.

What matters is to sift out the facts.

I didn't doubt Gina's report on Craig's aversion to guns.

So, in walking out to the playhouse, even if he saw a gun, he would be very unlikely to pick it up.

But he *did* pick it up.

That told me he must have had an overpowering reason to do so.

What if the gun lay near his wife's body along with a familiar beige sweater? And a police siren shrilled closer and closer?

Yes, then he'd snatch up both of them and run away.

I stood in the playhouse doorway. I stared down at the foul-smelling, darkly-stained rug.

Two minutes.

That would have made it six minutes after five. The dispatcher received the call reporting a body at six minutes after five.

Craig knelt by his wife, tried to help her.

That was when he'd seen the sweater. And the gun. His gun.

I plunged out of the playhouse, ran to the house, into the kitchen, through the hall, and out the front door.

Two minutes.

So there was just a tiny space of time for Craig to get in his car, stuff the damning sweater and his gun beneath the seat, drive around the house, and take the alley out before the police arrived at nine minutes after five.

It checked, it worked. If—a huge, enormous, unresolved *if*— Craig left that deli at twenty to five.

But if he left the store sooner, the prosecution would have lots of elbow room to argue that there was plenty of time for Craig and Patty Kay to engage in a violent quarrel. The D.A. would claim that Craig went directly to the kitchen, Patty Kay ragged him about the basket, it wasn't right, it wasn't the one, they quarreled, he threw the cheesecake (*But look at it, gentlemen, really look at it and explain why Mrs. Matthews bore no stains from that encounter*), then raced out to his car, got his gun from the glove compartment, and—

If the police were correct, what was Patty Kay doing while her husband armed himself?

If the quarrel reached that level of violence (which was so unlike the amiable Craig Matthews everyone described), surely she would have made an effort to protect herself?

Quickly, I walked back through the house and out the back door.

Patty Kay's car was parked outside the garage.

What was it Gina had said? *His and her guns.* For protection in their cars.

Patty Kay's blue Lexus was unlocked.

I opened the car door and immediately saw why I'd not found her car and house keys in her purse. Patty Kay'd left them in the ignition. Certainly an intruder on Monday afternoon could have used these keys to open the back door.

But why replace them in the ignition?

I was afraid—very afraid—I knew. After the search of the office, the intruder brought the keys out to the car, turned on the ignition—

I turned on the motor and popped open the glove compartment.

Patty Kay's glove compartment held maps, an unopened packet of Kleenex, insurance papers, vehicle safety receipts, a small bag of taffy.

But no gun.

No gun at all.

•   •   •

Desmond Marino's secretary put me right through.

"Patty Kay's gun is gone."

"Patty Kay's gun—"

"Everyone says she kept one in her glove compartment."

"That's right. I've seen it."

When? I wondered. I said, "The gun's gone."

He asked sharply, "Are you sure?"

"Yes. I looked everywhere. The playhouse. The yard. The shrub-bery. The swimming pool."

"What the hell do you suppose that means?"

"My best guess is that Patty Kay's murderer has that gun. Who else would have taken it?"

"I'll call Walsh. Immediately."

"Good. If I were Walsh, I'd announce this to the press, warn the community."

It was something to do. But not enough. I had a dreadful sense of urgency. The missing gun worried me terribly.

"We must warn everyone on King's Row Road. Call Cheryl Kraft and ask her to do it." ·

"Fine."

I wished there were something more to do. Then I realized Desmond was talking.

". . . could have been worse. Judge Lehman decided to grant bail, but he set it at a hundred thousand. The bad news is that Craig doesn't have ten thousand to put up with the bonding company. I talked to Braden Fairlee. The estate can't do it when the charge is murdering the legator. But I'm working on it. I think I can line up the money this afternoon. Craig should be home this evening. Now, about the other matters—"

Ah, the tasks I'd assigned Desmond this morning. I pulled a pad from my purse.

"None of the poker players have alibis between four and five on Saturday." He cleared his throat. "Including me. I've got a hammock out in my backyard. I was in it. Reading."

"What?"

"The new biography of Merton."

What you eat shapes your body. What you read shapes your mind.

"All alone, I suppose?"

"As a matter of fact, yes. . . . I didn't know I was on your list."

"Don't take it personally. Everyone's on my list."

"Yes, of course. Willis Guthrie says he was in the video store at Haycroft and Alexander. Nobody to confirm it. David Forrest was at his office. So what else is new. No confirmation there either. No other workaholics in his firm—"

"Firm?"

"He's a lawyer too. Anyway, David says he was there all day. No way to prove it."

Or disprove it. "And Stuart Pierce?"

"He was out jogging."

"Where?"

"In the neighborhood."

"King's Row Road?"

"Exactly."

I checked addresses in the phone book. Now I could put a face to every house in the neighborhood. I walked by the Hollis house. There were still a great many cars parked in the drive. The Neal house looked untenanted despite the light shining through drawn drapes. The Forrest house was of the kind of perfection celebrated in *Architectural Digest*—smooth rolling lawn, freshly painted Doric columns, and three-story magnificence. The Guthrie house was boring—a huge gray stone house, squat and bleak like an English fortress. Gina Abbott's white colonial looked a little shabby. Part of the guttering was missing along the second story.

The Pierces' French mansard home was around the corner from the Abbott house. It certainly had easy access to the alley that ran behind the homes fronting on King's Row Road.

I looked at the Pierce home for a moment. Did it harbor a murderer behind its elegant façade?

13

One of a reporter's toughest tasks when a story involves murder or scandal is to get anybody on the inside to talk.

After all, why should they? Not unless they enjoy being blazoned in headlines coast to coast. Most people don't, notwithstanding the constant parade of soul-barers on the national talk shows. Statistically the I-can-tell-more-than-you-can-tell folks are a tiny minority.

So I'd be on the outside looking in if I were trying to cover Patty Kay's murder.

But I wasn't trying to cover it.

I was Craig Matthews's aunt.

It worked one more time.

Pamela Prentiss Guthrie wasn't thrilled to see me. But she wasn't quite willing to be rude.

Everything about Pamela Guthrie bulged—her eyes, her bosom, and her butt. She was a fat Patty Kay without the appealing vigor and charm. Pamela's irregular mouth turned down at the corners, her greenish eyes were dull, her black hair indifferently combed. Yet it was eerie how strong was the resemblance to Patty Kay.

"Oh. Mrs. Collins." She didn't quite mask a pettish sigh. "Come in."

I followed my hostess into a living room that should have been declared a fire hazard. Heavy as she was, Pamela managed to find a path among the mahogany tables and needlepoint benches and massive glass-fronted cabinets crammed with collectibles. I followed, stepping carefully, afraid if I caromed into one piece, it might trigger an avalanche.

The room was like a curio shop stocked by Imelda Marcos: Hundreds of pieces of Liberty silver cheek by jowl with Chinese Lohan figures (always sizable), plus more than a dozen (two dozen?) alabaster, marble, and bronze statuettes of Pierrot, hand-painted porcelain cats, seventeenth-century Russian icons, antique jewel boxes, carved African wooden animals, cut-crystal vases, Mexican wooden angels, and more, much more, all reflected ad infinitum in Venetian engraved mirror panels.

The chintz-covered sofa with its dainty blue and yellow forget-me-nots seemed absolutely ordinary and out of place. It was also quite comfortable. "I'm so glad I caught you at home, Pamela." It was odd to address her by her first name, but it was appropriate for Craig's aunt in talking to Patty Kay's sister. "As you know, I'm trying to find out who might have been angry with Patty Kay. And since you are her sister—" I paused meaningfully.

Pamela Guthrie sank into an Empire chair. She gazed at me with bulging, unreadable green eyes that reflected no sorrow. "I don't see how I can help you. I hadn't seen her for a while." She picked a mint out of a cut-glass bowl and popped it into her mouth. She chewed for a moment. "But I'm not surprised someone killed her." Pamela's voice was light and high and sour. Like pink vinegar.

"Really. Why is that?"

She chose another mint. "My sister was absolutely impossible."

"How?"

"So stupidly pigheaded. She always had to have her way." Pamela gazed down at her right hand, held it so the light reflected from the rings on her fingers. Not one ring, of course. A half dozen. Ruby, pearl, diamond, amethyst, emerald, turquoise.

"When did you last talk to Patty Kay?"

Her dull green eyes passed over me without interest. They focused on a bronze elephant with upraised tusks. "I don't know. Last week probably."

Impulsively, I decided to see what a sharp poke might do. "Craig thought you were coming over Saturday afternoon."

But she remained as placid as an overfed dog. "Craig's mistaken. I didn't leave the house Saturday. Willis was here too."

Hmm. Not according to what Willis Guthrie told Desmond. Not according to what they'd said at Cheryl Kraft's neighborhood-alert session. I played out the line. "So you and Willis were both here around four?"

She nodded complacently.

Time to pull her in. "I thought he'd gone to the video store."

Those dull eyes widened. Her face hardened. "Not at four. He was home at four."

"Were you together?"

She thought just a moment too long, then, resentfully, snapped, "No. I was upstairs. Cataloguing buttons." Her face softened. "I have a wonderful button collection. Would you like to see it?"

"Perhaps another time."

Disappointment crossed her pudgy face. "Oh, well. I don't suppose you collect."

"No."

"Neither did Patty Kay." Disinterest was clear again in that light, oddly high voice.

I wondered if Pamela Guthrie was quite sane.

"What will happen now with the tract of land you want to develop?"

Pamela's thick lips curved into a slow, satisfied smile. "Why, the deal will go through. When it does, when it does, I think I'll go to India. There are so many lovely pieces there—and so much cheaper if you do your own buying. I can buy so much more that way. Won't that be *wonderful?*"

Louise Pierce barred the doorway of her elegant house. The second Mrs. Pierce listened patiently to my explanation of my presence. But that was all the patience she intended to show. "I'm just on my way out, Mrs. Collins." Her heart-shaped face and violet eyes reminded me of daguerreotypes in old lockets. Her slender, athletic figure was clad in immaculate tennis whites; she carried a white leather racquet case. A dark pink warm-up jacket was draped over her shoulders. Stepping out onto the porch, she shut the door firmly behind her. "I doubt I could be helpful. I saw very little of Patty Kay." She spoke pleasantly but briskly, as if she were discussing the weather.

"You didn't see her Saturday afternoon? About four-thirty?"

"No." Her smooth face remained unchanged, but her violet eyes were steely.

"Where were you then?"

"Here." She sounded untroubled. "Working on some needlepoint."

She started down the steps.

I kept pace.

That brought a tiny frown. She suddenly looked much less pleasant.

"Surely as Brigit's stepmother you had some dealings with Patty Kay?"

We were walking briskly around the side of the big house to the driveway.

"Some." All trace of a smile was now gone.

"I understand Brigit was terribly upset at the idea of being sent away to school."

"Nothing had been decided. I imagine Patty Kay would've settled down."

"Brigit might not have thought so."

A shrug.

No impassioned defense of her stepdaughter.

We reached the salmon-colored Mercedes; she opened the driver's door.

"Did you enjoy working in Patty Kay's bookstore?"

Louise slipped into the driver's seat. She looked up at me: There was no trace of warmth in those huge violet eyes. "Mrs. Collins—do you really want to know the truth?"

"I'd like that."

"No. I did not enjoy working there." She propped the racquet carrier in the passenger seat.

I rested a hand on the car door. "Then why did you do it?"

Her eyes glowed with hostility. "You'd have to live in Fair Haven to understand, Mrs. Collins. But—ostensibly—it was a sweet gesture by Patty Kay to invite me." A saccharine edge crept into her disciplined voice. "She was demonstrating that it didn't matter at all to her that Stuart dumped her."

"Did he? Dump her, I mean."

"You bet." Oh, how she relished saying it. "She was impossible to live with, she demanded attention all the time. It was ruining his life."

"Is that what he told you?"

Louise Pierce glared. "Yes. He certainly did. And everybody in town knew about it. It drove Patty Kay crazy. So she wanted to show what a good sport she was by inviting me to work in the store. So I showed what a good sport I am by accepting the offer. I could afford to. Stuart is my husband. Mine."

She turned the key in the ignition, and the motor purred.

Before the luxury car backed out of the drive, our eyes locked.

I knew that Louise Pierce knew that Stuart and Patty Kay were lovers.

But her triumphant smile never wavered.

Artists and architects reveal themselves to the world by the surroundings they fashion.

Light cascaded through floor-to-ceiling windows, turning the oak furniture of Stuart Pierce's office a glistening gold. Beautifully detailed models of office buildings and homes were displayed in deep shelves along one wall. Everywhere there was light and the color of light, as rich and luminous as a Vermeer painting.

The tall, handsome architect rose and came around his desk to greet me.

Patty Kay's great love.

It was certainly easy to understand why. I had the same sense I'd had upon meeting Stuart Pierce Monday evening at the Kraft house. Here was a compelling man, a man you wanted to know, a man most women would certainly find irresistible.

"You wanted to see me?" Unexpectedly, he was brusque. A tight frown pulled his face into flat, hostile lines.

I immediately understood. "You're very angry, aren't you? And helpless to change it. Which makes you even angrier."

"It shouldn't have happened." He spoke harshly. "Patty Kay should be walking onto a tennis court right now." His face might have been scored out of stone. "If Craig—"

"He didn't. You know Craig. Let me tell you more of what happened, more than was in the papers. Then you can judge."

We sat on an oversize white sofa.

His blazing eyes never left my face.

I was keenly aware of his bitter anger.

But when I finished describing the scenes I had found in Patty Kay's home, Stuart's headshake was abrupt and final. "No. That's not Craig. If he were angry, he'd run away." He pushed up from the couch and began to pace, head down. "Patty Kay knew her murderer. That's obvious. But she must have been taken by surprise. She didn't realize she was in danger. Why not? She was smart, plenty smart." He stopped and stared down at me. "But sometimes she wasn't smart about people's feelings. You know how she was—funny, quick, bright, kind in her own way. But she had a blind spot." Restlessly, he began to pace again. "She saw things the way *she* saw them. She must not have realized she had somebody on the raw.

"Okay, why the playroom? It's private. Somebody wanted to talk to her about something in complete privacy. Or maybe that was the excuse to go out there. Because the murderer must have planned to trash the kitchen. He couldn't shoot her"—a spasm of pain briefly tightened his handsome face, then disappeared—"in the kitchen and then throw that stuff around. It would have been obvious it happened after she died. And, if you're right—and I think you are—the entire stage was set to trap Craig. But why?" he demanded wearily. "For God's sake, why?"

His hopeless grief was painful to see.

"Do you know of a quarrel with anyone? Anything Patty Kay planned to do that someone would kill to prevent?"

He flung himself down on the couch beside me. "Christ, what could possibly be worth killing her? She and Pamela fought all the time. If it wasn't the land use, it would be something else. So that was nothing new. And Pamela doesn't really need any more money."

"Pamela will never have enough money."

"But not murder. Not even Pamela." He scowled. "But Patty Kay's dead. . . ."

"Patty Kay wanted you to send Brigit away to school."

Slowly he turned to face me, his handsome face both incredulous and outraged. "Oh, now, wait a minute. Wait a goddamn minute. That's crazy!"

It was definitely a new thought and not a welcome one.

"Sure, Brigit and her mom tangled. That's no big deal. A teenage girl and her mother. But Brigit's a nice kid. *No.*"

"It *is* a new development. We're hunting for something that happened recently."

"No. Never."

"Why did Brigit live with you? And not with her mother?" I waited a little tensely. Craig's aunt might be expected to know the answer to this.

But Stuart Pierce was focused on protecting his young daughter. "It seemed like a good idea last summer. Girls need to feel like their dads care. And she and Patty Kay—well, it was just that Brigit was growing up, wanting more independence. It wasn't a big deal. She spent a lot of time with Patty Kay."

I let it drop.

But I wasn't finished with Stuart. Or Brigit. Not by a long shot.

There was no graceful way to say it. "When did you and Patty Kay last—meet?" There could be no mistaking my meaning.

For a moment Stuart was utterly still. His voice was gruff when he demanded, "Does Craig know?"

"I don't know," I replied honestly.

"If he doesn't, I'd like to keep it that way. Because—" His eyes met mine gravely but without apology. He shook his head and broke off. "You won't understand."

"I might."

It was hard for him. The words came reluctantly, but with a painful raw intensity. "We didn't mean harm. We weren't going to mess things up for anybody. Craig depended on Patty Kay. And Louise and I—I love Louise. She's gentle and sweet. She helps me keep it all together. Patty Kay and I—it was always wild and a little insane. We were up and down but not at the same time. We couldn't live together. We tore at each other. We couldn't—we never could get a balance." Bleakly, he stared down at his interlocked hands. Then he added fiercely: "But I loved her the way I'll never love anyone else in the world."

I believed him.

I also knew that this kind of affair had to have brutal ramifications.

"Did you want Patty Kay to divorce Craig and marry you?"

"No. That was never a possibility." His deep voice was dismissive.

"Patty Kay wasn't pushing you to divorce Louise?"

"No." He looked startled.

"Did Louise know?"

"Absolutely not."

"How can you be sure?"

"She would've walked out."

Maybe. Maybe not. If she knew, Louise Pierce might have figured Patty Kay's death could solve her marital problem. Permanently.

Of course, every word Stuart Pierce said was suspect. Discovered as an adulterer, he could be putting on a clever performance designed to convince any interested parties that certainly neither he nor Louise had any motive to murder Patty Kay.

"When were you and Patty Kay last together?"

"Thursday. Thursday afternoon."

"How was she?"

"She was just like always." Anguish burned in his eyes. "It was so perfect. God, it was so perfect. And now, now—"

The cry came from his heart.

As it so understandably could, whether he was innocent or guilty.

But I wasn't concerned about that just now.

I thought about what it meant.

On Thursday afternoon Patty Kay's world was full of happiness. Stolen happiness.

She then had two more days to live.

"Why?" her lover cried. "Why?"

14

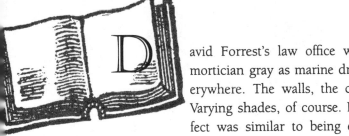

avid Forrest's law office was not so much
mortician gray as marine dress blue. Blue everywhere. The walls, the carpet, the chairs.
Varying shades, of course. But the overall effect was similar to being encapsulated in a
Norwegian fjord. The late afternoon sunlight streaming through a west
window merely emphasized the chill of the room.

He rose and gestured for me to take one of the leather chairs that
faced his desk. Blue leather.

"Mrs. Collins." He placed my card facedown on his desk. On it
I'd written: *May I have a few minutes of your time? We met at your
neighbor's home last night. Henrietta Collins.* "What may I do for you?"

He regarded me gravely. He was muscular, trim, fit. Forrest

hadn't lost his Corps shape. His black hair was cut so short, he looked like he'd been scraped. But nobody would have picked him for a recruiting ad. His long, saturnine face had a zealot's eyes and a taskmaster's stern mouth.

"I'd like to talk with you for a moment about Patty Kay. My nephew did not shoot his wife. I'm looking for the person who did."

He tapped the edge of my card against the polished surface of his desk. "That is the duty of the police."

"It is the duty of everyone who knew Patty Kay to provide information about who might have been angry with her. Or jealous of her."

He gave a final tap with the card, then tossed it down. "Certainly. But I'm afraid I know nothing that would be helpful to you, Mrs. Collins. I rarely saw Patty Kay."

"But you knew her."

"Of course. Fair Haven is a small town."

"When did you see her?"

"At social occasions. Usually for charity."

"Patty Kay was certainly active in promoting the arts. And extremely successful at it."

His face was a study in distaste. "She had no dignity. I'm glad my mother didn't live to see how Patty Kay cheapened the Revelry Club's annual Christmas dance."

"But it was all in fun—"

Cold gray eyes stared at me.

"—and it did earn a substantial amount for the scholarship program."

He glared at me. "It was merely an excuse for Patty Kay to parade her body in front of every man in Fair Haven. It was unseemly. Not befitting her position. I'm surprised her husband didn't take steps to stop it."

Now those icy eyes challenged me. Apparently, as Craig's aunt, I was to be held responsible for this flaunting of social mores by a member of the Matthews clan.

"Husbands aren't czars anymore, are they, Mr. Forrest?"

"A man with the proper kind of wife doesn't have to instruct her how to behave." The thin mouth closed tightly.

I recalled the tennis video and Patty Kay's teasing of Brooke. No wonder Brooke told Patty Kay not to joke about the tennis pro. Her husband David sure as hell wouldn't think it was funny.

But I doubted that beautiful, socially attuned Brooke Forrest engaged in any kind of improper behavior. According to Gina, Brooke had designed every aspect of her life to achieve social prominence. Did she ever question whether it had all been worth it?

Yet perhaps noblesse oblige was instinctive to Brooke. Certainly her overriding preoccupation this morning at Walden School had been to establish the proper memorial for Patty Kay.

"Your wife was a good friend of Patty Kay's."

"Brooke is extremely active—and properly so—in this community. She takes her duties as a Forrest quite seriously. This is, as I'm sure you are learning, a very small community—"

It's a small town, for chrissakes.

"—and the women who preside over our social and artistic endeavors form an elite group. Brooke, of course, maintains cordial relationships with everyone."

"So you wouldn't say your wife was especially close to Patty Kay?"

"No. They were social peers. And she and Patty Kay enjoyed playing tennis. Patty Kay," he added grudgingly, "was an excellent tennis player."

"And cook?"

"Yes. Yes, she certainly was that." Finally, a note of approval.

If Patty Kay's spirit lurked near earth, I could imagine her thumbing her nose and chanting, *Frigging stuffed shirt.*

"Did you like her cheesecake?"

"I never eat dessert."

"What did you think of Craig's limericks, the ones he composed the night you played poker?"

He shook his narrow head firmly. "As I told Brooke, it was a disgusting display of disloyalty."

"You didn't think—"

The phone rang.

"Excuse me, please, Mrs. Collins."

He lifted the receiver. "Hello." He picked up a pen and began to mark on a notepad. "That's no excuse, Dan." He made a series of thick, dark Xs—XXXXXX—on the sheet. "A Forrest never quits. You are to engage in the competition. And I expect you to do your best."

He didn't wait for a response. He didn't say good-bye. He simply replaced the receiver and looked at me.

I finished my question. "—think Craig's limericks were funny?"

"Most certainly not."

Willis Guthrie kept glancing at his watch.

To an accountant, time is money, but not when spent talking to a fellow poker-player's aunt.

". . . may have mentioned the cheesecake jokes to Pamela." He gave a quick, sniggering little laugh, then smoothed his wispy ginger mustache. "Or I may not. I don't recall."

His tight, spare face wasn't improved by that kind of laughter. Abruptly, he was serious again.

"I know this is a difficult time for you and Pamela."

The blankness in his pale blue eyes was so revealing. Finally, he got it. "Oh, yes, yes, of course. Such a loss." His voice was fairly high for a man.

Over the telephone, could it be mistaken for a woman's?

"You were shopping for a movie when the murder occurred?"

"I suppose so. I was out sometime that afternoon."

"Would you have any ideas about who might have shot your sister-in-law?"

"Not really." Those pale eyes slipped toward the clock on the wall.

I decided to shake his indifference. "How much money will your wife get from Patty Kay's estate?"

Instead of outrage, Willis Guthrie looked at me with suddenly alive and shining eyes. "A substantial amount, Mrs. Collins." Then he realized how callous it sounded. He added hastily, "Of course, my wife was already a wealthy woman."

"But now," I said softly, "she will be a *very* wealthy woman."

. . .

I found a pay phone on the ground floor of Guthrie's office building. It was almost five. I called Desmond's office. A recorded message came on. I hung up.

I called the Matthews house. Another recorded message, the husky, unmistakable voice I'd heard on the tennis and birthday videos. Patty Kay's voice.

"You have reached 555-0892. We aren't here. We may be on the Amazon or around the corner at the soccer field. We'll call back if you leave a number—and a good reason." A ripple of laughter, the buzz signifying other messages, and finally a beep.

I hung up the phone.

So Craig wasn't out of jail yet. Or, if he was, he wasn't home. My guess was that he would hurry to the house for a shower and fresh clothes, trying to put the feel and smell of a cell as far behind him as possible.

I wanted to talk with my honorary nephew as soon as possible. I had, in fact, some sharp questions to ask.

I redialed the Matthews number, listened again to Patty Kay's voice, so alive and vibrant and untroubled. This time I left a message. "Craig, please remain home until I get back. I should be there by six. I must talk to you." My own voice was crisp and, if I do say so, compelling. I can sound like a city editor when need be. Unless I was completely wrong in my estimation of Margaret's nephew—so unlike Margaret—he would dutifully stay put.

Of course, all things considered, perhaps I should be wondering if I hadn't misread Craig altogether.

Was he quite the innocent, hapless victim I'd thought him to be?

I drove again to King's Row Road. Craig wasn't at the house. I hesitated in the hallway for a moment, then went out the front door and walked swiftly down the drive, retracing my steps of the evening before.

Cheryl Kraft's black silk slacks hung on her bony hips. Not even the brilliant brocade of a mandarin jacket made her emaciated frame substantial. She brushed back that silver-blond hair. "Mrs. Collins— I'm so glad you've come. I've been dying to know what's happening. Come on in."

Once again we descended into the man-made rain forest. Cheryl headed straight for the wet bar. "A gin and tonic?"

I had to give her good marks for a noticing eye.

"That will be fine." And it was, tart yet sweet.

For herself, she fixed a martini as dry as the Sahara.

We settled on opposite redwood benches.

The high collar of the brocade jacket emphasized the reedlike thinness of her throat, the product of a sustenance-deprived body reduced to an almost skeletal frame. It's interesting how our society defines beauty. Heavy gold earrings glittered against scalpel-tightened skin.

"What have you found out?"

I took a sip of the gin. "That Patty Kay's life was quite complex."

She nodded approvingly. "Yes, oh, yes. That's certainly true. Stuart. And Louise. And poor, dear Craig. Of course, I've known Patty Kay for a million years. . . ."

It took only an occasional murmur to keep the flow going. I felt like a gold hunter with a sluice pan, hoping for a nugget, getting mostly gravel.

". . . known each other forever. Patty Kay was so upset when Stuart moved out. She couldn't believe he'd leave her. She was absolutely furious when he married Louise. She married Craig just six weeks later. Eloped to the Virgin Islands." A spurt of laughter. "I thought that was *so* funny. But it all seems to have worked. And then to have both Patty Kay and Stuart serving as Walden trustees! But they treat each other very politely at board meetings. Actually, I was looking forward to seeing Stuart at Patty Kay's house for dinner . . . that night. So far as I know, it would be the first time he'd set foot in that house since he walked out. But lately, it seems to me like they were almost *too* polite at board meetings."

Cheryl couldn't know that she was hot and getting hotter. But this was no longer a puzzle to solve.

". . . Patty Kay and Pamela never could get along. Pamela's such a pig, you know. About everything. So grossly fat." The throaty voice dripped disdain. "But she had enough of the Prentiss spunk that you can't count Pam out. None of them ever like to lose. Their great-grandfather was in a duel and everybody always said he shot before the count was up. But it couldn't be Willis." A moue of contempt. "He'd do anything for money, but Willis Guthrie was no match for Patty Kay. He was terrified of her and of course that's why I'm sure Craig didn't—" She clapped a hand to her crimson mouth.

I smiled. "That's quite all right. And *very* perceptive of you."

She downed half the martini. "Oh, of course, I suppose in a family things are understood, though I wouldn't for the world say the wrong thing." She leaned toward me, gesturing with her drink. "The truth is, Craig's very nice but he's not rugged. Not the kind of man to shoot anyone. Or any*thing,* for that matter. My husband hunts." Quiet pride underlined the declaration. "And I told Brooke when she described that mess in the kitchen to me . . ."

It's a small town, for chrissakes.

". . . that it certainly didn't sound like the Craig Matthews *I* know." She finished her first martini, popped up, and poured another.

I nodded, but I had the thought that though Craig might not be rugged, he was intelligent, and if he planned a murder, he might well set it up to look like something he would never have done. . . .

She plopped back on the bench and leaned toward me. "Of course, there is one thing I've wondered about."

I caught the faintly smutty tone to her voice. The gin was definitely loosening her tongue.

So I encouraged her. "It's better if all the truth comes out."

"Of course, since I work at the bookstore, I couldn't help noticing how *well* Craig and Stevie—she's our dear, *cute* little assistant manager —how *well* they get along." Her eyes gleamed.

Women notice a lot. Especially what goes on between men and other women.

If Cheryl had noticed, so might have others.

I was certain Craig and Stevie thought no one knew.

They were wrong.

Now I had my nugget.

Cheryl had picked up on Craig and Stevie. Other women who knew Patty Kay and Craig worked at the bookstore—Pamela Guthrie, Brooke Forrest, Edith Hollis, Louise Pierce. Women notice. And women talk.

It's a small town, for chrissakes.

And everyone who was anyone in Fair Haven shopped at Books, Books, Books. So the murderer could easily have taken Stevie's sweater, deliberately planted it beside Patty Kay's body, and hoped it would implicate Stevie or panic Craig.

As it had.

"Do you think Patty Kay knew?"

Cheryl considered it, turned the idea over and over, then rejected it, reluctantly. "No. I saw Patty Kay at the store when I was there last Thursday. She treated Stevie just as always."

I definitely caught a faint note of regret in her voice.

It was almost six when we started back up the atrium stairs, Cheryl, a little unsteady, using the handrail for support.

She said farewell, her thin frame leaning against the huge teak door. "Now, you be sure to come back, Mrs. Collins, if I can do anything else to help. And do give dear Craig my love. Such a *blow*."

I smelled cinnamon aftershave. His blue and white striped pincord slacks and yellow linen sport shirt were crisp and fresh.

But Craig's weakly handsome face was haggard.

And his glare sullen.

"Jesus, why do I have to answer *your* questions? All I've done is answer questions, talk, talk, talk about it. I'm sick of talking about it."

His hand flung out, struck the flank of a black carousel horse. The tinny music started, stopped.

"Stupid goddamn horse!" Craig snarled.

I opened the small refrigerator in the wet bar, grabbed a handful of ice for my glass. Plain soda this time. "Until Patty Kay's murder is solved, you're going to have to talk—and talk a lot." My voice was sharp. I was tired. A squabble with Craig was just one more problem. His temper tantrums were another. I was already dreading a call to Margaret.

Craig walked to the mantel, put out his hand, gripped it hard. He was dangerously close to exploding.

Maybe it was time to go easy. "Simmer down, Craig. I just want you to think about last week. Did Patty Kay say anything, do anything out of the ordinary?"

He shrugged impatiently. "Christ, I don't know."

I wondered abruptly just how much attention—real attention—Craig had paid to his wife's actions.

"How often did Patty Kay do things on the spur of the moment?"

He pushed off the mantel, walked to a barstool, and straddled it. His face was resigned. "All the time. She always said she wasn't a prisoner of a schedule, anybody's schedule. One time she saw a story in *The Tennessean* about white-water rafting in Idaho and we had reservations to go the next morning."

"What about her commitments? Like the class? Or parties?"

"Oh," he said vaguely, "I think that was in the summer sometime. But she'd just get a substitute or call and say we weren't coming."

It must have made Patty Kay a popular guest.

But as a hostess?

"So this last-minute dinner for the trustees wasn't that unusual?"

He shook his head. "One time she decided to have a New Year's Eve party and sent telegrams inviting everybody just the day before. But generally, she planned dinners ahead. Because she really loved to cook and she liked to think about the dinner and work on it and order special foods and things. Like reindeer meat for a Twelfth Night party."

Maybe the timing of that night's dinner didn't really matter. But there were regularly scheduled board meetings. If Patty Kay had something to present to the trustees as trustees, why not do it at a regular meeting?

I got my notebook out of my purse. "I copied down Patty Kay's appointments for Friday and Saturday. Does this suggest anything to you?" I handed it to him.

He scanned the notes, then pointed at *Friday - 9 a.m. Class.* "I don't know if it matters, but she left for school earlier than usual. Usually she left about a quarter to nine. Friday morning she left earlier. About eight, I think."

"Did she say anything?"

"No. She was in a real hurry. She looked grim, so I kept my mouth shut. That was the best thing to do when Patty Kay was frosted about something. She looked like she was spoiling for a fight." His brows drew down in a puzzled frown. "Hey, you know what's funny? The night before, she was fine. We played tennis, took a swim together. Everything was great." His eyes widened. "Hey, wait a minute, wait a minute. Okay, late Thursday night, we'd just turned off the TV and started upstairs and she said, 'Oh, damn, I forgot the files.' And she decided to run out to school and pick them up."

"What files?"

The eagerness seeped away. He shrugged.

"Did you see her after she went out to the school?"

"No. I didn't even hear her car. I went right to sleep."

"Do you know when she came to bed?"

"No."

"Okay, you didn't see her after she got back with the files. And you kept out of her way Friday morning. How about Friday night?"

"We went into Nashville for dinner, then to the symphony. She hardly said a word all night. Which was odd. Because usually the world knew if Patty Kay was mad. She was real upset about something. But she was real quiet."

"You didn't try to find out what was bothering her?"

He shrugged. "Why stir things up?"

"How about Saturday morning?"

"That was crazy. Everything was haywire. The daughter of some of our friends died Friday." For an instant he shifted his focus from himself. "Christ, she drowned herself in the lake!" He fell quiet. I knew that he had imagination, that he was envisioning the painful, choking finality as water clogged the desperate young girl's throat, poured into her lungs. His body jerked. "Somebody called to tell us the next morning. Patty Kay was knocked for a loop. I was about to go to work. I asked her if she was going to cancel that dinner. She kind of huddled in her chair. I wasn't sure she'd heard, so I asked again. She shook her head. She didn't say anything." He looked forlorn. "She was crying. . . . That's the last time I saw her."

"Until she was dead." I waited, then added deliberately, "Or just before she died."

His head jerked upward, as if I'd slapped him.

"Amy swears you left the bookstore at fifteen minutes to four."

He stared at me with desperate, frightened, angry eyes. "No, no. It was *four*. I know it was."

"Amy's sure. I'll tell you something, Craig. A jury will believe her. Not you."

"Dammit, she's just a kid. Just a stupid kid. It was four!" His voice was thin and reedy.

We looked at each other.

I knew he was lying.

One more time.

So what else was new.

Why a lie this time?

Because he knew how long it took to drive to the deli and from there to his house and he knew how long he spent at the deli. And he had an extra fifteen minutes he wouldn't—or dared not—account for.

I had some ideas about it.

He could have dashed by Stevie's apartment. Or stopped at a convenience store to call and see if his girlfriend was home. If he *was* innocent, he would have had no idea that it really mattered what time he got home that night with the fruit basket.

Or he killed his wife.

Either way, I'd been lied to too many times in Fair Haven.

"You found Patty Kay—and you found a bloody sweater. Tell me the truth about that sweater, Craig."

"Sweater?"

"The sweater you wrapped the gun in. The sweater the cops found in a roadside trash bin. The bloody beige Lands' End sweater."

He lurched off the barstool, jammed his hands into the pockets of his slacks. "It was a sweater?"

I've met five-year-olds who could lie more convincingly.

"Oh, hell's bells, Craig. Come off it. Yes, it was a sweater. A sweater that belonged to the woman with whom you're having an affair."

That got me a straight look.

A straight, wild, panicked look.

"What the hell are you talking about?" But the bluster ran thin and shrill.

"Stevie Costello. You know. I know. Others who worked at the bookstore know."

He yanked his hands out of his pockets, took a step toward me. His face was bone-white with rage. "Walsh. Christ, have you told Walsh?"

I could feel my heart thudding in my chest. Had I shot off my mouth one time too many?

He took another step.

"Walsh will get there." My voice was level. "I'm already there. Craig—it's time you told me the truth."

"You've got to *shut up.* Look—who asked you here? What the hell are you doing? Trying to get me convicted? Get out. Just get out. Okay? Get the hell out of here." His voice cracked.

I said nothing.

"You aren't my aunt. Just pack your—"

"It's a little late for you to say so, isn't it? What makes you think Walsh would even let me leave town now? Especially if you tell him we're not related. He might begin to wonder just what kind of story we rigged. And why. No, Craig. You lied and now you're stuck with it. I'm not going anywhere."

His hands tightened into fists. Color flamed on his face. "Dammit, dammit, keep your mouth shut, you've got to. *You've got to!*" Then, with a last furious glare, he turned and ran out of the room.

In a moment I heard the door slam. And, faintly, the motor of the Porsche.

Interesting.

Craig got mad—and he ran.

Just as Stuart Pierce predicted.

I walked toward the kitchen. I still had to eat. I wondered if Craig was hotfooting it to Stevie Costello's.

Not, I presumed, if he had a brain.

Because Captain Walsh surely was going to keep track of his prime suspect.

But maybe that's exactly what Craig would do.

That might truly put the fat in the fire.

At this point, I royally didn't give a damn what Craig Matthews did.

But I was still in the game. I wouldn't deal out.

Not because of Craig.

Because of Margaret.

Because I don't run.

And because of Patty Kay.

If Craig was guilty, I wanted to know. I would grieve for Margaret, but I had to know. In my mind I saw a young, graceful, vibrant woman in the peak years of her life, smiling, playing tennis, working for her community. And I saw her lying dead in her own blood.

I stopped at the telephone in the main hall.

No message lights.

Be interesting to know if Craig'd already had a call from Stevie.

I dialed Desmond's office.

This time he answered.

"You're working late," I said.

"Yeah. I just got back from getting Craig out of jail."

"I know. I talked to him."

"Tell him to keep a low profile. Walsh is determined to pin his hide to the barn door."

"I'll tell him." And so I would—eventually. "Desmond, who's going to chair the trustees meeting tomorrow night?"

Desmond sighed heavily. "I guess I will. I'm vice president." Papers rattled. "Brooke's already left me three messages, something about a memorial for Patty Kay."

Brooke certainly had an agenda.

So did I. Two, in fact. One I explained to Desmond. The other—mounting a search for the author of the letters that drove Franci Hollis to her death—would have to wait. But, in time, I would get to it. Cruelty cannot be permitted to triumph.

"Sure. Why not? Will I see you before then?"

"Yes. How about after the funeral?"

"After the funeral." Desmond's voice lost its buoyancy.

"Patty Kay's guild is bringing luncheon over to Pamela's. I'll look for you there." I put down the receiver.

I heated a frozen dinner. Not supermarket fare, but Patty Kay's marvelous cooking: sesame chicken, scalloped zucchini, carrots. As soon as I finished the dishes, I headed upstairs to Patty Kay's office.

Patty Kay's trashed office.

I stood in the doorway.

Surely this was proof of Craig's innocence. For he was in police custody when this office was ransacked.

But Patty Kay's death could have triggered panic in other quarters. What if she had letters from Stuart? Present-day, passionate letters? What if Gina had fired off an angry, threatening letter about the land zoning?

I couldn't assume this mess was made by the murderer.

But I was still glad young Dan Forrest hadn't sought out the source of the noise Monday afternoon. There was a viciousness to this devastation that appalled me.

I set to work. I couldn't put everything where it went, of course, because I didn't know. And many objects were too broken to be repaired. But I tidied up. And finally felt I had all the papers that belonged in Patty Kay's Walden School file.

I took the material, more than a dozen folders in an expandable brown file, down to the clubroom. I didn't want to stay in the office with the scarred desk and shattered bookcase glass.

Thursday night at bedtime Patty Kay was happy. She abruptly

realized she'd forgotten some files. She drove to Walden School, returned with—presumably—the file holder I now possessed. Friday morning at breakfast, Patty Kay's mood had altered completely. Friday afternoon she arranged a last-minute dinner for the school's board of trustees.

I glanced at the clock.

Half past seven.

At midnight I gave up. I'd read and reread every file in the folder: Budget, Physical Plant, Personnel, Recruiting, Sports, Academic Programs, Scholarships, Endowment, Land Use, Media, Board Minutes.

If there was anything the least bit odd, unusual, or suspect in that mass of material, I couldn't find it—and I'm damn good at finding odd, unusual, or suspect facts.

I was frustrated. Frustrated, confused, and exhausted.

I finally gave up and went to bed. After locking my door and wedging a chair beneath it. Craig had run away, true. But I couldn't be certain he was innocent. And I knew a great deal he wouldn't want Captain Walsh to learn.

I woke several times in the night and once was tempted to get up and have another go at the files.

Because the answer had to be there, hadn't it?

Patty Kay was her usual self Thursday evening.

She went to the school, got those files, came home.

And Friday morning she was very upset.

Why, dammit, why?

15

The Episcopal burial service is swift and merciful. A silk pall covers a closed casket. The liturgy emphasizes the promise that death is swallowed up in victory. Prayer asks that the deceased, increasing in knowledge and love of the Lord, go from strength to strength in the life of perfect service in the heavenly kingdom.

Sometimes there is a eulogy, often not.

There was a eulogy for Patty Kay.

". . . your servant, O Lord, who labored diligently to make this world better . . ."

The elderly priest quietly and lovingly recalled Patty Kay's impact on the lives in her community. Her good works. And they were many.

It was beyond the priest's skill to recall her gusto for life, her cocky disdain for the pretentious, her willingness to face abuse for unpopular causes.

It was odd, staring at the cross emblazoned in scarlet on the golden silk pall, how well I felt I knew a woman I'd never met.

The church pews were full. There were folding chairs set up in the narthex.

I sat with Craig. We'd exchanged only nods that morning. He came downstairs shortly before the limousine arrived. He'd avoided looking at me, hiding behind the newspaper with his coffee.

But he never turned a page of it.

We sat alone in the first black limousine.

A haunted-looking, red-eyed Brigit rode with her father and step-mother and the Guthries in the second limousine.

But despite my irritation with Craig and despite my newly kin-dled suspicions of him, the funeral made me glad I'd come to Fair Haven three days ago.

Because Craig would have stood alone without me. And that shouldn't happen to anyone. As the service began, I could feel his body shrink beside me, as if a heavy weight bowed his shoulders. He gripped the unopened prayer book so tightly, his fingers blanched.

It was almost as if an invisible wall surrounded him when we entered the church. So many eyes slid away from his glance. So few hands reached out to touch him. So many quick, covert looks followed after he passed.

As we walked out of that packed church, I could count on one hand those who even acknowledged his presence. Gina Abbott. Brigit. And yes, Stuart Pierce. And the Forrest family, Brooke, her husband David and son Dan. Cheryl and Bob Kraft.

But most eyes avoided contact. Most faces turned away.

Some of it might have been awkwardness.

How do you greet a man whose wife has been violently mur-dered?

It isn't the acceptable way to die. If Patty Kay had died of cancer, the handclasps would have come, the murmured condolences.

But this was murder, and Craig had been arrested for the crime.

And I wondered how many knowing looks had been exchanged in conversations across Fair Haven, how many silken whispers shared: *So much younger than Patty Kay . . . I've heard he and that girl, the pretty blond one, at the store . . . The gun came from his car. . . . Always thought he looked shifty . . .*

It was no better at the cemetery.

Craig sat stiffly beside me in the first row beneath the green funeral canopy. The bronze casket rested above the newly dug grave. The gravesite, part of the Prentiss family plots, was near the top of a hill. A sea of tombstones fell away below, sparkling in the soft April sunlight. Pine trees stood watch, sentinels to sorrow. But no observer would have noted heartbreak in the face of this widowed husband. Instead, Craig looked hunted, his eyes defensive, his shoulders hunched, his tightly clasped hands trembling.

Desmond Marino was in the front row of a semicircle of mourners facing the grave. The lawyer's monkey-bright eyes, somber and thoughtful, remained on Craig.

Marino wasn't the only person watching Craig. Captain Walsh stood deep in the shadow of the towering pine. His cool, dissecting eyes never left Craig's face.

The priest's resonant voice carried his words to us: "Almighty God, with whom do live the spirits of those who depart hence in the Lord, and with whom the souls of the faithful, after they are delivered from the burden of the flesh, are in joy and felicity . . ."

I looked at other now-familiar faces.

Chuck Selwyn, the headmaster, might have posed for Funeral Director, U.S.A. His black suit, bowed head, and somber face embodied decorous grief. Tonight at the trustees meeting, I intended to point out that there was nothing in Patty Kay's school files about an aeronautics program.

Mr. Selwyn, what was the real reason for her anger with you?

I couldn't wait.

"We give thee hearty thanks for the good examples of all those thy servants, who, having finished their course in faith, do now rest from their labors . . ."

Louise Pierce touched a dainty cambric handkerchief to her eyes. But her heart-shaped face was calm. I saw no tears. Her other hand gripped her husband's arm possessively. I remembered her tone so clearly.

Stuart is my husband. Mine.

"And we beseech thee . . ."

Stuart Pierce seemed unaware of his wife's touch. He stood with his hands clasped behind his back and gazed at the casket, his dark eyes empty, his face bleak.

Patty Kay and I—it was always wild and a little bit insane.

". . . that we, with all those who are departed in the true faith of thy holy name . . ."

The Forrest family was in the center of the semicircle. It would have been a focal point for a photographer. I supposed the Forrest family always automatically assumed pride of place. David Forrest's stern face was composed. His black pinstripe suit fit him perfectly. Of course. I would scarcely have expected less. Dan Forrest, slim and handsome in a crisp navy blazer and dark gray slacks, stood between his parents. The handsome teenager was definitely his mother's son, her beauty transformed into a young man's clear, resolute features. Dan stared fixedly, his eyes enormous, at the flowering rhododendron to the right of the gravesite. Death is difficult for any young person, and within the space of a day Dan Forrest had experienced both the death of a schoolmate and of a family friend. I hoped the counselors at Walden School were skilled. Brooke's lovely face twisted in sorrow. Tears slid down her cheeks. Her husband might say she and Patty Kay were merely social equals. There was more here than that.

It's so important to do the right thing.

". . . may have our perfect consummation and bliss . . ."

Gina Abbott's eyes were closed. Her bony face was drawn and frighteningly pale.

That's the last time we talked. We yelled at each other.

Gina's daughter Chloe clutched a prayer book. She stared at the casket with puzzled, frightened eyes.

". . . both in body and soul . . ."

Stevie Costello's arms were clasped tightly across her chest. She wore a boxy black suit that wasn't especially becoming. It made her look shorter, heavier. And black turned her pale face sallow. She, too, watched Craig.

". . . in thy eternal and everlasting glory . . ."

I almost didn't recognize the final member of the tennis foursome. I had yet to meet her, of course, other than in Patty Kay's videos of the tennis holiday and Brigit's birthday. I wished I could step forward, take her arm, cry, "I understand, I understand."

Edith Hollis looked twenty years older than the woman who had vacationed at the tennis resort. Her fair, freckled face was bloated with suffering; her chunky body—once a muscular threat on the court—sagged heavily. She clung to the arm of the man next to her. Her husband, I assumed. His face, too, bore the marks of sorrow. Balding and stocky, her husband looked my age. He was probably twenty years younger.

My heart ached, too, for their son, Walt, the dead girl's brother, the other nice-looking redheaded kid in the snapshots in Gina's store. Walt's sunken, splotchy face—so young, too young for so much pain —looked utterly dazed, lost, despairing. My Emily had grieved so long, so deeply for her little brother.

". . . through Jesus Christ our Lord. Amen."

One final prayer.

The funeral director caught my eye and nodded.

"Craig."

Those hunted eyes slid toward me.

"Time to go," I murmured.

Brigit was the first of the family to reach open ground.

Friends began to move toward her.

Pamela and Willis Guthrie walked in front of me as we filed away from those seats so close to the grave. Craig was behind me.

". . . a very nice service. I'll have to tell Father Burke that the family is well pleased." Pamela's voice was just one shade short of condescending.

"Quite nice, quite nice," Willis echoed.

Like well-rehearsed marionettes, they took their places beside Brigit and began to greet friends.

I moved to join them.

And realized Craig was standing motionless near the open grave. He looked from it to his wife's daughter and her aunt and uncle. Uncertainty flickered in his eyes.

Brigit, struggling for composure, looked toward Craig, saw the open space around him. Her eyes widened indignantly. "Craig!" she called out.

He took a step toward her, hesitated, his eyes dark with misery.

Brigit darted to him. "Over here, Craig. We'll say hello to everyone over here." She grabbed his hand and tugged.

In an instant it was a family receiving line headed by Brigit and her stepfather. Then came I and Pamela and Willis.

Craig Matthews became the widower.

Not the murder suspect.

Now came the handclasps, the murmured condolences.

It was like watching a water-starved plant respond to a rain shower. Craig stood taller, his shoulders back, his handshake firm.

Brigit stood beside him, clung to his arm. I admired the determined jut of her chin. But I didn't like the glint of satisfaction—and delicious pleasure—in her eyes.

Captain Walsh watched too.

So many kind words, so much sorrow.

I wondered how Patty Kay's murderer felt at that moment, that moment of finality and grief.

Was the murderer among us, pretending to grieve for Patty Kay?

The mourners were walking away now and our line broke apart, Brigit reluctantly loosing her hold on Craig.

I heard Pamela's calm voice. ". . . put out that lovely crystal punch bowl of Mother's. It is perfect for . . ."

And watched Louise Pierce stride briskly toward the cars, parked bumper to bumper on the winding gravel road.

Or perhaps the murderer was among us—and not pretending to grieve.

.   .   .

Pamela Guthrie, her heavy body molded into a black silk dress, might have been presiding at a spring social event, not the gathering following her sister's funeral. Candy-striped awnings and cloth-covered tables were set up on the patio behind the Guthrie house. A long table provided a substantial buffet. Almost a hundred people milled about.

I stood with Desmond near a gazebo. The lawyer stared down at the ground and didn't say a word.

I didn't mind. I had people to watch.

Volatile Gina Abbott sped directly to Brigit and held her close, then took both of Craig's hands and gave them a hard squeeze.

Cheryl Kraft shaded her eyes from the sun and listened as Brooke Forrest spoke earnestly. I'd have bet a bundle Brooke was presenting her plans for a memorial to Patty Kay.

David Forrest shook hands with Stuart Pierce. Then, in what I would guess to be a rare display of emotion, Forrest cuffed Stuart on the shoulder before he walked away.

Gina's plump, fair daughter carried two plates of food. Chloe came shyly up behind Dan Forrest and called his name.

He turned and took the plate, said casually, "Thanks, Chloe."

She stood beside him, toyed with her food, and watched him with glowing eyes. Dan ate briskly, oblivious of her scrutiny.

Ah, young love.

Better though than the hungry glances Brigit was wont to give her stepfather.

Speaking of . . .

Brigit clung to Craig's arm. Proudly. And almost as possessively as her stepmother with her father.

At least Captain Walsh wasn't here to see it.

But a small black woman in a lace-trimmed purple dress watched, her elderly face lined with worry. Jewel took a step toward Brigit and Craig, then her shoulders sagged, and she stayed where she was, alone, in the shadow of a flowering mimosa.

Cheryl Kraft's husband stood with one arm about the shoulder of each grieving Hollis parent.

No wonder his emaciated blond wife sped him bright, sweet smiles.

Willis Guthrie smoothed his wispy ginger mustache and glanced at his watch.

I was tempted to tell Guthrie he could charge this afternoon up as a financial success. Look how much money his wife was going to inherit.

Near the swimming pool, Walt Hollis stared stubbornly at the brightly colored tiles, making no response as Chuck Selwyn spoke to him, the headmaster's hands chopping in short emphatic gestures.

And threading in and out of those who had known Patty Kay well —and either loved or hated her—were those who had come to pay their respects. Well-dressed, articulate, charming, Fair Haven's elite.

Yet, I knew that they'd been talking, all of them: *You know, the sisters never did get along . . . I saw Patty Kay and Stuart in Atlanta . . . Somebody said Louise Pierce cut her dead . . . Of course he married her for her money . . .*

Pamela's plump cheeks glowed pinkly. She moved from group to group, receiving homage.

One small group hesitated near the French windows that gave onto the patio. I recognized Amy, small, dark, anxious-eyed. Oh, of course, the employees from the bookshop. Ill at ease, they clustered close to Stevie. The young assistant manager looked toward Brigit and Craig. Her face was shuttered.

Pamela crossed to them. "It is so nice of you to come. Very, very thoughtful. I know Patty Kay would have been pleased. Do be sure and have something to eat before you go back to the store." It wasn't the precise words that offended, it was her patronizing tone, her unconcealed assessment of them as social inferiors.

"Thank you, Mrs. Guthrie." Stevie's voice was wooden.

Beside me, Desmond abruptly growled, "Jesus, what a poisonous woman! Let's get out of here. Okay?"

.   .   .

It wasn't easy to follow Desmond's low-slung black Ferrari. He drove too fast. We made it from Pamela's house to Vanderbilt Plaza in Nashville in a little less than twenty minutes.

He was driving fast, but he wouldn't be able to escape the demons that rode with him.

I pulled into the hotel parking lot right behind him.

Desmond held my arm as we entered the cool, expansive lobby.

"The bar's this way."

Our shoes clicked on the sand-toned marble.

I was amused at his choice of bars. Certainly this one was refined enough for anyone's elderly aunt.

We settled on an overstuffed couch.

Desmond looked at me. "What would you like?"

"Iced tea, please."

Desmond looked up at the waiter. "One iced tea. One double scotch."

Inwardly, I was chafing to be back in Fair Haven. There was still so much to learn.

But sometimes you have to answer other calls. Desmond wanted to talk. I almost told him how the headmaster was squelching Gina's efforts to discover who drove Franci to suicide. But another look at his grieving face dissuaded me. Yes, Desmond needed to talk, but he needed more to talk about his childhood friend.

The lawyer looked down at his clasped hands. "You know about Junior Assembly, the dances for kids so they learn how to be ladies and gentlemen?"

I nodded.

"We were probably twelve, maybe thirteen. Patty Kay snuck in this tape of 'The Colonel Bogey's March,' you know, *da da tum tum tum tum,* and she'd sent word around in whispers, and when it came on we all started marching back and forth and the ladies in charge stood there, looking at us like we'd turned into Martians and everybody got hysterical, it was so funny."

Our drinks came.

He downed half of his and signaled for another. "Kid stuff. Maybe funny only when you're twelve."

Twelve . . . I held tightly to my glass.

A scowl twisted his forlorn-monkey face. "She shouldn't be in a casket." His voice was flat and cold. It held no trace now of the softness of reminiscence.

"No. She shouldn't."

Nor should Bobby. Or Franci.

"So I want to be straight with you. I spilled my guts to Walsh. I told him everything you've found out—and everything I know about these people. This may spell the end of my legal career in Fair Haven. But I fucking well don't care." A brief glance. "Sorry."

I reached across the table, gave his hand a brief squeeze. "I'm glad. Every piece of information puts pressure on Walsh to look harder."

"He's looking. Believe it, he's looking. The guy's not stupid. And he's scared now that maybe, just maybe, Craig didn't do it. Walsh doesn't want several million dollars mad at him. But every time he asks a question, he's stepping on expensive toes."

"That's not going to get any easier." I told him about Patty Kay's late-night trip to pick up her files on Walden School. "Next morning she's upset. And she invites the trustees to dinner. Cause and effect? I don't know. I've been through those files like the Golden Girls with a list of eligible men. I can't find anything out of order. But Patty Kay was terribly upset about something. Whatever it was, it set everything in motion, including the dinner. So what did she say?"

"I got her message on my answering tape." He concentrated, trying to recall. "She said, 'Desmond, I'm having dinner at my house Saturday night at seven for the Walden School trustees. It is essential that you attend.'"

"That's all?"

"Yes."

"She didn't identify herself, didn't call back, tell you what it was all about?"

"No."

CAROLYN G. HART   190

I sipped my tea. "Don't you think that's odd?"

"When Patty Kay made up her mind, she moved fast. She assumed I knew her voice. She assumed everybody'd come. And I'm sure—"

"No. I'm not talking about the dinner party. Why didn't she contact you *before* the dinner to pitch her plan or campaign or whatever it was she wanted? Why was it *essential*? To her? Or to the school?"

He finished his second drink, gestured again to the waiter. "I don't have any idea."

"But she arranged a dinner. There had to be a reason. She was upset, so she must have had something serious to discuss with the trustees. Here's a woman who's used to running all kinds of groups. What's the first precept of success in an organization?"

"You rally your troops long before there's open discussion. You never make a motion unless you're sure it will carry."

"Right. Why didn't she?"

"I don't know." He picked up his new drink, took a greedy gulp. "Maybe she called later but didn't get me. She wouldn't leave another message. Besides, she knew she could count on my vote—if it really mattered to her."

I looked in his eyes.

He met my gaze.

And it was there, love and grief and deepest hopelessness.

Abruptly, I understood. Desmond had never married. Now I knew why. Desmond, too, had loved Patty Kay. Had he ever told her? Did it make any difference? Would he have been upset by her secret rendezvous with Stuart? What did he really feel about Craig?

He downed the rest of his drink and grimaced. "So if I knew what she wanted, I'd tell you. You're right, Patty Kay'd definitely line up her ducks. You can find out tonight from the others."

It was just past three when I got back to the house. My conference with Desmond frustrated me—we'd rehashed everything we knew or imagined but got nowhere even though my instinct said we were close—and I was desperately impatient for that evening's meeting of the Walden trustees. Some of them surely would know what Patty Kay wanted, enough at least to carry a vote.

I slammed out of my car, then stopped to take a refreshing breath. A frisky breeze stirred the blooming jonquils, dazzling gold in the spring sunlight.

I decided to jog. Not only did I need the exercise, I could take another survey of the neighborhood, perhaps spot where the murderer might have awaited Craig's arrival. If that was what had happened . . .

The note on the front door stopped me cold:

Henrie O,
Amy called at 2:25. Wants you to call her at the store. Said it's
important. Gone for a drive.

Craig

Amy. The little clerk was so certain when Craig had left the bookstore on Saturday. Had she changed her mind?

I used the hall phone.

"Books, Books, Books." The voice was pleasant and masculine.

"May I speak to Amy, please?"

". . . She isn't here."

"With whom am I speaking?"

"Todd Simpson."

"I had a message asking me to call her. Is she supposed to be there?"

"She certainly is." He sounded puzzled. "From noon to six today."

"She didn't leave word where she was going?"

He was silent for a moment. "Who is speaking, please?"

"Henrie O Collins. Craig Matthews's aunt."

"Oh, Mrs. Collins." Todd rushed now to confide. "Listen, we

don't know what to think. Amy's been absolutely dependable. She even came in a few minutes early today. She was here, unpacking boxes, doing some phoning, other stuff. Then we had a real rush around two. When I looked for her later, I couldn't find her. I've even called her apartment and there's no answer. You'd think she would've told me if she was sick or had to leave."

A dreadful wave of coldness swept through me. I thanked Todd and hung up hastily, battling nausea.

I drove too fast, all thoughts of spring beauty and a jog gone. I didn't like the thoughts I was having.

Amy's message asked me to call; she'd said it was important.

I parked at the curb directly in front of the store and hurried inside.

I spotted a stocky blond young man, still in the navy blue suit he'd worn to the funeral.

He walked swiftly to me. "Mrs. Collins?"

"Yes. Are you Todd?"

"Yes, ma'am. Listen, it's awfully nice of you to come, but I've looked again. Everywhere. Amy's definitely not here."

"I hope not."

"What do you mean?"

I didn't take time to answer. I plunged past him, gave only a cursory glance at the open floor of the store and the easily seen mezzanine, then hurried to the stockroom.

Todd followed. He quickly got the drift of my search. His eyes widened.

It didn't take long. There weren't that many places to check.

Some large cupboards in the storeroom.

The shipping crate that had held a new refrigerator for the coffee bar.

The dark shadows by the closed loading dock.

The dank old cellar no longer in use.

And, in the bricked alleyway, the dumpster.

The heavy rusted top shrieked when I propped it open.

I looked at the worn soles of low-heeled pink flats. And at thin grayish ankles. The blood had drained to her upper torso. I was glad I couldn't see the congested, dark, purple skin.

Quick anger shook me. Damn, oh, damn, damn, damn. "Call the police," I told Todd, and didn't recognize the harsh voice as my own.

16

The lights overhead spilled down on the coffee area where we waited, capturing us in a sickly yellow pool of fluorescence. The only sound was the quiet murmur as the policewoman, Sergeant Roman, took down the names, addresses, and phone numbers of the employees and customers who were in the bookstore when we found Amy.

I, too, scribbled the names down. Not quite surreptitiously, but without advertisement.

I could hear the slight scratch of my pencil against the pad, feel the pressure of my fingers against the pencil.

I was alive, able to feel—and raging at myself.

Because poor little Amy with her oversize glasses and anxious eyes was dead in an alley dumpster.

And it could be my fault.

Mine.

I'd told Craig Amy was absolutely positive of the time he left the bookstore on the day Patty Kay died.

Goddammit, *I* told him.

The tip of the pencil snapped beneath the pressure of my fingers. I found another pencil, completed the list, and dropped pad and pencil into my purse.

The store around us, lights glaring down on untenanted aisles, was somber, and vaguely threatening.

Occasionally someone rattled the locked front door, puzzled at the prematurely posted CLOSED sign.

Police came and went through the entrance to the stockroom. Those of us sequestered in the coffee area miserably watched them in silence.

One of the clerks, a plump girl with a wide mouth meant for smiling, snuffled noisily into a damp wad of tissue. Todd Simpson, his face sympathetic and bewildered, patted her shoulder.

Restless, I walked over to the coffee bar, poured chocolate mocha coffee into a mug, and splashed in a generous amount of cream. The coffee did nothing to warm the hollow coldness in my stomach, but I sipped it as I glanced around the coffee area.

I didn't know any of the other clerks. Except, of course, Cheryl Kraft, the afternoon's designated socialite. She kept brushing back silver-blond hair from a suddenly gaunt face, and her huge pagoda-shaped silver earrings gave an eerie tinkle. The harsh light betrayed the telltale traces of plastic surgery.

A siren sounded from the alleyway.

Every head turned.

Captain Walsh came through the storeroom door. He glanced at a card in his hand. "Todd Simpson?"

Todd gave the plump girl another pat, then stood. "Sir?"

"Come this way, please."

About five minutes later Todd returned. He was sweating heavily.

I knew why. To identify the body of someone you know is a sickening experience.

Now the police could close the body bag on poor Amy.

I figured it would be at least an hour before Walsh interviewed those of us detained. The captain and his small investigating team had plenty to do: a painstaking examination of the actual scene, note-taking, sketching, photography (more than likely videocam taping too), the careful, tedious collection of physical evidence.

A mumble of voices drifted through the open stockroom door. Try as I might, I couldn't understand what was being said.

Suddenly the door swung shut. Now we couldn't hear anything.

I probably had an hour at most before I'd see the police chief.

I had a decision to make.

If I told Captain Walsh about my talk with Amy and my report of it to Craig, I'd be hand-delivering a class-A motive for Craig to commit murder.

The probable result: Craig's instant arrest.

But maybe that's exactly what I should do.

Only two facts held me back.

The search of Patty Kay's office.

Craig ran away when I confronted him.

But, nonetheless, the fifteen minutes that Amy would have sworn to was enough to put Craig back in jail.

The decision was mine to make.

The businessman who'd been pacing up and down by the psychology shelves swung toward the policewoman. "Look, I'm missing clients. I just dropped in here to buy *Fortune*. I've given you my name and address. My office is just across the street."

"I'm sorry, sir. No one can leave until Captain Walsh says so."

"Well, ask him, will you?"

"The captain requested that everyone remain here until further notice. He will speak with each of you as soon as possible."

"Dammit to hell, I've got a new client coming in at four-thirty. He's—"

Todd pushed up from the straight chair he'd straddled. He was a big young man, the kind who plays lineman for his high school team

—trunk legs, a barrel chest, a big head. He wasn't large enough for college ball, but he made the businessman look small. His face still glistened with sweat. "Look, mister, Amy's dead. You may not care, but we do. And maybe you can help. Don't you want to help?"

Every face turned toward the complainer. He had the grace to turn fiery red. Then he slumped silently into a chair.

I had the clerks sorted out by now: Jackie, the plump, snuffling girl; Paul, cadaverously skinny, his long black hair in a ponytail, a golden ring in his left earlobe; Candy, serious gray eyes, a cheerful pug nose, a sprinkle of freckles that stood out now against shock-paled skin.

Cheryl Kraft, of course, didn't look like a clerk. Not in that turquoise floral silk jacquard dress. She was uncharacteristically subdued. The jeweled hands in her lap trembled.

The other customers made no complaint. A nursing mother turned her back to the group and cuddled a baby to her breast while she played a rhyming game with her restless toddler. Two well-dressed middle-aged women exchanged anxious whispers. A distinguished-looking man about my age calmly read a paperback of Suetonius.

Todd once again straddled the straight chair. He rested his sweaty face on his crossed arms.

I walked over to him.

"Todd, where's Stevie?"

"Ma'am, the captain said no talking." The policewoman was pleasant but firm.

I nodded, returned to the coffee bar, and sat on a stool. I got out my notebook again. Okay. No questions now.

But I'd damn sure ask questions later.

I'd just started sketching down my thoughts, when the front door opened.

We all turned to look.

A patrolman ushered in Craig Matthews and Stevie Costello.

Craig looked at me, looked quickly away. He took a seat at the periphery of the café area.

Stevie slid onto the stool next to mine. "Tell me—"

"No talking, please." The policewoman stepped toward us. Stevie nodded jerkily. She didn't look toward Craig.

Across the room, ignoring us, Craig wiped his face with a handkerchief.

I stared hard at him. I didn't care now that he was Margaret's nephew. That concern seemed long ago and far away. What I had to know, what I must discover, was whether he'd murdered a helpless young girl because I'd talked too much.

The pitiless overhead light emphasized the weakness of his face, the self-indulgent mouth, the uncertain eyes, the defensive expression. He'd changed from the black pinstripe suit he'd worn to Patty Kay's funeral into olive linen slacks and a cotton sport shirt with brilliant red, green, and blue vertical stripes. He wore brown alligator loafers. Fine clothes. Expensive clothes.

Craig Matthews could dress this way because he'd married an older woman with a great deal of money.

He must have felt my glance.

He looked at me, and in his eyes I saw both defiance and terror.

It was Craig who looked away.

The storeroom door opened again. A trim young woman carrying a large square black attaché case walked briskly toward us. She placed it on one of the tables. "Hello, I'm Lieutenant Margaret Berry. I'm here to take your fingerprints." Her voice was matter-of-fact. "These are called elimination prints. It's customary to take the prints of all persons on the premises of a homicide so that investigators can quickly identify and discard those that are irrelevant."

It was the very best butter—and no hint that these prints might send someone to the electric chair.

Lieutenant Berry was pleasant, professional, and thorough. She took finger and palm prints. It was a tedious process. She took Stevie's first, Craig's second.

The businessman looked at the ink in distaste. "I just came here to buy a magazine," he complained in a voice used to being obeyed.

"I understand Captain Walsh will begin the interviews as soon as the fingerprinting is completed." Lieutenant Berry held up the roller used for palms.

He glared at her, then stuck out his right hand. "I've already missed my appointment."

Todd shifted forward in his chair, his face pugnacious. The antagonism between them had become electric. "So who cares?"

I, too, was aware of the passage of time and beginning to watch the clock in earnest. It was almost five. The school board meeting was in two hours.

Each person in turn was directed to the bookstore's main office on the mezzanine in the order in which their fingerprints were taken.

Mine were taken last.

That it was deliberate, I had no doubt.

But why?

It was almost six-thirty when I was finally ushered into the main office on the mezzanine. Captain Walsh sat behind a paper-littered desk.

An attractive redhead nodded to me from her chair next to the desk. She had pulled a swivel chair away from a computer work station to face the door.

Walsh didn't get up. He jerked his head toward the woman. "Assistant District Attorney Susan Nichols," he said brusquely.

She nodded again.

"Hello, Captain, Ms. Nichols."

Captain Walsh no longer looked movie-star handsome. The bristle of the day's beard was dark on his cheeks; lines of tension were etched in his face. And he didn't give a damn who I was related to.

Or maybe he did.

"I'd like to have your movements today." He jabbed a blunt forefinger at a tape recorder on the desk. "Whatever you say will be recorded. If you wish to speak with a lawyer first, you can use the phone."

It was decision time.

And I still hadn't decided.

The police chief's glance sharpened.

I'd taken just a little too long to answer.

So I delayed an instant longer. "That's not a Miranda, Captain."

"No."

"Very well. I've no objection to being recorded." I ignored the straight chair directly in front of the desk and instead chose a comfortable armchair. I quickly sketched my activities. Today's activities. But nothing—yet—about my session last evening with Craig.

"You found the message asking you to call Amy Foss on the front door of the Matthews home?"

"Yes."

"When?"

"At approximately three o'clock."

"You came directly here?"

"No. I went inside and called the bookstore. When I was told she'd disappeared—"

Walsh held up his hand. "Nobody said she'd disappeared. Todd Simpson said she couldn't be found."

"That's correct. She couldn't be found. In my judgment, Captain, objects or people who cannot be found may reasonably be considered to have disappeared. That's when I got worried. I arrived here about three-twenty."

"Describe your actions."

I did.

The police chief's cold, suspicious eyes never left my face.

The assistant D.A. made notes.

Walsh abruptly boomed: "How did you know she was dead?"

"I didn't *know*. I was afraid she was." I kept my voice relaxed. If he'd hoped for a nervous start, he didn't get it.

"You went straight to the body."

"No."

"You started looking for a body. Simpson said so."

"Yes."

"Why?"

Zero hour.

To speak. Or not.

He hunched forward in his chair, his face forbidding.

When I confronted him, Craig ran away.

I took a deep breath. All right. Jewel said it best, with a black woman's painful wisdom: It's a lot harder to get in jail than get out.

So for now, one more time, I was in Craig's corner.

I'd give it—and him—twenty-four hours.

If I didn't know the answer by then, I'd come clean with Captain Walsh.

"We can't be sure, Captain, why Amy was killed. But there's one critical point to remember: Amy took the message Saturday that instructed Craig to go to the delicatessen and then home."

"So?"

"I told her to be sure to call me if she remembered anything about that call, anything at all. I think she did remember something about that call, something that made her extremely dangerous to the murderer. And so she called me."

It might be true.

Or it might be that I'd put Amy in terrible danger.

I would—before God—find out.

The chief's handsome face curled into a sneer. "Oh. I suppose she had a sudden recognition of the caller's voice." The sarcasm was thick.

"I don't know what it was."

His tone became accusing. "How much money do you have, Mrs. Collins?"

"Sufficient, Captain Walsh."

"Are you next of kin to Craig Matthews?"

Oh, what a ticklish, interesting, revealing question.

I smiled at him. "It would take a bit of genealogy to figure that one out, Captain. I'm more of a distant cousin treated as an honorary aunt."

He leaned back in the chair, crossed his arms over his chest. "Just where were you, Mrs. Collins, when Patty Kay Matthews was killed?" His eyes were lethal as stilettos.

"Late Saturday afternoon I was en route to Monteagle."

"You can't prove it."

"No." I smiled gently. "But you can't prove otherwise."

"And you don't have an alibi for the murder of Amy Foss." Again that piercing stare.

"When," I asked quietly, "was Amy killed?"

He didn't have to check his notes. "Between two-forty and three this afternoon."

"At that time, I was driving back from Nashville to my nephew's home."

"Alone?"

"Yes."

His eyes said it all: *Same song, second verse.*

"Was Amy shot?" I asked abruptly. Where was Patty Kay's gun now?

There was a flicker in his chilly eyes. He gazed at me thoughtfully, then shook his head. "No. Somebody knocked her unconscious. Then he—or she—strangled her."

Oh, God. Poor Amy. Poor kid. "It's hideous," I said angrily.

But Chief Walsh wasn't interested in my expressions of concern.

Instead, he snapped, "Was Craig Matthews's arrival at your cabin Saturday evening prearranged, Mrs. Collins?"

It's always nice to be able to tell the truth. "No." I thought it had a ring of veracity.

"How did he know you were there?"

This was tricky.

"I always keep my family informed of my vacation plans." Which I do.

Captain Walsh rubbed a bristly cheek; his eyes never left my face. "I want a copy of recent letters you and Craig Matthews exchanged."

"I don't keep letters, Captain."

The assistant D.A. scooted her chair forward. She studied me like Bacall eyeing a bad guy. Her tone was cool as she spelled it out. "Craig Matthews is going to be extremely rich if he inherits his wife's estate. He won't inherit a cent if he's convicted of her murder. And you've come to Fair Haven and repeatedly tried to divert police suspicion from him. We have to wonder if the circumstances of his wife's murder weren't arranged to look as though someone was trying to place the blame on Matthews."

I met her gaze steadily. "Interesting thesis. But you're going a little fast, aren't you, Ms. Nichols? There are still some items to be explained. To whom did the beige sweater belong, the one Craig wrapped the murder weapon in?"

Walsh didn't need to consult his notes. "Mr. Matthews said it was his wife's sweater."

Damn Craig. He was going to wrap a noose of lies around his own neck.

I handled it as well as I could. "Really? I suppose most men don't pay too much attention to clothes. In fact, he could have made a mistake." I looked at the assistant D.A. "I imagine you know quite a bit about clothes, Ms. Nichols. Suffice it to say, the bloodied sweater came from Lands' End. If you check Mrs. Matthews's closet, you'll find a lot of far more expensive designer outfits."

Captain Walsh looked faintly bewildered, but quick understanding flickered in Nichols's eyes.

"Actually, Captain, Ms. Nichols, I recommend that you take a look at the clothing worn by others who knew—or worked for—Mrs. Matthews."

"More distraction, Mrs. Collins?" Walsh sniped.

I was pleasant but crisp. "I'm not into conspiracy, Captain Walsh. I'm just trying to get at the facts. I suggest you do the same."

17

I was grateful I had the second Baby Ruth in my bag. I made it out to Walden School with two minutes to spare, the candy wrapper crumpled on the car seat, a surge of sugar in my blood.

I was torn.

I desperately wanted to know more about Amy's last day at the bookstore. To whom did the girl talk? What did she do? I wanted to know what the others in the store had seen. I wanted to ask each of the customers when they last saw Amy, if they talked to her.

I didn't know a damn thing. The last to be interviewed, the last out the door, I was left with all the unanswered questions and nobody there to ask.

Did Amy have a desk, a drawer, a cubbyhole, anything where she kept her things?

Where was Stevie when Amy disappeared?

Where, most important, most emphatic, was Craig?

Twenty-four hours, that's all I'd give him.

And I keep my promises.

But I couldn't miss the meeting of the trustees of Walden School. Amy was killed because she was a threat to Patty Kay's murderer. To avenge Amy, I had to find out why Patty Kay was furious on Friday, the day after she went out to Walden School for her files. Walden School—its trustees were invited to a dinner canceled by Patty Kay's murder. Walden School—its headmaster knew more than he was telling.

Walden School. Suddenly every path led to it.

Light spilled cheerfully from the tall windows on the first floor of the beautiful Greek Revival mansion.

I hurried up the steps, opened the front door—and cannoned into Chuck Selwyn.

The headmaster jerked back. Again he wore the navy blazer, Oxford cloth button-down shirt, khaki slacks, and tasseled oxblood loafers. But there was nothing boyish about the look he gave me.

"Mrs. Collins, the school is closed to visitors at the moment. I'll have to ask you—"

"Henrie O, glad you could make it!"

Desmond's welcome was warm, loud, and genial. He ducked around the headmaster, hand outstretched, to greet me, then looked toward Selwyn. "Mrs. Collins is here to represent the Matthews family tonight." His tone was pleasant but final.

Brooke Forrest hurried in. "Oh, I hope I'm not late." Her smile faltered. The dark smudges beneath her eyes emphasized her paleness. She actually looked ill. Her apple-green silk blouse was elegant with the charcoal linen skirt, but not perhaps the best color choice for her wan face.

"Hello, Brooke. I was telling Chuck that Henrie O's here to give us some help on an appropriate memorial for Patty Kay."

"Oh, yes, yes. I'm so glad you could come." Her hand touched my arm. "It's *so* important."

Every word Desmond and Brooke said made it more difficult for Selwyn to object.

The headmaster nodded grudgingly. "Very good of you to take the time, Mrs. Collins," he said stiffly.

As the grandfather clock in the corner chimed seven, Stuart Pierce and Willis Guthrie entered together. Cheryl Kraft was the last to arrive. For once she didn't appear elegant. Her silk dress was crumpled, her too-thin face distressed.

"God," she said to me, "you made it too. God, what a dreadful thing." If the others heard her husky, subdued voice, they gave no sign of it.

Selwyn waved us toward his office. "Please find a comfortable chair. And I have coffee—"

I slipped up beside Desmond. "I've been at the bookstore. Did you—"

He cut me off. "Yes. Craig's home now. I think he's okay."

That wasn't my first concern, but Desmond had no way of knowing that.

"—and sodas if anyone would like one."

Selwyn had no takers. This was one board meeting that would have no aura of a social gathering.

Desmond quickly brought the meeting to order.

The somber-faced trustees watched and listened as Desmond spoke.

". . . a double toll on our faculty and students and patrons. I know that we . . ."

Selwyn was trying hard to appear appropriately sorrowful, yet calmly in charge. But it was a struggle. He gave me a final sharp glance, then looked away. His mouth turned down. He looked more like a petulant schoolboy than a schoolmaster.

Desmond paused, his voice choking. ". . . all of you know that Patty Kay and I were such old and . . ."

Desmond's grief was reflected in Stuart Pierce's grim face. Patty

Kay's lover and former husband stared morosely down at his tightly clasped hands, his gaze bleak and despairing.

". . . difficult for our students to cope with the demise of a classmate. It is very important that we emphasize how all of us—students, faculty, parents, trustees—are available at any time to those in despair. We can't . . ."

Willis Guthrie smothered a yawn. It was probably as well for him that neither Stuart nor Desmond was looking his way.

". . . at the assembly tomorrow I will describe the counseling services that . . ."

Brooke watched Desmond with anguished eyes. Once again I recognized a mother's terror, the unspoken fear that one young suicide might trigger another and another and another. Everyone in this room knew the turmoil and uncertainty and depression that tumultuous hormone levels can create. All too well we knew that no teenager could be considered immune, no matter how outwardly happy or well-adjusted.

The passions and fears and heartbreaks of the young burn brighter and fiercer than those tempered by age and experience.

I hoped that experienced eyes were watching all the young people in Fair Haven for the next few weeks.

". . . necessary for all of us to present a reassuring face to the world."

Cheryl Kraft broke in sharply. "That's easy enough for you to say, Desmond! I can't believe what's happened to our lovely, lovely town. Two hideous murders in Fair Haven in less than a week—"

At the shocked looks from around the table, her eyes blazed. "The poor dear little clerk at Patty Kay's bookstore, found this afternoon in a *dumpster*! I feel that we must *demand* more capable police protection, and I intend—"

"Dumpster!" Stuart's handsome head jerked toward her.

The meeting halted as Cheryl described the afternoon.

Selwyn's face puckered in distaste.

Brooke pressed a slender hand hard against her mouth.

Even Willis Guthrie appeared shaken.

Finally, Desmond interrupted firmly. "Wait, please. We're all appalled at what's happened, but, please, let's focus on Walden School's situation. There's nothing we can do about the murder at the bookstore except support Captain Walsh in his investigation. And certainly we will do that. But we have extremely serious matters to discuss tonight. Before we get into our work, I want to welcome Mrs. Collins, who is visiting us tonight to represent Patty Kay and Craig."

"Thank you, Desmond." I looked at each trustee in turn. "I'll be brief. I know the board has much to discuss. But I understand a memorial to Patty Kay is under consideration. Both Craig and I believe the finest memorial Walden School could make would be to honor Patty Kay's last request. The problem, of course, is that although we know she considered the dinner meeting at her house to be very important, we don't know why. So, I'll ask each of you to help if you can."

Selwyn jumped in. "I can't be certain, of course, Mrs. Collins, but I do think it was the flying project. I'd told her I was absolutely opposed to it. We'd had a sharp exchange about it Friday morning, and it was Friday afternoon that my secretary took the message saying the dinner was scheduled." He flipped that boyish lock of hair back from his forehead. "I'll have to admit I wasn't happy with Patty Kay." His voice oozed the regret of hindsight. "I felt she should at least look into the aspects I'd brought up. Especially the legal liability. We all know how little waivers can mean. But once Patty Kay got an idea in her head, it was hard to get her attention." A rueful smile. "As everyone here well knows."

Stuart Pierce scowled. "She didn't say a word about flying to me. Her call came just as I was going into a meeting with out-of-town clients. She said, 'Stuart, I'm having the trustees for dinner Saturday night at seven. We've got a problem out at school.' Before she could continue, I said I had to get into a meeting, but I'd come."

The anguish in his eyes told me he was recalling that conversation as the last time he'd spoken to Patty Kay—as the last time he would ever speak to Patty Kay.

"A problem out at school," I repeated. I looked at Selwyn. "That doesn't sound like a disagreement over a course. And I find it quite interesting that there was not a single mention of a flying course in *any* of Patty Kay's papers. I know. I looked."

"Of course not." Selwyn was bland. "I told you. She'd come up with this plan only this week. And of course she saw it as a problem." Irritation sharpened his voice. "Anytime anyone disagreed with Patty Kay, it was a problem. The *problem* was that I opposed her."

"What Patty Kay wanted or didn't want doesn't matter." Willis Guthrie's tone was querulous. His pale blue eyes skewed me with dislike. "What matters is that you're causing trouble for all of us. You're running around town stirring things up, Mrs. Collins, telling the police lies."

"I'm glad to hear it." I gave him stare for stare. "I hope to cause a lot of trouble. I'm going to find out who killed Patty Kay and why. I thought those close to her would not only understand but approve my actions."

"I certainly applaud them." Cheryl Kraft's earrings made their ghostly chime. "And I must say I think it's very odd—odd indeed—that no one knows why Patty Kay called this meeting. She wouldn't tell me. I asked her and she said the matter would be made clear at our dinner. But I certainly stand behind your efforts to find out what happened, Mrs. Collins. We *owe* it to Patty Kay." She gave a determined nod, and the earrings tinkled.

"So you want to encourage this old woman to stir up trouble, send the police after us?" Guthrie's voice was savage.

Cheryl lifted a finely penciled eyebrow. "Mrs. Collins should do whatever is necessary." Her gaze was imperious.

"Well, my wife and I don't appreciate being treated like suspects." Guthrie slammed a hand on the table.

I knew that the police inquiry that prompted Guthrie's outburst was caused by Desmond's honesty and not my probing, but I was quite willing to take the responsibility. And I was delighted at the uneasiness I sensed. Good oh, as an Australian friend loved to shout when news conferences turned rowdy.

I pressed on. "The truth is, Willis, your wife and her sister were quarreling, and Patty Kay's death brings a lot of money to Pamela."

"That didn't mean a thing," he sputtered. "I told Captain Walsh you're nothing but a troublemaker. It's obvious what happened. Craig got mad and shot Patty Kay. Everyone knows it."

"No!" Stuart Pierce shoved back his chair. It crashed to the floor as he surged to his feet, his eyes blazing. "Everybody *doesn't* know it, Willis. The whole setup stinks. Patty Kay never ran from anybody. Especially not from Craig. And that stuff was thrown around the kitchen after she was dead. That lets out Craig."

"Unless it's a double bluff." Willis's face flushed an unkind hue. "Be just like him. Thinks he's so damn clever."

So that was where Captain Walsh had gotten his theory.

During this heated exchange Brooke had looked from Willis to Stuart to Willis as if at a tennis match. Now she shook her head decisively, a touch of color in her pale cheeks, her lovely black hair swirling around her face. "No, no, it can't be Craig. We'd have known if Patty Kay and Craig weren't happy. Women know these kinds of things about their friends," she explained earnestly.

Stuart leaned down, jerked the chair upright, then stalked to the mantel. He faced the wall, his back to the others.

There was no hint that Brooke knew about Stuart and Patty Kay's secret trysts. So much for feminine intuition.

Of course, Brooke was right on one count. Patty Kay and Craig hadn't been unhappy. But they hadn't been passionately in love either. Perhaps that made for a certain kind of happiness. But that wasn't my focus right now.

Willis Guthrie was angry and flustered. So I kept after him. "Mr. Guthrie, what did Patty Kay tell you about the Saturday evening dinner?"

"I didn't talk to her." He bit off the words, his sallow face twisted in a furious frown. "My secretary took the message. I didn't want to go —but Pamela thought I should. Patty Kay kept trying to give that land from the estate to the school. We've given Walden School a great deal —but there are limits." His pale eyes locked with Selwyn's.

The headmaster fingered his rep tie. "Mr. Guthrie, this school owes its very existence to the Prentiss family. Certainly we understand that you and Mrs. Guthrie have other interests too. But I wonder if it would help achieve peace in your hearts—at the loss of Mrs. Guthrie's sister—if you might be willing now to agree to reserving that land for Walden School. Why"—eagerness lifted his voice—"we could agree tonight—I know the board would be happy to do so—to name the wilderness preserve the Patty Kay Prentiss Matthews and Pamela Prentiss Guthrie Nature Preserve. Such a gift to our present students and to future generations of Walden students . . ."

I hoped Selwyn wasn't holding his breath on this one.

Guthrie didn't even bother to answer. Instead, he glared at me. "I don't have any idea what my sister-in-law had in mind. But I know for sure it had nothing to do with the land. That deal's been cooking for a year. Nothing new's happened."

"Actually, Mr. Guthrie, that's not accurate."

The derisive note in my voice caught their attention.

Stuart Pierce turned to listen.

Brooke Forrest's hands trembled, and she caught them together in a hard grasp.

Chuck Selwyn brushed back that lock of hair.

Desmond's dark eyes were puzzled.

Patty Kay's weedy brother-in-law tensed. "What do you mean?"

"The situation is profoundly different—because Patty Kay died. That land is now in the sole control of your wife."

Guthrie couldn't quite keep the gleam of satisfaction out of his eye. But he said nothing.

I persisted. "Isn't it?"

"Actually"—he used the word as a taunt—"I'd not even thought about it until you brought it up. My wife and I have been much too upset over Patty Kay's death to have given any thought at all to the disposition of her estate."

I wouldn't have wanted to be Willis Guthrie at that moment.

They all looked at him in disgust. Desmond, Stuart, Brooke, Cheryl, even Selwyn.

Guthrie smoothed his skimpy ginger mustache. Even he realized that his insincerity was sickening to those who had loved Patty Kay.

Stuart Pierce strode across the room. "How much is that land worth now, Willis? Two million? Three?" But Stuart's question had nothing to do with money. "How much did you and Pamela want that money?" His voice had a dangerous edge.

Guthrie swallowed nervously, leaning back in his chair. "That is an extremely unwarranted inference. Very unfair. We have every right—"

"Sure. You sure do. Especially now that Patty Kay's dead." Pierce wheeled around, moving away, and I knew he didn't trust himself that close to Guthrie.

Guthrie knew it too. He licked his thin lips, nervously smoothed his mustache.

"Willis, when did Pamela and Patty Kay last talk about that land?" I inquired.

Guthrie didn't answer.

I let it go. I figured I'd had my run at him. I said, "Brooke, what did Patty Kay say to you?"

"About the dinner?" Her aquamarine eyes clung to my face.

"Yes."

Brooke sighed and wearily massaged her temple. "I was late for tennis when she called Friday morning, so when she said she was going to have a special dinner meeting, I said sure, what time, and that was it." She spread her graceful hands helplessly. Her diamond wedding band—which had the look of an antique—sparkled. "I'm so sorry," she said unhappily. "I could tell she was bursting to talk." Her eyes closed briefly. "And I didn't take the time. . . ."

"So," I summed it up, "am I to understand that only Cheryl asked Patty Kay why she was having you trustees to dinner?"

Their silence was an answer.

It wasn't the answer I'd expected.

Patty Kay Matthews knew the ins and outs of organizations,

boards, groups, and committees. She certainly knew, as all skillful organizers know, that nothing happens in a committee unless the wheels are greased.

Patty Kay called a meeting about something that mattered enormously to her.

Why did she keep her reason a secret?

18

I stepped inside. The first floor of the Matthews house was swathed in darkness except for the feeble glow from a single golden-globed torchère all the way down the hall in the dungeonlike entryway. Too little light to illumine the saucy moosehead. Clearly this was a night light indicating the householder had retired.

Craig's car was in the drive. I assumed that meant he was there. I doubted that he customarily went to bed at nine-thirty. But I didn't doubt at all that he was eager to avoid talking with me.

In fact, I wondered how soon he would try again to send me on my way.

And what would he do when he found out I'd nudged the police toward Stevie in their investigations? I was sure the assistant D.A. had picked right up on the information I'd given her about the sweater.

Well, it didn't matter that he would want me gone. I had no intention of leaving.

Amy's death settled that.

He would continue to afford me his hospitality. He was in no position to disclaim me as his aunt. That was his story, and he was stuck with it.

At this point I doubted his veracity on almost all counts, but my commitment to find out who shot Patty Kay remained strong.

For Patty Kay herself.

And now Amy.

Especially Amy.

I flipped on lights as I went. The kitchen, though sparkling clean, thanks to me, was not a cheerful place to be. Memory held another, darker picture. The faint acrid smell of burned chocolate lingered. But I was hungry, and I had much to do this night. I fixed a peanut butter and jelly sandwich, thankful for pantry staples. I checked the date on the milk carton. It was still good. I poured a tall, frothy glassful.

All the while, I puzzled over my unsuccessful quest—so far—to discover the reason Patty Kay had abruptly summoned the Walden School trustees and its headmaster to dinner.

Was my basic assumption wrong? Could Patty Kay have merely been indulging her fancy for last-minute entertainments?

No. That didn't fit with the unconcealed anger that had consumed the last two days of her life. Still, the dinner might have had nothing to do with that distress. I had no proof that Patty Kay was upset about her Walden School files even though that connection once seemed clear.

But I'd found nothing out of order or provocative in those files.

Of course, *caveat emptor:* the linkage of Patty Kay's distress to her late-night jaunt to the campus was provided courtesy of Craig Matthews.

Craig lied a lot.

Maybe I needed to rethink the matter entirely. Could the dinner

be a smoke screen for some other agenda? Could it be a way of bringing one particular trustee to her home?

Why?

Patty Kay could see the headmaster anytime she was on the campus.

She'd played tennis with Brooke on Thursday, no doubt planned
to play with her the next week. She was certainly on close enough
terms to give Brooke a call at any time.

According to Stuart Pierce, he and Patty Kay were together on
Thursday afternoon.

I finished half the sandwich, gulped some milk.

Okay, what if Stuart lied? Oh, not about their tryst, but maybe
that Thursday parting was—as far as he was concerned—final. Would
Patty Kay, desperate to see him, have used the trustee meeting as a
pretext?

It would be, in my judgment, an ineffective way to attempt to talk
intimately with a reluctant lover.

So, not to see Stuart.

Cheryl Kraft? I needed to probe more deeply there. Was there a
hidden disagreement between Patty Kay and Cheryl? If so, I'd not
heard a whisper of it. And this was such a small town. In any event,
they lived next door to each other. It would be absurd to go to the
effort of a dinner party if Patty Kay's objective was to speak with
Cheryl.

I licked an escaping dollop of blackberry jelly from the sandwich
edge.

That left Patty Kay's brother-in-law Willis and Desmond.

She could pick up the phone anytime and call Willis Guthrie. As
for Desmond, she'd known him for years. She could easily arrange to
see him.

I was left once again with the assumption—surely the natural
assumption—that the dinner was exactly as billed, a gathering of the
school trustees. So there had to be a purpose, a purpose linked to
Walden School.

Yet the argument against that conclusion was strong. No one

knew better than Patty Kay that you don't broach important matters cold. Not if you want a group to vote your way.

I wiped a trickle of jelly from my chin, finished the milk, and shelved my obsession with the board of trustees. I have a reputation for stubbornness, but I also face reality. My pursuit of the dinner party may have been off track from the start.

Because there was another focal point in this murder case.

Books, Books, Books.

I jabbed the bell to Stevie's apartment. Fingers of light splayed around the edges of the drawn drapes.

The peephole opened.

"Stevie, I need to talk to you. About Amy."

The disembodied voice was high and slightly shrill. "It's late and—"

"Captain Walsh is looking for the owner of a beige Lands' End cardigan. Would you know anything about that? It's the sweater with Patty Kay's blood on it."

No answer.

"Did you know cloth can hold fingerprints?"

A chain rattled. The door opened.

In a gold-striped T-shirt and jeans, she looked younger. Younger and scared.

I stepped inside.

She closed the door behind her, leaned back on it as if for support. "What sweater are you talking about?"

"The one Craig found bunched up by his wife's body Saturday afternoon. Bunched up against her and drenched with her blood."

"Oh, my God!" It was a thin, anguished whisper. "Oh, no. No."

I felt sorry for her, but not sorry enough to ease up. Not as long as I remembered the dumpster and those upturned pink flats. And not sorry enough to tell her that it wouldn't be long before Walsh, prodded by the young assistant D.A., had some very brutal questions for her.

"Yes. Craig wrapped the gun in the sweater, threw the gun away, then got rid of the sweater. But the police found it. They have it now. They're looking for its owner."

"I wore it to work Friday . . . and somebody took it."

I waited.

"You've got to believe me. When I went back to the storeroom, it was gone. Not on my hook. I haven't seen it since. You've got to believe me!"

It came down to her word, of course.

But that was her problem.

"Captain Walsh will be interested to hear what you have to say. And I suppose he'll also be curious as to why Craig should have chosen to remove the sweater from the murder scene."

She licked her lips.

Psychologically, I had her where I needed her to be.

"You have keys to the store." It was not a question.

"Yes."

"Let's go."

We turned on all the lights. We had full access to the main floor of the bookstore. Yellow police tape marking a crime scene barred us from the storeroom. And, I was sure, from the portion of the alleyway directly behind Books, Books, Books.

I wasn't interested in the storeroom. Or the alleyway.

I wanted information.

First, I left a call on Desmond's home and office answering machines.

Stevie stood rigidly next to the desk, her eyes dark with fear.

I hung up. "Okay. Let's take a look at Amy's personnel file."

She led the way to the main office where Captain Walsh had interviewed us that afternoon. Stevie pulled open the top drawer of the second file cabinet.

The impersonal application form didn't tell me much.

Amy Alice Foss. Home address, social security number, birth date. I looked at the latter. Nineteen years old. She was a sophomore at Fair Haven Community College, majoring in English. Her previous job had been with a Waldenbooks in Nashville. The manager gave her an excellent recommendation.

Bookstores.

Such lovely, civilized, safe places to work.

Damn, damn, damn.

We went downstairs to the history and politics sections. "Amy was learning these books," Stevie explained. "Three times a day she checked and straightened the shelves. She was at the information desk from one to three. The rest of the time she unpacked books or worked the floor or was at the front checkout desk, depending upon the customer flow."

We walked to a semicircular counter in the middle of the store. "Today she was supposed to double-check next week's schedule for the daily workers. A lot of Patty Kay's friends work in the store one day a week. Monday through Friday. They weren't interested in weekends, of course."

Stevie pulled open a shallow drawer and lifted out a ring-binder notebook. She put it on the countertop and opened it.

I saw monthly side tabs.

She flipped to April and the second sheet in that month. It was titled *Daily Schedules, April 5–9*. The names of the clerks ran horizontally, the days of the week vertically. The resulting grid gave a quick confirmation of who was scheduled to work when.

I checked back a few weeks. The ladies hopscotched around.

Brooke Forrest customarily worked Mondays, but the prior week she switched with Edith Hollis on Thursday.

Pamela Guthrie was down for Fridays, but she'd worked every other day in the week but Friday for the past month.

The other single-day workers were Cheryl Kraft, who'd been at the store today, and Louise Pierce, who worked Tuesdays.

There was a red *X* by each name for this week.

I pointed.

Stevie tapped an X. "That means Amy checked last week and had definite commitments for this week."

"So today"— I flipped to the next sheet. *Daily Schedules, April 12–16.*

Crimson Xs neatly marked each name. Next week Brooke would be in both Monday and Thursday. Louise and Cheryl had switched. Pamela was on schedule for Friday.

Stevie touched the Thursday column. "Next week I'd better call Mrs. Hollis. She may not want to continue. But we have a waiting list. It's a prized job in town."

"I'm sure it is. But it still surprises me that Pamela Guthrie does it."

Stevie's eyes glinted. "That woman."

"If she doesn't enjoy it, why does she do it?"

"To keep an eye on the bookstore, I suppose. Or maybe she just doesn't want to be left out of something that *the* women in town do."

"Does it have such a social cachet?"

"Oh, yes. It's even harder than getting into Talking Leaves."

"Talking Leaves?"

"*The* book club in Fair Haven. Been in existence for more than a hundred years. You practically have to inherit an opening. Simply being rich isn't enough."

It's a small town, for chrissakes.

Stevie's voice wasn't hostile. She was merely reporting a fact.

She fidgeted. "Is this what you wanted to see, Mrs. Collins? Are we finished?"

I didn't answer at once. I was looking toward the front door. Amy could have seen anyone who came through the front door.

And been seen.

"No. Tell me about the store today—from the time Amy arrived."

She shivered. "We didn't open until late, of course. Because of the funeral. I told everyone to come in at one. Amy came in a few minutes early. I was in the employee lunchroom. She got a cappuccino and a big oatmeal cookie from the café and sat with me. I teased her, said she wasn't eating enough for a growing girl. A cookie for lunch isn't enough." Her eyes flashed. "None of us ate anything at Mrs. Guthrie's."

"How did Amy act?"

Stevie closed the notebook, slid it back into a drawer. There was a pause before she replied, as if she were considering her answer. "Just as usual. She never had a lot to say. But she was pleasant. Nice. There was nothing different this afternoon."

"When did you last see her?"

"Right before I left, about two-forty. I walked by the information desk. She didn't see me. She was on the phone. That's all I noticed."

"So Amy was alive at two-forty." I got out my notebook, flipped to a fresh page. "You didn't see her again?"

"No."

"You weren't here when we found Amy." I'd not thought about Stevie's absence until the policeman ushered her and Craig into the bookstore. Ever since, I'd thought about it quite a bit.

"No. God, I'm glad. It's so awful."

"Were you off work?"

"I wasn't feeling well. I had a headache. So I went home for a while. Then I felt a little better and I decided to go to the park." Very glib, very quick. She'd thought about this.

"Park?"

"Cravens Park. It's a mile or so from here. I sometimes take a picnic lunch to the park."

"Did the police find you there?"

"Yes."

"When?"

"About four."

"With Craig?"

"Oh, no. I mean, we didn't go there together. We just happened to run into each other."

She didn't lie nearly as well as Craig.

"Oh." I let it hang.

Her eyes flickered away from me.

"Did you see anyone else at the park?"

"I didn't pay any attention. We—I was walking in the rose garden, and I ended up in the little amphitheater. It's at the end of a path and rather secluded. No one else was there. Until Craig came."

"When was that?"

"I think it was around four."

So she wasn't alibiing Craig—or herself—for the time when Amy was killed.

"I was so surprised to see him," she said hastily.

And I entertain Venusians before sunrise every Tuesday.

I refrained from saying it. I needed her cooperation.

She wasn't thrilled at my plan.

But she agreed.

We each manned a telephone. That was one reason I'd wanted to come to the store. More than one phone line. We split up the list. I gave her the clerks. I took the customers. But I tried to listen to her questions and responses even as I talked.

At this point I didn't trust anybody.

It was like wearing a Walkman with a different talk show in each ear.

Stevie got more willing responses than I, of course. She was, after all, the boss. I was an unknown woman calling late in the evening to ask about a traumatic event. I had one hangup and one threat to report me to the cops. "Be my guest," I replied. "There's no law against asking questions—and I hoped you would want to find the person who strangled Amy Foss. She was nineteen." That got me cooperation.

Stevie and I each asked the same questions:

Did you talk to Amy?

When?

About what?

When did you last see Amy?

Who did you notice in the store from two-thirty to three o'clock?

We made the last call shortly before eleven.

By eleven-fifteen we worked it out:

Amy was last seen at two forty-five by Jackie. "She was walking toward the storeroom. I never saw her again."

At two-fifty, Paul realized the information desk wasn't manned and there were several customers waiting. "I thought maybe she'd gone to the bathroom. But she didn't come back. So I took over."

At three, Todd started hunting for Amy.

"Okay. It seems clear enough. She was killed between two-forty and three. So, let's see how many people we think were in the store then."

This was where it broke down. No one could say with any great certainty. We did get the names of three longtime customers. Stevie could call them tomorrow to see if they'd noticed anything helpful.

The rest of the list was indeterminate. An older man, a redheaded woman, a young guy in a navy hooded sweatshirt and pants, a couple of elderly women, two teenage girls. And, of course, the clerks, Todd, Jackie, Paul, Candy, and Cheryl Kraft.

On a fresh sheet, I listed these names:

Craig Matthews
Stevie Costello
Brigit Pierce
Stuart Pierce
Louise Pierce
Desmond Marino
Willis Guthrie
Pamela Guthrie
Brooke Forrest
David Forrest
Gina Abbott

One fact argued against the appearance of any of these: Cheryl Kraft knew each of them.

Of course, it was possible that one of them had managed to enter the store and escape notice.

Or what if it was someone who wouldn't excite notice at all, such as Craig or Stevie?

Or what if someone called and asked Amy to be in the storeroom or the alley at, say, two forty-five? That way the murderer might not have come into Books, Books, Books.

Surely Amy hadn't been that foolish.

"Stevie, what about the door to the alley. Was it kept locked?"

"No. Not during the workday. We would be in and out, tossing cartons, receiving deliveries."

That door would have been kept locked in a larger city. But this wasn't a city, this was a small town. No one worried about thieves or street people coming in from an alley in Fair Haven.

"So anyone could have come in, waited in the shadows near the delivery dock, knowing Amy would come into the back area at some point. Is that right?"

"I suppose it is."

I felt confident everyone connected with Patty Kay knew the bookstore well enough to be aware of that alley entrance.

So the murderer didn't have to be among those in the bookstore.

All right. Go at it another way. Amy knew something. That's why she called the Matthews house. That's why she left the message for me.

What did she know?

Was it connected with the phone call asking Craig to pick up the fruit basket?

Or was it simply that she knew—and would swear—that Craig left the bookstore at a quarter to four on Saturday?

Stevie leaned back in her chair and sighed.

I looked at her. The sweatshirt she'd pulled on when we left her apartment was oversize. Not the kind of thing she'd wear to work. No, she wore cotton cardigans to work. She claimed someone had taken hers from the bookstore on Friday.

What if—somehow—Amy knew better?

What if Amy saw Stevie with that cardigan Friday night or Saturday morning?

"Is Amy's apartment near yours?"

Stevie gave me a guarded, cautious look. "Nothing's far from anything in Fair Haven."

"Did you and Amy shop at the same grocery?"

"What are you getting at? Why are you asking me that kind of question? I didn't have any reason to—"

A brisk knock sounded at the front door.

We both turned to look.

I moved first. "Good. It's Desmond."

Stevie unlocked the door.

"Henrie O, I got your message. I talked to Susan Nichols."

We stood near the front checkout counter in a yellow pool of light. The lawyer looked desperately tired. His face was haggard. Dark circles shadowed eyes numb with misery.

"Good. We've narrowed things down at this end. Amy was killed sometime between two-forty and three. What did you find out?"

"Susan said Amy was hit on the head, probably stunned, then strangled. The police found a tire iron in the bottom of the dumpster. No prints on it, but traces of Amy's blood and hair."

The attack was taking shape in my mind. I could see a figure in those dark shadows by the closed delivery door, Amy walking by, the brutal blow that struck with no warning.

"Why hit her, then strangle her?" Stevie asked.

I knew. "Strangling is quieter. The initial blow would make noise. Repeated blows would make more noise."

Stevie turned away.

A tire iron. It could possibly be traced to a particular make and model of car. But it could be linked to a particular car only if fibers clung to it. Surely this crafty and careful killer cleaned the murder weapon thoroughly before bringing it to the bookstore. "What was used to strangle her?"

"A navy scarf with a red diamond pattern."

"Oh, my God." Stevie's hands clutched at her throat. "Someone took my scarf. Someone took it!"

19

The MG headlights swept over the blue Lexus and green Porsche. I parked beside the Porsche, turned off my lights.

It was dark indeed, midnight-dark.

Craig hadn't left on any outside lights to welcome me home. When I stepped inside, I saw that even the torchère down the hall was off. I used my small purse flashlight to illuminate my way to the stairs.

In the upstairs hallway I hesitated. I wanted to bang on his door, demand to know where he'd been when Amy was murdered.

But why would Craig strangle Amy with the scarf belonging to the woman he loved?

A double bluff? But he didn't have that kind of gambling instinct. I would have sworn to that.

God, how it went round and round in my mind.

Yes, it's Craig.

No, it can't be.

I turned away.

In my room I slipped into my T-shirt and shorts, raised the window wide, and turned off the light. I was exhausted. I fell almost immediately into a restless, uneasy sleep. A mind on overload doesn't make for sweet slumber.

Images tangled: grayish ankles, Patty Kay atop an elephant, the bruised shadows beneath anguished aquamarine eyes, a single-engine plane twisting and turning against a stormy sky, a monstrous ginger mustache, the glisten of earth at a gravesite, the sonorous piety of an evangelist's radio spiel, the dizzying smell from a gas pump . . .

Gasoline.

My eyes snapped open.

I breathed the harsh, unmistakable stench of gasoline.

I rolled out of bed, hurried to the window.

No moon. No light.

And wafting through the window on the silky night breeze, the acrid scent of gasoline.

Below, I heard the scuff of hurrying footsteps—and the sound of liquid sloshing, splashing.

Whirling, I grabbed up the flashlight from the nightstand. I ran out of the room and down the hallway.

I flung open Craig's door.

"Craig, Craig!"

My flashlight danced across the empty bed. The silken spread was thrown back, a pillow bunched against the headboard.

My late husband, Richard, always cautioned me not to jump to conclusions.

I jumped to this one fast and pounded down the main staircase.

I was mad.

That sorry, no-good, murdering bastard!

I did have wit enough to click on the main hallway light, grab the phone, punch in 911, and yell, "Fire! 1903 King's Row Road," before I slammed out the back door, flashlight in hand.

"Craig! Craig!"

The stench of gasoline was overpowering here.

My thin pencil of light swept the back of the house.

I caught a glimpse of a dark, running figure.

A heavy piece of metal clanged on the drive.

And my brain caught up with my emotions.

The green Porsche wasn't in the drive.

Someone had Patty Kay's gun.

I flicked off the light, jumped to the ground and ran behind the Lexus.

Over the thud of my heart in my chest, I listened as hard as I've ever listened in my life.

A dog yapped hysterically.

But I didn't hear the sound of a car starting.

Then the night was alive with sirens.

I had on the outside lights around the pool and playhouse when the fire engine roared into the drive behind the house. Firemen jumped to the ground, dragging heavy hoses.

The others arrived hard on the heels of the fire truck: Captain Walsh, two patrol cars, and sketchily dressed neighbors hurrying up the drive or across the backyard.

The Jessops first, then the Forrests. The Krafts, in matching black silk pajamas, arrived next, followed by the Guthries. Stuart Pierce wore warm-up pants. He jogged up the drive, Brigit close behind him, a heavy cardigan pulled over her pink pajama top. A breathless Gina Abbott trotted up the drive with her daughter, Chloe. Last to arrive, their eyes dull and exhausted, were the Hollises.

I shouted above the spate of questions, pointing to the gasoline tin lying in the drive near the end of the house.

The fire chief herded all of us to the deck by the pool; two firemen began to hose down the house, washing away the gasoline from the thick ivy.

Gina Abbott's uncombed black hair stuck out on her head in sprigs and tangles. Chloe Abbott kept pulling down her shortie night-gown and glancing shyly toward Dan Forrest. The Hollises stood side by side, silent and somber. The Jessops ranged uneasily up and down the deck, chattering nervously.

Brooke Forrest clung to her son's arm. She stared at the house, her beautiful face a mask of fatigue. Dan's cheeks were pink with excitement and his eyes darted from the police cars to the fire truck to the house, but the teenager stood there decorously with his mother. David Forrest's navy-blue robe fit him like a uniform. A scowl creased his face.

"Things like this don't happen in Fair Haven," Carl Jessop insisted.

Bob Kraft looked at the tree limbs sighing in the night breeze. "If this house burned, the fire could easily have spread to us." Cheryl shivered and stepped closer to her husband.

A fireman turned his hose from the roof—the wooden roof—back to the ivied wall.

The ivy quivered beneath the force from the hose. If the ivy had caught on fire, the flames would have danced up to the wooden shingles.

Some of the spray misted over the Guthries. Willis skipped nimbly backward. "Watch it, watch it!" But Pamela didn't move. She simply stared at the drenched stone of her dead sister's house.

Captain Walsh, unshaven, his shirttail bunched in his trousers, once again stood beside me with his arms folded, his face impassive.

I shook my head. "No," I said quietly. "I did not."

That's when Brigit broke away from her father. She ran up to me, grabbed my arm. "Where's Craig? Where is he?"

"I've no idea."

Brigit whirled toward the police chief. "Something's happened to Craig. Why aren't you looking—"

And the green Porsche slewed around the fire engine, jolted to a stop. Craig jumped out. He ran toward us.

"My God, what's happened? What the hell's going on?"

"Somebody tried to set the house on fire." I wished I could see him more clearly, but the revolving light on the nearest police car washed over his face like a laser show, distorting his delicate features.

"I can't believe it!" Nobody ever sounded more shocked.

Or more scared.

Craig swallowed, stared at the house with frightened eyes. "I sleep like the dead. If it had caught fire—"

The fire chief unsnapped the clasps of his heavy asbestos coat. He shook his head grimly. "If the roof caught, the house would have gone up like wildfire."

Patty Kay's cupboard offered an assortment of coffee beans. I chose Colombian, in my mind always the best. The last drops were seeping into the carafe when Craig poked his head into the kitchen.

"Are you making coffee?" He looked toward the kitchen clock.

It was a quarter to three. In the morning.

We were alone. Finally. The police gone. The firemen gone. The neighbors gone.

"Yes. I've got some thinking to do."

He rubbed his eyes and looked absurdly young and vulnerable.

I gazed at him coolly. I hadn't heard a car leave when the arsonist fled. But Craig could have parked on the next street.

"Yeah. God. I can't believe everything that's happened. And the way Walsh talked, it sounded like he thought one of us tried to burn the house down."

"It's occurred to him."

"Why in the hell would we do that?" The outrage in Craig's voice sounded genuine.

I added two scoops of sugar and stirred. I needed energy. "Oh, Captain Walsh can see where I—your doting aunt, of course—would do it to divert suspicion from you." The coffee tasted magnificent.

Craig slumped into a chair. "Maybe we ought to tell him you aren't my aunt."

"Maybe."

"Is that why he thinks I'd try to set the house on fire?"

"Perhaps. Of course, if you did it, that isn't the reason." I held his gaze. There wasn't a flicker of understanding in his weary eyes. "No, Craig. If you did it, it would be because I know that Amy—very stubbornly—insisted you left the bookstore at a quarter to four on Saturday." My hand tightened on the mug of steaming coffee.

I could throw it in his face and be out of the kitchen and down the drive in an instant.

But Craig sat unmoving, his face petulant and angry.

"She was wrong. That's all. Wrong."

"Where did you go Saturday afternoon, Craig? What were you doing during that extra fifteen minutes?"

He shook his head. His mouth closed in a tight line.

"Same place you went tonight? To Stevie's?"

"I didn't go anywhere." He realized that was no answer. "I mean, I couldn't sleep. Hell, I just went for a drive. That's all. A drive."

He jerked to his feet and shoved through the door into the hall.

In a moment the stairs creaked.

Once again Craig ran away.

He appeared upset by the attempted arson, frightened, shocked at the suggestion he was behind it.

When I'd awakened and smelled gasoline, I'd immediately believed it to be Craig's effort to silence me.

But I could simply be a bystander. Perhaps the house was to be set ablaze to kill Craig. Certainly the person who splashed the gasoline couldn't have known Craig wasn't in his room. Though surely a mind bent on murder would notice the absence of Craig's Porsche.

A mind bent on murder . . . I'd talked with all of them now, the men and women who knew Patty Kay Matthews well enough to entice her into her playhouse to her death.

Craig Matthews. Definitely under the thumb of his strong-willed wife. Had he tired of Patty Kay's domination? He was involved with Stevie Costello. Whether he would admit it or not. Did he want both Patty Kay's money and Stevie as his wife? Was the flung-about cheesecake a daring effort on his part to appear the victim of a frame?

But was there time for him to arrive home, shoot Patty Kay, trash the kitchen, and be gone before the police arrived at 5:09?

Oh, yes. Especially if he left the bookstore at a quarter to four— and had a little help from his girlfriend.

Stevie wasn't at the store Saturday afternoon. She could have made the calls to Craig and to Amy. Perhaps that was the cause of Amy's murder. Certainly Stevie would have tried to disguise her voice. But something—some intonation, some phrase—may have betrayed her.

Stevie's sweater could also be part of the elaborate double bluff. Who'd be dumb enough to commit murder and leave her sweater behind? That would be the defense claim.

But that wasn't the only possibility. Craig could be innocent as a lamb, the hangups fortuitous, the deli call actually from Patty Kay. A neighbor could have found Patty Kay's body and made an anonymous call that brought the police.

Because the murderer could be Stevie. It would surely be much nicer to be married to Craig than to be his mistress. And there was all that money Craig would have—if Patty Kay died.

The cheesecake? A little harder to imagine a rationale here. It was surely intended to incriminate Craig. But Stevie might have been a little too clever. She could have thrown the cake, confident all the while that Craig was at the bookstore, well alibied. Yes, of course. Should she ever come under suspicion, the accusation would be weakened because Stevie of all people would not want Craig arrested.

Complicated. Maybe too complicated.

The sweater?

If Stevie and Patty Kay struggled, the sweater might have fallen or been pulled off. It would be hard for Stevie to pick up her sweater if it was steeped in Patty Kay's blood.

Committing a murder could rattle even the coolest head.

In a way, I was playing a macabre game of paper dolls, slipping in place each time a different face for the dolly with the gun.

Brigit Pierce?

So young and so old at the same time. Almost a child, definitely a woman. And crazy about Craig.

Could that girlish infatuation for her stepfather have turned to an ugly hatred if she thought Craig agreed with her mother that she should be sent away to school? Had Brigit tried to set the house ablaze to kill Craig? Brigit hungered for her stepfather's touch. Her mother had laughed. Worse, Patty Kay had threatened to send Brigit away. Youthful passions burn hot and bright with no thought for tomorrow.

I'd come to like Patty Kay. I admired her courage, her humor, her competitiveness, her brashness, her refusal to knuckle under to what she believed to be wrong.

But she was far from perfect. She was a woman who had been unable to imagine how others felt. She was so certain of her course, it didn't occur to her that what seemed so clear, so obvious, so right to her might be impossible for another to accept.

Even Desmond Marino, who'd loved Patty Kay, knew that she had a fatal lack of perception. Yes, Desmond had loved his old friend. Unrequited love can turn bitter and dangerous. In a twisted way, I could see him eager to destroy the man who had the woman he wanted. Had it galled the clever, ebullient lawyer that Patty Kay was content with a man Desmond considered ineffectual? For a highly successful lawyer, Desmond had mounted a lackluster defense for his client until I arrived to prod him.

Gina Abbott. Quick, intense, passionate. She claimed she'd quarreled with Patty Kay over the latter's liaison with Stuart. Why should Gina care? Was the true quarrel over rezoning land? Gina saw the rezoning as a ticket to college for her children. How desperate was she to remove Patty Kay's opposition?

Brooke Forrest. It was so terribly important to Brooke to do the right thing. Appearances were the reality to her. She didn't seem to be able to focus on her friend's murder as much as the necessity for the trustees to choose the proper memorial for the dead woman. An upside-down world view?

David Forrest. He didn't like Patty Kay. Her disregard of social standards—his social standards—deeply offended him. But surely the world was full of people who offended David Forrest?

And they were quite alive and well.

Stuart Pierce. His emotion over the loss of his former wife seemed genuine. But he might have grown restive since succumbing once again to her charm. Had she threatened to tell Louise about their relationship, to ruin his second marriage?

Louise. A smug, satisfied woman, happy with her life. I didn't think she'd stop at anything to protect it.

Willis and Pamela Guthrie. Both worshiped at mammon's shrine. They loved things, not people. Would either of them have been willing to destroy Patty Kay's house and its beautiful contents?

Chuck Selwyn. Gina called the headmaster Mr. Eternal Youth. It was hard to separate him from his uplifting twaddle. How much of it did he believe? He thought Walden School was an Eden. He'd do anything to protect it.

But how could burning down Patty Kay's house protect his precious Walden School?

Why try to set this house on fire?

I drank deeply of the coffee. That was the important question.

Why did someone want this house to burn?

To scare me? To kill me? To kill Craig? But what a hit-and-miss, uncertain method of murder.

There was nothing hit-and-miss about the gunshots that ended Patty Kay's life.

So why a fire?

To destroy the house.

That was the obvious, quick, immediate answer.

Take the obvious answer first.

The house, the house—how could it be a threat . . .

I sat very still.

Because the searcher hadn't found what he or she sought in Patty Kay's office Monday afternoon.

Yes. Oh, yes.

That search had been so violent, so desperate, so furious.

Yes.

Something in Patty Kay's office . . .

The Walden School files.

My shoulders sagged. I'd been through those files, through them and through them.

Craig linked Patty Kay's unhappiness to the files she'd brought home late Thursday night.

If Craig was telling the truth about that.

But if Patty Kay arranged that last-minute dinner because of a matter she wanted to bring before the trustees, why hadn't she lined up the necessary support?

All right. Toss the dinner. It didn't matter.

Yet, she died only a few hours before the trustees would come to her home.

I looked at the clock.

Almost half-past four.

The darkest watch of the night.

Images flickered in my mind.

Patty Kay. Brave, obtuse, generous, stubbornly unforgiving. Patty Kay fiercely playing tennis, Patty Kay laughing as she teased Brooke, Patty Kay atop an elephant, Patty Kay facing down the sanctimonious minister, Patty Kay lightly dismissing her daughter's first passion, Patty Kay driving out to school for her files . . .

Everything was fine until Thursday night, when she went out to Walden School.

Walden School, an enclave of privileged youth. I thought of the magnificent grounds, the fine buildings, and manicured playing fields. Even a beautiful lake. But now the lake had served as the background for such a needless young death. These students were pampered and protected and offered the finest education. But not even world-class cosseting could protect one young girl from ugliness and despair.

The serpent in Eden.

That was the kind of injustice that would inflame Patty Kay.

I imagined her driving there Thursday night, going to her office . . .

Thursday night.

Night. When no one is about. Or, if about, sometimes those who slip quietly through darkness are up to no good.

Abruptly I saw the trees and not the forest.

Quickly, quickly I ran through the idea in my mind, the shocking, explosive, quite possible idea.

Oh, yes, yes, it could be.

God, it could be.

Patty Kay would indeed be upset, outraged, determined to take action.

I pushed up from my chair, began to pace.

Think, Henrie O, think.

Patty Kay would have to be sure.

Perhaps somewhere in the house was proof of my theory.

But there might be an easier way.

If Patty Kay had acted as I thought she would, done what Patty Kay Prentiss Pierce Matthews would have had to do to be certain, there might yet be proof!

20

I t was an odd time to be in a school.

The antique clock mounted midway down the hall read fifteen minutes past five. Not even the earliest scholar was here yet.

Two aspects of this hallway differed from any school hallway I'd ever visited.

This hallway was clean.

The lockers had no locks.

The fingerprint technician brushed black powder in gentle, even, curved strokes on the surface of locker number forty-five. And on the handle. So far, Lieutenant Berry had been the most pleasant person on this somber outing. She'd made no complaint about the hour.

Fragments of prints overlapped on the gray metal in a bewildering array. But I knew enough to be patient.

Captain Walsh took turns glaring at me, then at the locker.

Desmond leaned against the peach wall. His face was deeply lined with weariness. He, too, stared fixedly at the locker.

Chuck Selwyn, outrage clear in every taut line of his body, stood with his legs apart, his hands jammed in the pockets of his khaki slacks. Unshaven, in a gray sweatshirt, he didn't look quite as boyish.

Berry took her time, used a magnifying glass. I wondered if she realized how tensely we waited, how lightly we breathed.

Her answer—when it came—was matter-of-fact. "Bingo." She gave me a swift glance. "I've found seven prints made by Patty Kay Matthews." Berry pointed at several spots, at the top of the locker, midway between the top and the handle, and on the inside top rear of the handle ". . . a fragment of the second finger, right hand . . ." The technician used the wooden tip of the brush to pull the handle up and ease the locker open.

I looked at the locker's contents. A school pep sweater hung from a hook. Books and papers were piled haphazardly. There was nothing especially notable about this particular locker except that its owner had touched the sweater and the papers less than a week past, but would never touch them again.

Berry began to brush the powder on the interior of the locker door.

But I was on the homestretch. It didn't matter whether there were prints inside the locker, though now I knew there would be. What mattered was that even a single fragment of one of Patty Kay's fingerprints had been found on the handle of this locker.

Walsh rubbed a bristly cheek.

Selwyn stared at the locker like he was watching a cobra undulate from its basket. The serpent in Eden, I thought again.

I concentrated on Walsh. I still had a selling job. "There is no reason for Patty Kay Matthews's fingerprints to be on this locker."

The police chief shrugged. "Mrs. Matthews was a teacher here."

But the headmaster's brow creased in a tight, puzzled frown. "Not in this building." Like me, he knew it was odd, inexplicable.

I was willing to be generous to the opposition. "Let's imagine for a moment that Patty Kay was in this building—perhaps to talk to another teacher—and let's even imagine her walking down this hallway and reaching out and happening to touch this particular locker. That still can't explain the print *inside* the handle. There's only one reason Patty Kay would have gripped the handle: to open the locker."

"From a partial print on the inside of the handle, from that you jump to murder?" Walsh demanded.

"Yes." I knew I sounded grim. I felt grim. Grim and angry, so angry. The snake in Eden had been so deadly, had brought so much harm and pain and needless suffering. "Here's what must have happened. She drove into the campus Thursday night." I looked at Desmond. "Are the gates locked at night?"

He shook his head. "We've never had a problem with security. We close the main gates unless there's a program or reception. But there's no lock." No, there had never been a problem with security in Fair Haven.

"So Patty Kay arrives. It's quite late. Nobody's here. She probably parked close to the languages building. I'm guessing it's right next door?"

Desmond nodded.

I didn't know the campus. But I knew what had happened, what must have happened. I met Walsh's unwavering gaze. "Patty Kay came out of her building in time to see someone entering this building. Or she arrived just as someone came into this building. Something about that figure attracted her attention. Being Patty Kay, what did she do?"

Desmond knew. He'd already figured it out. "She was never afraid of anything. She'd go look."

I watched a jigsaw of prints materialize on the inside panel. "She saw someone, and she knew it wasn't right. Being Patty Kay, she came to investigate. We'll never know exactly what happened, but we can be sure of one fact. She saw a student at this locker, a student who shouldn't have been at this locker. Maybe the student tried to brazen it out, claimed to be here to get a book, something of that sort."

"It's all assumption. What student? Why a student?" Selwyn's voice was shrill. He was protecting his students. He would always protect his students, no matter what the cost. "If we're going to pretend, let's pretend it was an adult she knew."

I ignored him. "Or it might have happened quite differently. Maybe the student ran away when Patty Kay came in. But whatever happened, Patty Kay saw enough to link the person to this locker. We know that because she came to this locker, opened it, and found what the student had left."

"You can't be sure of any of this." Walsh didn't like me very much. I was making his life too complicated.

"Yes, Captain, I can. This locker belonged to Franci Hollis."

"Hollis." Captain Walsh hunched his shoulders. His dark eyes were bleak. "The kid who committed suicide last week."

"Yes." Hounded to death. So young and so terribly vulnerable. "You know why. The anonymous letters. Dreadful anonymous letters. No one's told us how they reached her. Surely her parents would have noticed if she'd started receiving mail at home that upset her. It makes a lot more sense to assume she got those letters at school. How could she receive them anonymously? Very easily—if someone slipped them into her locker."

"Sure." Walsh looked at the headmaster.

We all did.

Selwyn's face was rigid. "This is all supposition. Every bit of it." He stared at us defiantly.

"No." The police chief spoke quietly. "Franci Hollis is dead. We found the letters in her bedroom. All right, Mrs. Collins. What's the connection?"

I put it on the table. "What do you think"—I looked at each of them in turn—"that Patty Kay Matthews would do if she knew who was writing obscene notes to Franci Hollis?"

"Oh, Christ." Desmond pushed away from the wall, his face sick.

"I think I know." I was sure I knew. Because in these last days I'd come to understand Patty Kay Matthews, her strengths and her weaknesses. And her courage. "She set up a meeting of the board of trustees. She told the letter writer that he or she must confess and take public responsibility before that meeting—or Patty Kay would reveal the writer's identity."

Selwyn's look of incredulous dismay was world-class. "You can't mean—surely you aren't intimating—you can't possibly think a *student* shot Mrs. Matthews to prevent her speaking out!"

"Right on all counts, Mr. Selwyn."

"You're accusing a child of *murder!*" The headmaster swung toward the police chief. "This is absurd, patently absurd!"

Walsh ignored him. "That dinner party at her house. That's where she was going to spring it if the kid didn't own up. Is that how you see it?"

"Exactly."

"Captain Walsh, I strenuously object to this absurd deduction." Selwyn practically danced with impatience. Edging on panic. "It's ridiculous. Why, it's *libelous!* Walden School is already suffering great trauma from Franci's death. It has cost us her brother Walt, one of our finest students. Walt is magna cum laude. He's been accepted at Yale. And now he has withdrawn from this school. I'm hoping to persuade him to change his mind. But if any kind of public revelation is made about this tragic situation, it may drive even more students away—"

My temper finally snapped. "You prefer to hide a murderer from prosecution?" I demanded.

The headmaster's face flushed. "I'm appalled, simply appalled at the unconscionable coupling of this school with Mrs. Matthews's murder. There are many who might have profited"—he slid me a quick look—"from Patty Kay's death. To make this jump, this absurd connection merely because she went out to the school on Thursday night—"

I pointed at Franci Hollis's powder-smeared locker.

"—is totally unreasonable and may do grievous damage to Walden School."

Walsh nodded politely. "I understand your concerns, Mr. Selwyn. However, it will be necessary to interview your students."

"A student assembly is scheduled at ten this morning." I like to be helpful.

Selwyn was horrified. "Under no circumstances will I agree to police invading the campus."

Even Desmond was concerned. "Captain, parents will be upset if police address the students about murder. This has got to be handled carefully."

Walsh rocked back on his heels. "Would you gentlemen prefer for these kids to be interviewed at the police station?"

It was the optimum moment.

"Gentlemen," I said, "I believe I have a solution that will satisfy everyone concerned."

It was just past seven A.M. I punched the bell at Gina Abbott's house. Not a proper hour to call. But I still had things to discover before the assembly at ten.

The door opened. The decorator was shrugging into a seersucker robe. Her expressive face looked both worried and weary.

"Gina, I need to talk to your daughter. About those letters Franci received. Patty Kay knew who wrote them."

"Oh, no. If Patty Kay knew, she'd have done something about it."

"She did."

Gina's face was abruptly very still. Her dark eyes widened. Sudden comprehension gave way to horror. "Oh, no. Do you think . . . Oh, God. You'd better come in."

The living room was a nice mixture of periods, a comfortable, embracing room lightened with lemon and accented with plum.

"Chloe!" Gina stepped into the main hall. "Chloe!"

Chloe Abbott was midway into the living room when she realized her mother wasn't alone. She stopped, her cool gray eyes surveying me. "I'm not dressed. I'll . . . ."

Gina shook her head. "It doesn't matter, honey. You know Mrs. Collins, Craig's aunt. She wants to talk to you about those letters Franci got."

Chloe remained in the doorway, her face blank, her eyes wary.

Gina looked at her daughter sharply. "What's wrong?"

The teenager's plump face was sullen, withdrawn. "Nothing. I just hate talking about it. Can't you understand that?"

Her mother wasn't fooled. She reached out her hand. "Chloe, what do you know?"

"Nothing. Nothing!" But she wouldn't look toward her mother.

"Actually, Chloe," I said quietly, "I'm interested in anything you can tell me. What you think, what you guess."

Reluctantly, Chloe came in the room. She perched on the arm of an easy chair. "I hate thinking about it. I *hate* it."

"We all hate it!" Gina yanked a package from her robe pocket, frantically pulled out a cigarette, and lit it. Her hands were shaking. "But we've *got* to think about it. Please, Chloe. Tell Mrs. Collins what you can."

"I don't know much. And now everybody's blaming me because I didn't tell anybody. But I didn't know what Franci was going to do . . ."

Again I tried for reassurance. "Nobody's blaming you."

"*Mother* is." The accusation was hot and swift.

"Chloe, no. It's just—if you'd just told me!" She drew deeply on the cigarette.

"If I had, what would you have done? Call Mrs. Hollis. And that's why I think Franci did it. She didn't want her mother to know."

"Let's not worry about that right now, Chloe." I almost asked Gina to leave us alone, but one glance at the woman's strained face told me I'd get nowhere. "When did Franci tell you about the notes?"

Chloe pushed her hair away from her face with both hands. "She didn't exactly *tell* me. It was last week. Wednesday afternoon. After field hockey. I was walking back to the girls' gym and I saw Franci underneath one of the evergreens. Kind of hiding there. I thought it was odd, so I ducked under the branches. She was lying on the ground, in a ball, sort of. I thought for sure she was sick. I asked her what she was doing. She said she was waiting until everybody left before she started home. I asked why. She said she didn't want to see anybody. She started to cry. She said she didn't have friends anymore and she never wanted to see anybody ever again. I told her that was dumb. I was her friend and she had lots of friends and whatever made her think she didn't have friends? And she held up this envelope. I took it and—" She stopped, didn't look at us.

Her mother understood instantly. "It's all right. You didn't write those words. But you have to tell us. We know it isn't you, Chloe."

Haltingly, Chloe repeated what she remembered.

Nasty, yes.

Worse than that, spiteful and cruel.

And cruelest of all—

". . . ended up saying if Franci ever told anybody about the notes, Walt would get one telling him all about Franci and he'd be so disgusted he'd say she wasn't his sister."

"Oh, Jesus." Gina's hands clenched into fists.

"And then she got real upset and made me swear I'd never, never, never tell anybody. And I *had* to promise, she was so upset."

"Describe the notes to me, Chloe. Handwritten? Typed? Computer?"

"Square pink envelopes. The message was from cut-out letters pasted on white paper. Dumb stuff. I told Franci it was just junk and she should ignore it. Either that or tell a counselor, like Mrs. Watkins. But she wouldn't listen to me."

"How did she get the letters?"

Her body stiffened. "She didn't say."

Gina looked sharply at her daughter.

"Who do you think wrote those notes?" I asked.

"I don't know. I don't have any idea." But her eyes wouldn't meet mine.

"Chloe, who disliked Franci?"

I didn't miss the slight easing of tension in the girl's shoulders. "Everybody liked Franci. She was always happy. Bubbly and cheerful and a little bit silly. Lots of times she didn't have a clue what was going on, but nobody cared. And she was so honest. She'd come up to some guy in her class and tell him she thought he was wonderful and it was nice—like somebody liking their dog or moonbeams or roses, and the guy would grin and pat her on the shoulder and say thanks. It wasn't like she had a crush on him or anything. I mean, she wasn't trying to push him, get him to pay attention to her. She just thought he was great and wanted to tell him. She made people feel good because she was always saying something nice—without trying to get something for it." She looked at me doubtfully.

"I understand. So you don't believe someone wrote the notes because of personal dislike."

"*Nobody* disliked Franci." She said it firmly.

"Somebody didn't like her."

Chloe stared down at the shiny pink polish on her toes. "Sometimes Franci could be irritating. Like when she'd sing the same song over and over. Or giggle too much. She made Brigit nervous."

"So she irritated Brigit?"

"Yeah. But look, we've been in school together since we were little kids. Everybody was used to Franci. She was part of things."

"When did Franci stop being happy?"

Chloe slid off the chair arm, took one step back. Her eyes flicked toward her mother, then, abruptly, her young face squeezed into misery. She yanked her hands up to her eyes. "I don't want to talk about it. I don't want to!" Sobs racked her voice. She whirled and ran from the room.

The blood drained from Gina's face as she stared after her daughter. "Mrs. Collins, if you don't mind . . ."

I was already moving toward the front door. I'd learned all that I could here.

I had one last glimpse of Gina's frightened eyes before the door closed.

I understood her fear.

I wished I could have followed Gina up the stairs. Because her daughter's voice may have shaken with sobs.

But when Chloe whirled to run from the living room, her eyes were dry.

When I see a slovenly woman, makeup askew or no makeup at all, unkempt hair, raddled stockings, I know I'm seeing a creature numbed by pain.

Even the outside of the Hollis home looked disconsolate, the accumulation of several days' newspapers, a brown plastic garbage pail lying on its side, a trail of litter across the lawn dragged there by a scavenging dog.

I pressed the bell, knowing it was still too early to call, especially at this house of mourning, but knowing, too, that I had no choice.

I rang again.

And again.

Finally, the door swung open.

Walt Hollis wore a faded T-shirt and jeans. In the photos pinned up at Gina's shop, he'd appeared round-faced and cheerful with an easy, good-humored smile. This drawn, white, too-old face didn't look as though it'd ever worn a smile.

"Yes." He stared at me dully, without interest.

He'd been at Patty Kay's funeral and at Pamela Guthrie's after the funeral. I couldn't tell whether he recognized me. I didn't think it mattered. This young man's world was down to bedrock. So that's where I'd start.

"Walt, I'm going to find out who wrote those notes to your sister."

The slack muscles in his face tightened.

I've seen that same look before in the African veldt, on a battleground, during a boxing match, the intense, unwavering stare of a predator.

Silently, he held the door open and admitted me.

This was a house where grief had suspended living. No light. No movement. Dust.

He led the way into the living room, switching on lights. He gestured toward an easy chair.

I took it.

He stood stiffly by the mantel.

"Is your mother—"

"She doesn't get up." The boy's voice was flat. "Maybe this afternoon. But she probably wouldn't see you."

I didn't ask, but he answered anyway.

"My dad's gone, left on a business trip a little while ago. I don't blame him. If I could go somewhere, I would too. Not that it would make any difference. Maybe it would. Maybe if I could just start walking and not stop, maybe that would help."

I could have told him it wouldn't, but he'd find out soon enough. Some wounds close over, but they never heal. No matter what happened—whether we ever found the poison pen writer, the person who shot Patty Kay—Walt Hollis's world would never be the same.

His eyes bore unrelentingly into mine. "Those letters—you think we can find out who did that to Franci?"

"Yes." I told him about Patty Kay's fingerprints on Franci's locker.

"So that's why Franci was so upset Friday morning. I saw her when I was on my way to French. She was crying. See, things haven't been right for a long time. But I couldn't get her to tell me." Anguished eyes stared at me. "Franci always told me everything. But this year everything was wrong. She wouldn't talk to me. It started the week after I won the election. In September." He glanced at me. "Class president. And I kind of wondered—she'd never, ever been jealous of me. Never. But I thought maybe that was it. Because nothing was right from that time on. But I never thought that it could be something like those letters. Do you know we found a whole box of them under her bed?" His mouth quivered.

I leaned forward. "Walt, where are they?"

"Mother burned them."

Damn. I understood why. If only we'd known in time. But if that line of investigation was closed, this one wasn't.

"Did you talk to your sister Friday morning?"

He turned away from me, rested his head on the mantel for a moment. His shoulders shook.

I waited.

Finally, his face splotchy, his eyes glistening, the boy faced me. "No. The last couple of weeks, it seemed to be worse. I asked and asked her what was wrong and she wouldn't say. I'd told Mom we had to do something, maybe get a counselor, but Mom was real stubborn about some things. She thought it meant admitting Franci wasn't . . . wasn't right and everybody's always acted like she was just fine. And actually she was fine. She was always sweet and gentle and great to have around." He shot me a sharp look. "So she couldn't do math or anything, there's no law you have to! At school she was in the special classes. And that was okay. She was proud of what she did." His fists clenched. "Maybe that's what was worst in the letters, talking about how stupid she was and how everybody pretended to like her paintings but everybody really laughed about them, silly blobs of color. And she was always so proud of her pictures. But she stopped painting before Christmas. She wouldn't paint anymore. She wouldn't tell me why. Then Friday morning, it made me mad because she saw me and she ran the other way. And I had a meeting—student council—so I just went on to it. I can't stand thinking about it, that I just walked the other way. For a stupid meeting—at a school where someone would treat Franci that way. I'm not *ever* going back there." He said it harshly, and I knew he meant it.

"So you don't know what Franci did next?"

"Not exactly. We figured it out. She cut classes for the rest of the day. She must have ridden her bike home—we found her books in her room—and she got her diary and rode her bike back out to the lake. On the last page of her diary, she wrote that she had to drown herself because then she wouldn't have to tell anybody about the letters." He stood stiff and straight, young and bitter. "If I ever find out who—"

"We'll find out, Walt. And when we find out, we'll make sure the world knows. Now, the thing is, you do know the letter writer."

His head jerked up. His eyes blazed. "What do you mean? If I knew—"

I held up my hand. "Think about it, Walt. You *do* know the writer —because it is someone at Walden School. Now, I want you to think. Who—out of all the students—who would do something monstrous like this?"

Walt gripped the mantel and thought. I waited patiently. Finally, he gave me two names.

One name I didn't know:

Larry Brown, a high-strung classmate of Franci's. "He's a wreck. His mother's been married three times. I think one of his stepdads— well, something kind of bad happened. And Larry got upset last summer because Franci won an art contest."

One name I did know:

Brigit Pierce. Walt stumbled over the name. "But it's true, Brigit's kind of mean. And she always picked on Franci."

I posed the last question, the cruelest question. "Okay, Walt. Who might have it in for you?"

21

The Walden School parking lot overflowed. Lots of sporty Hondas, smug Volvos, sleek Mercedes, svelte Jaguars, jaunty Range Rovers, nouveau Cadillacs. MGs have many nice qualities. One is size. I squeezed next to a fir tree in a slot too small for most cars.

I slammed the door and hurried toward the auditorium. Students, many accompanied by parents, were streaming past me. Near the auditorium I saw the slender young policewoman who'd taken down names at the bookstore. Good. Captain Walsh was taking me seriously at last.

I was halfway across the jammed parking lot when Dan Forrest loped to my side. "Mrs. Collins, Mr. Selwyn sent me to find you. He would appreciate it if you could come to his office. The trustees are gathering there before the assembly."

Dan thoughtfully shortened his stride to walk with me.

I wondered what mischief Selwyn intended. But I would find out soon enough. Right now I intended to capitalize on this unexpected opportunity. Selwyn would be appalled at my quizzing a student. He should have thought of that before he sent one to fetch me.

I prefaced it with a friendly smile. "I suspect there isn't much that goes on around here that you don't know about."

"Oh, well, I'm pretty active. And I know a lot of people."

We passed a group of girls. One of them called, "Hi, Dan. See you at lunch?"

He gave her a warm smile, and replied, "Sure, Lynne," yet managed to be attentive to me.

I looked up into sapphire-blue, courteous eyes. "You're vice president of the senior class?"

"Yes, ma'am. Actually, it looks like I'm going to be president. Walt Hollis has quit school. His sister died and I guess he doesn't want to come back because it reminds him of her."

His voice was casual. There was no sense that he had any understanding of Walt's despair.

"Tell me a little about Walt. Are you friends?"

"Oh, sure. I've known him forever. His mom and mine play tennis together. Walt's okay. Wants to be a doctor. So everybody treats him like he's special."

"Because Walt wants to be a doctor?"

"I guess."

"Does he make good grades?"

"A four point. But so do I. I mean, what's such a big deal if a guy beats you out by only a couple of points on tests?"

"No big deal," I agreed. "Unless you think it is."

Dan's stride didn't check. But his quick sideways glance was startled. "Well, we're both honor society."

"So you're taking Walt's place as president of the student council."

"The vice president automatically becomes president in the event the office is vacated." Dan's handsome young face creased in a frown. "Of course, we're all hoping Walt will change his mind." He looked down at me earnestly. "Nobody can believe the stuff people are saying. About a bunch of letters. But nobody's seen any, so it kind of makes you wonder . . ."

We turned up the sidewalk toward the lovely old house where Selwyn officed. "Makes you wonder what?"

Dan shrugged. "Well, whether these letters ever happened. Maybe it makes Franci's family feel better to blame somebody."

"The letters happened."

We reached the top of the steps.

Dan opened the door for me. "Nobody's seen them."

"Someone has."

I looked hard, but I didn't see any reaction at all. He gazed at me with nothing more than polite interest. "Oh. Who's that?"

"Another student." I thanked him and walked into the headmaster's office.

Selwyn stood by the door. As I came inside, he closed it. When I saw his satisfied smirk, I knew I had a fight on my hands.

Despite the abundance of elegant Chippendale chairs, everybody was standing, staring at me. I'm sure there are lepers who've received warmer welcomes.

Selwyn launched his attack. "Mrs. Collins, we've had a change in our program for the assembly."

Brooke Forrest, her lovely face haggard, nodded emphatically.

Willis Guthrie folded his arms across his chest, trying, I suppose, for an I'm-captain-of-this-ship stance. He merely looked bovine.

Stuart Pierce rubbed his temple. If he thought he had a headache now, wait a minute.

Cheryl Kraft's face was flushed. "I am absolutely opposed to the board's decision, Mrs. Collins."

Desmond lifted his hands in a gesture of resignation. "Maybe you can make them see."

"A change?" I asked.

Selwyn's reply was smooth. "I've explained to the board members the irresponsible allegations you've been making. As an experienced educator with a thorough grounding in psychology, I know—I *know*—we have no student in our school with the requisite emotional temperament to have planned and carried out the heinous crime that took the life of Mrs. Matthews."

"Really?"

He ignored my sarcasm. "Indeed, I've explained how hurtful it could be to our program and to the future of Walden School if you are permitted to invite students to carry tales of others' behavior to you. Why, it would suggest to our students that we favor a big-brother kind of mentality. Moreover, it clearly would suggest a link between the school and Mrs. Matthews's murder, and that would surely frighten parents."

Stuart Pierce's eyes were somber and thoughtful. "Patty Kay loved this school. I don't want us to do anything that would hurt it."

Brooke shivered. "The whole idea's dreadful. Children don't shoot people."

An almost unbelievable statement to make in this last decade of the century, a time when shootouts in school corridors and classrooms are commonplace, where violence real or imagined is an everyday companion to young lives. But this, after all, was Fair Haven, if not Eden, surely a very safe place.

"Children do kill," I replied mildly. "But the real point here is that we've got to follow up every possibility. Certainly a Walden student may not be guilty. In fact, there are several other persons who had reason to murder Patty Kay. But a student may have killed her. This board has an obligation to find out the truth."

"Not on the campus." Selwyn shoved back that lock of hair. "It would be catastrophic to our image. Parents don't pay seven thousand dollars a year to have their children subjected to grillings by strangers."

"I'm not a stranger. I won't be presented as a stranger. I'm representing the Matthews family. I assure you I'll couch my questions carefully, taking into account the sensibilities of your students." I didn't bother to point out that this Rambo-inculcated generation had been drenched in television and film blood since they were toddlers. "I give you my word on that. I feel confident the board will enthusiastically approve my appearance here today."

"Oh, no, Mrs. Collins, you're wrong about that." Selwyn yanked the door open. "We've already voted. The board members support my position. Except for Mrs. Kraft and Mr. Marino."

"Very well. I'm sure the board members will enjoy having Captain Walsh contact students directly." I spoke pleasantly. "It will be such an interesting experience for your students, unaccustomed as they are to contact with police conducting murder investigations. A real civics lesson. And I'm absolutely positive this board—and the parents of your students—will enjoy the newspaper headlines tomorrow."

I turned toward the door.

"Headlines? What headlines?" Selwyn sounded like a bleating sheep.

I paused in the doorway, smiled at them all. "Why, the headlines —on radio, TV, print—that will naturally flow out of the news conference that I will call for"—I glanced at my watch—"eleven A.M. All about the little girl driven to suicide by obscene letters at her school and the refusal of those in charge to find out who caused her death. An eleven o'clock conference will give plenty of time to hit the deadlines for the major media."

Students were filing in the main doors. The occasional parent looked serious and concerned. The only sounds were the quiet shuffle of feet and the faint rumble, like a faraway avalanche, of muted voices.

I led the way up the short flight of steps to the stage.

Two lines of chairs awaited us. In the back row sat the three students I'd seen on my first visit to the campus. Dan Forrest nodded gravely at his mother, politely at the rest of the trustees.

I took the seat nearest the podium. Selwyn, his face flushed and grim, sat next to me, then Brooke, Stuart, Willis, and Cheryl.

Desmond stood beside the podium. He glanced at his watch.

A bell rang.

Ten o'clock.

The students moved restively in their seats. Grave-faced parents looked at the stage. The low buzz of conversation quieted.

I looked out at the sea of fresh young faces and wondered if one hid a violent, cunning, dangerous nature. I scanned the rows.

Chloe Abbott, her face sullen and pinched, slouched beside her mother. Gina's sharp-featured face was set in a stony mask.

A few rows farther back, Brigit Pierce whispered animatedly to the pensive girl sitting next to her.

Desmond didn't need a microphone. No lawyer ever does. "Good morning. I'm Desmond Marino, president of the Walden School board of trustees . . ."

I listened with only half an ear. I was busy thinking about my own presentation.

But I wasn't first on today's agenda.

". . . a chance today to present a special memorial to one of your classmates, Franci Hollis. To make the presentation I would like to call on Dan Forrest, president of the student council."

Brooke's troubled face softened as she watched her handsome son stride toward the podium.

Dan started off with a quaver but kept going, and his voice steadied. ". . . at three o'clock this afternoon everybody's invited to attend the dedication of the Franci Hollis Memorial Rose Garden which will be planted between the girls' gym and the lake. We had hoped that Franci's brother Walt would be here today." He cleared his throat. "Walt has decided to withdraw from school—"

Exclamations of surprise and dismay sounded among the students.

"—and I know all of us will urge him to come back." He glanced down at the notecard tightly gripped in his hand. "Walden School will miss Franci, and all of us deeply regret her loss. Perhaps if everyone would write Walt a note—just to let him know how we feel—maybe then he will come back. I know we want him to be our class president. I see my taking the job as temporary." He looked earnestly out at the audience. "I hope it's just temporary. I promise I will make every effort to do the best job that I can. Thank you."

There was a ragged burst of applause, led by Chloe. No one knew quite what was proper here.

Dan returned to his seat.

Desmond stood with his hands clasped behind his back. "As many of you are aware, Walden School also suffered the loss this past weekend of Patty Kay Matthews, a teacher and a longtime member of the Walden board of trustees. A representative of the Matthews family, Mrs. Collins, will now speak to you."

I have no traffic with New Age concepts. Channeling, to me, is a rather sad attempt at self-importance. I see crystals as the modern equivalent of the rabbit's foot, and good karma, bad karma as an exotic means of escaping responsibility.

But maybe strong emotions do reach across time and space. Because—just for an instant—as my audience quieted, I experienced a wave of fear—sharp, immediate, profoundly disturbing.

Someone in this auditorium was desperately, wildly, dangerously frightened.

I felt it, then it was gone.

It shook me.

Because fear can be dangerous. Fear led to the murder of Patty Kay and of little Amy at the bookstore.

I was tempted to speak out frankly, to warn that there was terrible danger present—here and now—on this lovely campus.

But I'd promised.

And if I spoke that openly, it might simply increase the pressure on the murderer, increase the danger.

I've spoken in a good many difficult and trying circumstances. I can assume whatever tone I must. There was no echo of distress in my voice. "I appreciate the opportunity to talk to you this morning. My request is simple. The family hopes to learn—perhaps through Mrs. Matthews's conversations last Friday—information that might be helpful to the authorities. I am asking all persons in this room who saw Mrs. Matthews on Friday to write down when they saw her and with whom she was speaking. Of course, if you happened personally to speak with her, that's even better. Now, please take a sheet of paper, respond to these questions, put your name on it, sign it, then pass it to the right. Remember, it's important for us to know every single person Mrs. Matthews saw that day."

I worked fast in the lobby outside the auditorium. The young policewoman, Sergeant Roman, stood a few feet away, watching. I wanted to be in position to set up interviews by the time the assembly ended. Even though the doors were closed, I heard Selwyn's smooth tenor as he urged students to talk with counselors and teachers about the untimely events of the last week. I suppose that man could make the Second Coming sound pedestrian. The smooth-tongued headmaster certainly had no trouble with a suicide and murder. And yet I hoped his message was being heard. It is so desperately important to listen when children speak. Despair and depression strike the young as well as the old.

It didn't take me long to separate the sheets. Many I discarded at once. Others went into a pile signifying a brief, unrewarding glimpse of Patty Kay.

The gold lode contained sightings of Patty Kay in conversation.

And one report was a chart buster—written by a very smart student. I read it twice, put that student's name at the top of the list, then swiftly added the others I wanted to see.

I felt a flicker of irritation. Surely Walden School had an extra office at its disposal. Obviously Selwyn intended to cooperate as minimally as possible. All right, I could conduct interviews in the now-shadowy and cavernous—with most of the lights dimmed—auditorium.

Actually, the auditorium had the advantage of the adjacent lobby, which provided a place for the students I had selected to wait.

My first interviewee strode purposefully down the aisle. Short, stocky, and athletic, Barbara Phillips got right to the point. "I didn't see Mrs. Matthews at all on Friday, but I gathered you want to know about everyone who talked to her. Of course, I don't know that it will do you any good, because Franci's not here to tell you about it. But I know that Franci talked to Mrs. Matthews sometime Friday morning."

It was as satisfying as watching the third lemon click into place in a slot machine.

Finally, I had proof that Patty Kay and Franci had connected on that fateful Friday.

"Yes, that's terribly important, Barbara. I want to know all about it, whatever you can tell me."

Barbara's squarish, good-humored face was troubled. "I feel terrible about Franci. I mean, I guess I should have done something. But I had a physics quiz at ten and I was in a hurry. It was just a fluke I even saw her. I went by the girls' gym after my nine o'clock class Friday. Normally, it's empty then. The first phys ed class is at eleven. Anyway, I dashed into the locker room to get some stuff I'd left the night before. And I heard somebody sobbing in the rest room. It sounded awful. So I called out. And the stall door opened and Franci stumbled out. She looked awful. I thought she was sick. I asked what was wrong."

Barbara's face puckered in a puzzled frown. "Then she didn't make any sense. Franci said something like Mrs. Matthews said there wouldn't be any more letters but she'd had one this morning and it told her she'd better say she'd written the letters or Walt would die. I couldn't get it straight what letters she was talking about and how she could say she'd written letters she'd received. And I didn't have time! And she kept crying about Walt, so I told her that was the silliest thing I'd ever heard, Walt wasn't going to die, and she should do whatever Mrs. Matthews wanted. But Franci moaned and said she didn't know what to do. The warning bell rang and I had to go." Her eyes pleaded for understanding, for forgiveness. "Mr. Jeffers won't let you in class if you're late. I told Franci to go see Mrs. Watkins, the counselor, and I ran out of the gym. Later, during lunch, I hunted for Franci. But I couldn't find her anywhere." Tears filled her eyes. "I'm so sorry."

After Barbara left, I sat for a moment, thinking it through. And realized that Barbara's shamefaced contribution was critically important:

Patty Kay not only talked to Franci, Patty Kay had confronted the student who wrote the poisonous letters.

Panicked, the letter writer had threatened Franci.

All of this happened between Patty Kay's arrival on the campus Friday morning and nine fifty-five, when Franci sought refuge in the rest room of the girls' gym.

I whipped through my sheets.

I discarded the contacts that appeared fleeting.

But there were three persons who'd been observed talking to Patty Kay before ten o'clock Friday that I wanted to see.

Her daughter Brigit.

Dan Forrest.

Chuck Selwyn.

I stared at the headmaster's name. My chest felt tight. Oh, my God, of course.

I almost jumped to my feet and charged to Selwyn's office to confront the sorry, obtuse, tunnel-visioned idiot! Obsessed with protecting the reputation of his precious school, he'd hidden the fact that Patty Kay had talked to him about the letters.

Of course she had.

It would be the very first thing she would do. He was the headmaster. Selwyn was the first person she would tell.

He'd lied to all of us, claimed she wanted to start a flying program.

And he'd kept on lying.

I wondered if Selwyn had any idea how lucky he was that the letter writer didn't know about his chat with Patty Kay. I intended to make that clear when I spoke to him. As well as the possible results of his hiding that knowledge.

Such as poor little Amy's murder.

But I wanted to have all the ammunition I could before I faced Selwyn. I carefully rechecked the student reports. Yes. Only two other persons were observed talking to Patty Kay before ten A.M. that day. So the chances were very good that I'd narrowed the search for the letter writer down to a choice of two:

Dan Forrest.

Or Brigit Pierce.

Brigit followed me down the shadowy aisle. When we reached the front row, I took the second seat. My purse sat on the floor by my feet. I reached down, opened the flap, and flipped on my tape recorder.

Brigit plopped down next to me, dropped her books carelessly on the floor. "I don't see what difference it makes who my mom talked to on Friday. She didn't know somebody was going to shoot her Saturday." She spoke of her mother's murder without emotion.

"I understand your mother was angry?"

She thought about it, gave me a sideways glance. "Hmm. Yeah. I guess. She was in a rotten mood Friday morning. I know she was hacked at Mr. Selwyn."

"Was this when she gave him an icy look?"

"Yes. He was coming out of her office as I went in. He was going fast, like he couldn't wait to be outta there."

"Why did you go by your mother's office?"

She thought about it just a shade too long. "I had a note in my locker."

"Why did she want to see you?"

She looked at me blandly. Entirely too blandly. "Franci. Mom asked me how Franci'd been acting lately. I couldn't see why she'd care, but I told her Franci was weird, glopping around like the world was coming to an end. But Franci was always kinda weird." Brigit chattered on, disdain in her voice. ". . . 'course, I didn't know about those notes then. I mean, you talk about weird! I've heard those notes are real sicko."

"Do you have any idea who might have written them?"

She shrugged. "No." She frowned. "Somebody who's not very nice."

"Is that all you and your mother discussed?"

She was gathering up her books. "Hmm? Yes."

"She didn't talk to you about going away to school?"

Her eyes skidded toward me, then away. "No." Her voice was harsh. "Not a word."

If you've ever watched a duel with swords, you'd have a sense of my joust with Dan Forrest.

I edged my purse and the silently whirring recorder a little closer to his chair. Surely I could get something—even if it was just the tone of his answer—to buttress my suspicion.

Like his mother, Dan was undeniably attractive. Crisp, short black hair. Finely chiseled features. Smooth skin. Deep-set dark blue eyes. Clean-cut enough for a Norman Rockwell cover. He didn't appear to have a care in the world. A smiling face.

Ted Bundy smiled a lot.

It would take rock-solid proof to ever convince a jury of Dan's guilt.

"You talked to Mrs. Matthews Friday morning."

He was smart enough not to deny it. "Yes, ma'am. About a paper I'm doing." He was relaxed, casual, smiling, his sapphire eyes courteously attentive.

"What kind of person wrote those letters to Franci?"

"How should I know?"

"I'm asking you to give me an idea. Do you suppose it was a nerdy little creep?"

The smile looked iced on his face.

I gave him a swift, thorough scan. His hands were loose in his lap. There was no room for a gun beneath his blazer. He did have on a backpack. There would be plenty of room in it for Patty Kay's missing gun. Before he could get to it, my Mace would be out and in use.

But I was very glad that the young policewoman wasn't more than a shout away.

However, if I could somehow entice Dan to attack me . . .

He still smiled, but it wasn't reflected in his hot, angry eyes. And was he really so handsome? Wasn't there a hint of cruelty in his mouth? A feline secretiveness in his polite gaze?

"A second-rater, somebody who isn't good enough to succeed. A coward, of course."

One eye flickered. A nervous tic.

I jabbed again, hoping to draw more blood.

"Maybe somebody like you. *Vice* president. Not president. Not on your own steam. You're jealous of Walt, aren't you? Walt always beats you. In grades. In sports. In elections. They don't like you as much as they do Walt."

Glittering blue eyes never left my face.

"You decided to tyrannize Franci because you knew it would upset Walt. She didn't really cooperate, did she? It would have been better if she'd told him. But you really got to Walt finally—because poor Franci killed herself and that drove Walt out of Walden School. You couldn't have hoped for a better result, could you? Now you're class president. Well, I can promise you, Dan, you won't be class president for long."

He pushed up from his chair, stood, glared down at me.

Oddly enough, I wasn't frightened.

How did Patty Kay feel when she looked into her murderer's eyes?

"Where were you at five o'clock Saturday afternoon, Dan?"

"Home. I was home."

"How about yesterday afternoon, Dan? Around three o'clock."

"I'm on the cross-country team."

"Out running by yourself?"

"Yes. Yes, I was."

"You wrote those damn notes."

"You can't prove a thing. Mr. Selwyn said—"

He broke off.

I reached down for my purse and stood, facing him. "Yes, Dan. What did Mr. Selwyn say?"

Panic swept that handsome face. Dan turned and ran up the aisle.

I looked after him. Then I clicked off my recorder.

22

T he bright sunshine stung my eyes. But I wasn't particularly aware of my surroundings. There was too much turmoil in my mind.

I was certain Dan Forrest came to the Walden campus late Thursday night to put yet another nasty pink note in Franci's locker.

Patty Kay had seen Dan.

All the tragedy of this week flowed from that moment.

Dan wrote the tormenting messages. He was bitterly jealous of Walt and desperately wanted to hurt him. Dan saw Walt as vulnerable through his sensitive, gentle sister.

I stepped onto thick grass to angle my way across a broad sweep of lawn to the path leading to the old house and Selwyn's office.

Yes, Dan wrote the notes. My description of the letter writer infuriated him.

But Dan made no move to attack me.

Of course, he must have realized a policewoman waited in the foyer of the auditorium.

Yet he was angry and upset, surely as threatened by my knowledge as by Patty Kay's.

Perhaps Dan felt all he had to do was deny any knowledge of those letters. I had no concrete proof. Not like Patty Kay, who had actually possessed—

I stopped short.

The trashing of Patty Kay's office. The attempted arson.

Of course. Dan did both.

And how it must have amused him to tell me about the open back door and the sounds he'd heard upstairs Monday. His lies would cover his presence behind the Matthews house if he had been observed that afternoon.

It was Dan who rifled through the files and, when he didn't find the note, he'd angrily damaged the office. It was Dan who splashed gasoline against the house and escaped into the darkness.

But I was still surprised that he'd run away now, making no attempt to silence me.

He must feel as long as I had no visible proof, it was his word against mine.

After all, Dan was a Forrest.

I smiled grimly and began to walk swiftly across the lawn.

Dan didn't know I had recorded our conversation, including that terribly revealing "Mr. Selwyn said . . ."

Chuck Selwyn. I couldn't wait to face him down. The sorry jerk. Dan's artless comment meant Selwyn knew that Dan wrote the notes that drove Franci to suicide. The headmaster had done nothing about it. Just as I had surmised before I talked to Brigit and Dan. But the critical difference was that Dan Forrest *knew* that Patty Kay had told Selwyn about him.

Why kill Patty Kay and leave Selwyn to tell the tale?

How could Dan have counted on the headmaster keeping quiet?

Would a murderer take that chance?

But the desperate gamble had succeeded, hadn't it? Publicly, the headmaster had given no hint he knew the identity of the writer of those cruel notes. But he'd talked to Dan.

I didn't understand.

Was I wrong on all counts? Did Patty Kay's discovery about the notes have no connection with her murder?

I stopped in the shadow of a huge fir.

The lovely campus brimmed with life and movement. It was almost noon. I shaded my eyes. The cafeteria, a low-slung one-story building, sat to the west of the auditorium.

Think, Henrie O.

Patty Kay told Selwyn about those letters.

What then?

I felt confident the headmaster's immediate instinct was to object to any public revelation.

The Patty Kay who stood up to a fundamentalist attack against her efforts to provide a public forum for AIDS education certainly wouldn't yield to Selwyn.

Patty Kay called the meeting of the Walden trustees. She told the headmaster she intended to bring the matter before the board.

Just how determined was Selwyn to prevent her from passing along what she knew to the board?

Or was it deeper than that? Did Patty Kay give Selwyn an ultimatum: Agree to public punishment of the letter writer or I'll demand your resignation?

Selwyn had angrily insisted Patty Kay's murderer wasn't a student.

Perhaps he had the best reason in the world to be sure of that.

Okay, Chuck baby, time for a showdown.

But first I'd find the policewoman and get in touch with Captain Walsh.

I stepped out on the path.

Birds chattered cheerfully in the blooming redbuds. Soft running steps sounded behind me.

"Mrs. Collins."

She looked almost like a young boy in the hooded navy sweat-shirt and sweatpants and mirrored sunglasses. But I instantly recognized that soft, silken voice.

"Hello, Brooke." Brooke Forrest was the last person I wanted to see. She'd been so distressed at the ugliness of the notes. She would be devastated when she knew what her son had done.

"Chuck Selwyn wants to see you."

"I'm on my way there just now."

"He's not in his office. He wants us to meet him on the other side of the lake. At the pavilion." The shiny mirrored sunglasses glittered in the sunlight. She stood a foot or so from me. A nylon jacket was draped over her right arm. "I'll show you the way."

Sometimes I'm a little slow on the uptake.

But nobody's ever painted me as stupid.

I kept it casual. "Why over there?"

"He didn't say exactly. Something about Franci." The words flowed from her quite-perfect lips, touched so lightly with a subtle pink, lips with tight lines etched at each corner. "Something they found. He and that Captain Walsh."

Clever.

The only giveaway was the rigidity of her face, the skin tight over her cheekbones, those harsh indentations by her mouth.

And the jacket-draped hand.

I rested my fingers on the flap of my purse.

I lifted my left arm, glanced at my watch. "I need to make a phone call, Brooke. Why don't you wait here for me? It will take me only a moment."

"They want you to come directly."

I shrugged and started toward the administration building. "Oh, they can wait."

"Stop, Mrs. Collins." She briefly pulled back the jacket to provide a quick glimpse of the gun in her hand. "I'll shoot you now if I have to."

My right hand still rested atop my purse.

But I couldn't get the purse open and reach the Mace on my key ring before I would be dead.

Unless I was very careful and quick indeed.

I faced her. I spoke quietly but firmly. "It won't do you any good to shoot me in front of witnesses—and that's what you'll have to do. Because I won't go with you, Brooke."

"Yes, you will." Brooke's soft, silky, lovely voice contrasted eerily with the hard, intractable words that spewed from her mouth. "Do you see the policewoman coming toward us? I'll shoot her and then I'll move so quick and put the gun right up against you and shoot and scream and then I'll tell everyone *you* had the gun and you shot the policewoman because you thought she was coming for you, that they'd found out that you killed Patty Kay, that you planned it with Craig."

She said it all so fast, the words blurred in my mind, but I understood.

Brooke was desperate.

She would do whatever she had to do.

I might possibly be able to save my own life.

But the young policewoman would die.

It was a wild and dangerous gamble on Brooke's part. But it was the only chance she had.

It could work.

"You were listening—when I talked to Brigit and Dan."

"Yes." A brittle smile. "I was on the stage behind the curtain. All right, let's start walking toward the lake. That's right—stay a little in front of me and to my left."

She prodded me forward.

"You shouldn't have talked like that to Dan." Her voice shook with anger. "It was a prank. That's all it was. He didn't realize how serious it was."

"To write obscene letters? To brutalize a gentle, helpless spirit?" I heard the tremor in my voice. "He didn't realize?"

The young policewoman came closer, nodded hello, passed us by.

Brooke set a fast pace. We were even with the lovely old mansion. Only a few yards more and we would reach the path by the lake. The path soon plunged into trees.

If I ducked away . . .

A little boy—a sandy-haired little boy about twelve—ran past us, calling to a friend. I stumbled to a stop.

There was something about the high, happy sound of his voice that brought back a bright, quick, poignant memory:

"Mom, Mom, look at the *key*!" His eyes dancing with delight, Bobby held up the massive iron key that was six inches long at least.

I could smell the dank, dark corridor in the centuries-old monastery that had been converted to a hotel, see the massive oak door, and hear the happiness in Bobby's voice.

The barrel of the gun gouged my back. "Do as I say. I'll shoot. And not just you."

I began to walk. The little boy broke into a run.

"Hurry. Hurry!"

The sandy-haired little boy was well past us now. Safe. And alive.

We turned onto the path. Our shoes scuffed little bursts of dust.

Brooke was watching my every move.

I gripped my purse. How could I open it? When?

"Hurry!" We walked faster and faster.

Soon there was no sound or sight of the school. The chinkapin oaks towered above us. It was cool and shadowy and quiet.

Now I couldn't be held hostage by the lives of children.

But would I have any chance to open my purse when we reached the place where Brooke intended for me to die?

I had no illusions. My death was to be the finale.

Now there was no subterfuge. The gun was in the open, pointed directly at me.

I know what kind of damage a .38 does at the range of two feet.

If I tried to open my purse, Brooke would shoot.

No. Not yet.

Fronds of willow trees wavered in a soft breeze. Greenish water glistened ahead of us.

We came to a fork in the path. "This way." Brooke's once-lovely face was as hard and unfeeling as porcelain.

"Brooke . . . you can't do this. You can't get away with this."

"Yes. Yes, I will. You see, you're the last person who knows."

I almost contradicted her. Chuck Selwyn knew. Surely she realized that. She'd overheard my talk with Dan.

But if Brooke didn't know, I wasn't going to tell her.

The path led uphill. A white pavilion crowned the gentle rise. Benches overlooked the shimmering lake water.

We climbed the steps.

Funny to think I could be so aware of the muscles in my legs. The sense of mobility, the awareness of existence.

"It's your own fault," she said bitterly. "If you hadn't come to town, they'd have been sure it was Craig. And my Dan would have been safe."

We reached the white iron benches.

"You've got a notebook in your purse. You carry it around."

"Yes."

"All right. Get it out."

So I had a few minutes left, the time it would take to write the words signing away my life.

But I could open my purse.

We sat down.

I lifted the purse flap, got out the notebook and—behind it, pressed against the back—my keys with the Mace canister. And I flicked on the tape recorder as I set the purse down, still open.

I placed the notebook on my lap and looked at her merciless face. "So Dan would have been safe—at the price of Patty Kay's life and Amy's life and Craig's."

"I had to. I had to." It was a deep, tortured cry. "Don't you understand? Patty Kay was going to ruin Dan's life. *Ruin* it. All because of a prank. He didn't mean for Franci to be so stupid. It was just a prank."

"A prank? Do you know what was in those notes?"

Her mouth quivered. "Boys talk that way. It means nothing. Patty Kay wouldn't listen to reason. She wanted Dan to resign from all his offices and teams and apologize in an assembly. It would have been so awful. And Stanford—he's been accepted. They'd want to know why he quit all his activities. He wouldn't be accepted anywhere."

"He might have learned something about being human."

Brooke wasn't listening. The gun never wavered as her voice rose. "David—I don't know what David would do. He would be so angry. It's terrible when he's angry. His voice drops and drops and drops. So deep and cold and hateful. He would disown Dan. I know he would. And what could Dan do? Where could he go?"

I understood now what drove her to the horrors she'd committed. David Forrest held high standards. Perhaps impossibly high standards. He expected so much of his wife and his son. It might have been pressure from his father that corroded Dan's soul. It was certainly that pressure which led Brooke to murder.

"Patty Kay was your friend."

She drew a ragged breath.

"She wouldn't *listen.* You don't know how Patty Kay was. She didn't care what kind of scandal it caused. She was going to make Dan pay. But it was too late. I tried to make her see. She called me that morning, asked me to come over to her house after lunch. That's when she told me she'd seen Dan—and found the note. I said I knew it was a mistake, some kind of dreadful mistake. She insisted that it wasn't. She told me she'd seen Dan go into the building. She looked inside and saw him open a locker and put something in it and that the look on his face was spiteful and mean. She called out and he looked up and saw her and ran away. And she got the note. She showed it to me. I kept telling her that it was a joke. Not a nice one, but sometimes these things happen. They're kids—they don't mean it. I tried to make her understand. Why destroy a boy's life? But she wouldn't *listen.* Then, the next morning, when we learned about Franci, it was like talking to a stone wall. Dan didn't mean for Franci to do what she did. And no matter what Patty Kay did to Dan, it would never bring Franci back."

"When did you decide to kill her?"

"I couldn't sleep. Not all night. I lay there and listened to David breathing. I knew he would turn Dan out. Just like that. His only son. You don't know how harsh he is. I had to stop Patty Kay. She'd promised not to say anything until the trustees met. I was to talk to Dan. I said I'd have him come with me to the meeting Saturday night.

I told her he would apologize. She finally agreed that if Dan came before the board and apologized to the Hollises and quit his offices, that would be enough. She said it could all be kept within the board. But I knew better than that. People love to talk. When you're from a family that matters, they can't wait to tear you down.

"When I left I'd made up my mind. I drove straight to the bookstore. Craig lets the staff use his car to run errands. I waited until nobody was watching and I got his keys—they hang on a hook in the main office—and I went to his car and got his gun. When I put the keys back in the office, that's when I took Stevie's sweater. Everybody at the store knew about Stevie and Craig. I wish now I'd told Patty Kay." Her voice was sharp, vindictive. "I knew that if the police found out about Stevie and Craig, they'd arrest Craig. So that's why I got the sweater. I worked it all out, how much time it would take. But up until the last minute on Saturday, I kept thinking it would be all right, that Patty Kay would listen. Things like this don't happen in Fair Haven. I gave her every chance. Right up to the last minute in the playhouse, I *begged* her."

"You didn't give Amy a chance."

"I couldn't. She recognized my voice. She called Thursday afternoon. About our schedules. And her tone changed, right in the middle. I knew. So I went to the bookstore." The mirrored sunglasses hid her eyes. "I didn't have any choice."

"She was nineteen years old."

"I didn't have any choice." Now her voice was peevish. I was bothering her.

The lake sparkled in the sunlight.

"All right now. The note." She'd thought it through, solved her problem. She sounded so confident.

I looked into the dark hole of the gun barrel.

Then my eyes widened. I looked past her, back toward the way we'd come. My mouth opened.

Her head jerked to look back.

I took a deep breath, whipped the Mace canister toward her, and jammed my finger on the button.

Mist spewed over her.

A choking, guttural scream.

A shot.

But I wasn't there.

As the Mace spewed, I'd bolted to my feet and jumped over the side of the pavilion. I dropped into a crouch and began to run.

Her wavering angry scream rose.

Another shot.

Leaves crunched beneath my thudding feet.

I plunged into the woods.

The gun sounded one more time.

23

rooke Forrest's funeral was two days later. Private services, of course.

There could be no doubt of her guilt, thanks to my tape recorder.

But there was no public revelation.

Charges against Craig were dropped.

The final stories in the media about the shocking series of incidents in Fair Haven were oddly incomplete, simply a statement from the Fair Haven police chief that Brooke Forrest's suicide closed the investigations into the deaths of Patty Kay Matthews and Amy Foss.

The inference was unmistakable, but no motive was revealed.

I kept in touch with Desmond Marino. Margaret, of course, spoke every so often with Craig.

I'd been wrong about one thing.

Dan Forrest remained as president of the student council at Walden School.

It didn't especially surprise me. The power of wealth and privilege may disappoint me, but they never surprise me.

However, I subscribe to the old-fashioned view that people ultimately receive what they deserve.

Of course, when the truth isn't revealed, imagination takes over. Desmond wrote me about the gossip and innuendos and ugly rumors clouding Patty Kay's name.

I decided that Patty Kay deserved better. I was not in thrall to David Forrest, the Forrest name, or Walden School. Fair Haven's precious reputation meant nothing to me.

And I wanted to tell the world about Franci Hollis, who laughed so often and told people nice things and loved to paint. I wanted to give the Hollises a happy portrait to remember, as I remember my sandy-haired Bobby. The sum of their lives is more, much more, than a truck careening out of control or cold, unforgiving water.

I wanted to remind all of us that when we see a child—or adult— withdraw and there are only tears, no more laughter, we can't simply hope it will go away. We must recognize depression for what it is. We have to know that help must be given.

As soon as the spring semester ended, I set to work. It took most of the summer. I put down the truth about Patty Kay Matthews and Franci Hollis and Dan Forrest and Brooke Forrest and what happened at Walden School.

In one respect, my book differs from most books about true crime. There are no photographs of Patty Kay dead in the playhouse. The portrait of Patty Kay playing tennis is on the cover. The book has a great many photos of Patty Kay and Craig and Brigit in happier days.

One photograph is my favorite—a summer shot of a vibrant Patty Kay with an arm around Franci Hollis, both happy and smiling at the camera.

It is my first true crime book and I'm proud of the story it tells, the story of a woman who would not be swayed by power or privilege, a woman who did what she felt she must do.

The story of Patty Kay Prentiss Pierce Matthews.

I feel she deserves no less.

Oh, the title?

Scandal in Fair Haven.